I DON'T LIKE MONDAYS

WAKING UP IS ONLY THE BEGINNING OF HER NIGHTMARE

MARIA FRANKLAND

AUTONOMY PRESS

First published by Autonomy Press 2025

Copyright © 2025 by Maria Frankland

All rights reserved. No part of this publication may be reproduced, stored or transmitted in any form or by any means, electronic, mechanical, photocopying, recording, scanning, or otherwise without written permission from the publisher. It is illegal to copy this book, post it to a website, or distribute it by any other means without permission.

This novel is entirely a work of fiction. The names, characters and incidents portrayed in it are the work of the author's imagination. Any resemblance to actual persons, living or dead, events or localities is entirely coincidental.

Maria Frankland asserts the moral right to be identified as the author of this work.

First edition

Cover Design by David Grogan www.headdesign.co.uk

'The mind replays what the heart can't delete.' – *Unknown*

JOIN MY 'KEEP IN TOUCH' LIST

To be kept in the loop about new books and special offers, join my 'keep in touch list' here or by visiting www.mariafrankland.co.uk

THE BROTHER IN LAW

KEEP YOUR ENEMIES CLOSE...

Maria Frankland

PROLOGUE

I PULL into the station car park, unable to recall the journey. Hands trembling on the wheel, I glance in the rearview mirror. My hair is a mess, and the shadows beneath my eyes are darkening by the day as I become more and more marked by insomnia. I rummage in my handbag, searching for my hairbrush and makeup compact. Some quick fixes are essential – I can't look like this for my pre-interview presentation.

Dragging my wheelie case from the boot, I sigh, breathing clouds of vapour into the freezing dawn air. *It's as though you can't wait to get away from us.* It's not the argument I've just had that's needling me the most, it's more what my husband said as I searched the hallway for my keys. His words play on a loop in my mind, as relentless as the rumble of passing trains.

My eyes ache with the fluorescent light inside the station, and my stomach growls as I'm hit by the scent of coffee and warm croissants. I check my watch – I have ten minutes to spare, so there's enough time to grab something to eat. Food might settle the growing unease in my gut.

As I wait at the counter for my order, my phone vibrates in

my coat pocket with a message. For a moment, I hardly dare to look. Is it a friend or a foe?

> Stay away from him, do you hear? Just bloody stay away. I'm watching.

It's swiftly followed by another one. At first, I think it's *her* again but no, it's a different sender. It seems that everyone's out to get me this morning.

> May the best woman win. And just for the record, it won't be you. Good luck, Cathy – you're going to need it.

The words sting, as sharp and biting as the frost outside. Tears well up, blurring my vision. This Monday morning has hardly begun, and already, it feels unbearable.

It's as though you can't wait to get away from us.

His voice again. It won't leave me alone. Even two hundred miles from home won't be far enough today. Guilt at this thought twists my stomach into knots.

'Can you spare some change, please?'

The voice draws my gaze to a man wrapped in a filthy duvet, huddled against the wall. His gaunt features and hollow eyes remind me of my brother. Without thinking, I hand him my coffee and croissant. His smile is startling, brimming with gratitude that feels out of place in this chilly, indifferent concourse. I peel the cover from my phone, retrieving the emergency twenty-pound note tucked behind it.

'Here.' I thrust it at him.

'Are you sure?' His voice lifts like I've handed him a lifeline, instead of what, to me, is small change. For a fleeting moment, I feel lighter. But then the whispers return.

It's as though you can't wait to get away from us.

Stay away from him. Just bloody stay away.

Good luck – you're going to need it.

I squeeze my eyes together, desperate to block it all out. Perhaps I *am* as bad as they all say. My head swoons, so I quickly reopen my eyes. I'm woozy from not eating since yesterday morning, but there's no time to fix that now.

'The next train to arrive at platform six will be the 7:02 service to London King's Cross.'

The announcement jars me back into the moment. I join the tide of passengers moving toward the platform as I fumble around on my phone to find my e-ticket. The crowds feel thicker today, and they're pressing in on all sides. How can it be this busy so early in the morning? The thrill I used to feel at embarking on my weekly commute has gone and has been replaced by a suffocating loneliness. I feel like people are staring at me – as if they can somehow sense what an awful person I am inside.

The ticket gate doesn't budge as I try to scan my barcode. A weary attendant smiles kindly, presses his card to the machine and waves me through the barrier. His small act of generosity feels oddly significant, a faint warmth against the chill of the morning. I've got to hang on to whatever positivity I can find.

I home in on a familiar face which dots the throng, trying to push my way closer. Then I see one I *don't* want to see, so I backtrack, keeping my head down while I pretend to scroll through my phone. With a bit of luck, I'll blend into the crowd and not be noticed. I can slip onto the train and just pretend I'm engrossed in my reading. I really can't take any more this morning.

'Back to the grind?'

I glance up, startled. A woman I vaguely know smiles. She works further down the South Bank.

'Um, yes. I guess so,' I mumble.

'Are you okay?'

'Why wouldn't I be?'

Her fingers brush my cheek, and I flinch. They're wet with

tears I didn't realise I'd shed. Embarrassment flushes through me, but the crowd surges forward, shoving us apart.

'The train shortly arriving at platform six will be the 7:02 service to London King's Cross. Please stand back from the edge of the platform.'

The robotic words feel distant, muffled by the buzz of voices and the chaos of movement. I should have eaten something – I really don't feel too good. A shout rings out, sharp and commanding:

'Stay back behind the line!'

But the crowd presses forward. My feet lose contact with the ground, and I'm carried by the surge, weightless and powerless.

Then, suddenly, I'm alone.

Falling.

And the last thing I see are the headlights of the oncoming train.

1

'OPEN YOUR EYES, MUM.' The voice belongs to a child – a boy, I think.

'Please, Mum.' It's a different child this time – an even younger boy. 'It's time to wake up.'

The voices, soft and urgent, stir something. *Mum?* Who are they talking to? It can't be me.

A warm hand rests over the chilly skin of mine. 'Stand back, boys.' It's a deeper, more commanding voice, adult and steady, but still, someone I don't recognise. The sharp bleeps of monitors punctuate his words. Hospital. I'm in a hospital. *But why?*

The scrape of chairs beside me grates against the pounding ache in my head. I try to lift it – just a little – but pain locks me in place. With effort, I force my eyelids open, and slivers of light slice into my darkness.

The first thing I see is my arm, swathed in bandages. The next are three faces, hovering expectantly over my bed.

Strangers.

I open my mouth, desperate to explain their mistake. They've got the wrong person. But the sound that escapes is a rasp – dry and raw, like something clawing its way up my throat.

'Don't try to talk, Cathy.' The man leans in closer, his voice calm but firm as his hand remains over mine. What the hell is he doing? What gives him the right to touch me? 'You've been intubated for the past week. The doctors said it might take a day or two before your voice returns.'

I tug my hand from under his, relief seeping through me at freeing myself from physical contact with him. But hang on – what did he say? *A week*? No – that can't be right. I'd know if I'd been unconscious for that long. Wouldn't I?

'Is she trying to talk?' Another figure moves into view – Emma. Relief floods my body. My stepsister's face is familiar and safe. She takes my hand, her grip steady as she addresses the man. She can hold my hand – he bloody well can't. 'This might mean there won't be any lasting damage.'

Lasting damage from *what*?

I try again to speak, but my throat feels like it's in shreds. Instead, I stretch my fingers towards her, silently pleading for her to understand. She has to tell these strangers they've made a mistake and that they must be looking for a different woman.

Emma turns to the man. 'We should let the staff know she's waking up – they'll want to check her over.'

'Mum?'

As the man leaves the room, my attention is drawn to one of the children. He's young – maybe six – with sandy hair, a sprinkling of freckles and teeth which are too big for his mouth. Cute, sure. But he's not mine – he can't be. Brad and I agreed we'd wait, travel, and live a little before even *thinking* about kids.

Brad.

My chest tightens as I turn my head from side to side, searching the shadows around the edges of the room for my husband. The machines hum and glare in the dim light, but there's no sign of *him*. Instead, the man reappears, his presence filling the doorway. He looks at me with an intensity I don't understand – like he knows me better than I know myself.

'The doctor will be through in a minute.' The man drifts back into the room, and Emma moves to the side as he approaches my bed. He's already gripping my hand again before I've had the chance to tuck mine beneath the blanket, out of his way. 'He's just finishing up with another patient.' I want to tell him to get off me. I *need* him to get off me.

'She's awake sooner than they said.' Emma shuffles around to the front of my bed, her face etched with concern.

'Everything's going to be alright, Cathy.' The man entwines his fingers with mine and I look towards Emma, hoping she'll read the panic in my face. I can't move my hand. I can't release myself from him. I want him to get the hell off me. He shouldn't even be in here. 'Sit back down, boys. We need to let the doctor check her over when he comes in. He'll need room to see what he's doing.'

'But when will she want to talk to us?' The freckled boy asks, his voice quivering. 'When will she be coming home?'

'I want her to come home too,' says the other boy.

'It's not that she doesn't want to speak,' the man replies. 'She just *can't* right now after that horrible tube. But maybe in a day or two.' Relief seeps through me as he lets go of my hand and heads over to the children. He crouches and brushes a hand over each boy's hair. 'I say we go for a drink and some cake in the cafe to celebrate that your mum's going to get better. It won't be long before she's home and everything can get back to normal.'

That's it. Just go, go, *go*.

'Auntie Emma, can *you* come with us?'

'Of course she can,' the man replies, his gaze flickering from them, to Emma and then back to me. 'Come on, let's leave the doctors to do their jobs. We won't be long, love.'

I feel sick at the way he smiles at me, as they all file out. None of this makes sense, and I can't even ask for an explanation.

Who are these boys, and why are they calling Emma their auntie?

Who is this creepy man?

And why the hell are they all acting like they know me when I've never even seen them before?

2

'CATHY?' A middle-aged man dressed in blue scrubs approaches my bed, his feet clicking against the floor. An identically dressed woman follows him in, her greying hair scraped into a bun on the top of her head. She tilts the blinds at my windows before arriving at his side. 'I'm Dr Mike Glover, and this is Sister Carrie Layton.' He points at his colleague's name badge. 'We've been looking after you since the paramedics brought you in.'

I want to reply, but obviously, I can't.

'Don't try to speak.' Sister Layton rests her hand on my good arm. Well, I say good; it's peppered with cuts and bruises, but at least it doesn't seem to be broken – not like the other one. 'It can take a while after the tube's been taken out for your voice to fully return, so just take it easy.'

I look at her with eyes that hopefully convey my unable-to-be-spoken questions – *what happened to me?* And *how the hell have I ended up in this bed?*

'You're in the intensive care ward of Leeds General Infirmary,' she says. 'You've been here for the last seven days.'

Intensive care? *Seven days*? An army of questions marches through my mind. Questions I'm unable to ask.

'You might not feel lucky right now, but you really *have* been in so many ways,' Dr Glover continues. 'Most of your injuries are superficial cuts and bruises that have already begun to heal. However,' – he closes the gap between us, – 'according to the CT scan we carried out when you arrived, you'd sustained severe swelling to the brain.' He points at his own head. 'This required an immediate craniotomy to relieve the pressure.' The way his voice falls as he describes my head injury suggests I haven't been quite as lucky as he first made out. 'Without the surgery, there was a chance you wouldn't have made it.'

Instinctively, I raise my hand to the site of the pain in my head. The skin feels smooth where my unruly dark curls have been shaved away, and all I can feel is the coarse zig-zagging of the surgical stitches. I probably look like something out of a horror film. No wonder Brad isn't sitting beside my bed.

'You've also suffered some broken ribs and three breaks in your arm from when you landed on the track,' the nurse adds, with sympathy swimming in her eyes.

The track! What on earth is she talking about? What track?

'Additionally, you may have suffered some nerve damage in your back.' The doctor glances at a machine to my left. 'How are you for pain right now, Cathy? Raise your hand if you need more pain relief.'

I keep my hand flat on the bed. I feel woozy enough as it is without them giving me something that might send me floating back off again. I have no chance of working out what's going on if I'm out of it.

'We do need to ascertain as soon as possible what the chances of getting you up and walking again are.' His voice takes on a more sympathetic edge. 'So we'll be trying to get you walking as soon as possible.'

Oh my God – is he trying to tell me there's a chance I could never walk again? Is this what he means? I blink back tears. I can't get my head around what's happening here – I've still got my whole life ahead of me. If they're going to tell me I won't be able to walk, I might as well be six foot under in a box.

'We'll know as soon as we try getting you up and about whether the accident's led to any problems with your walking, and we can take action from there.'

'Just nod or shake your head, Cathy – can you recall *anything* about that morning?' Sister Layton's hand remains on my arm. 'Last Monday?'

I close my eyes, but all I see is the reddish glow of the lamp over my bed and some dark shapes swimming around behind my eyelids.

'Can you remember how you ended up in the path of that train as it was slowing into the station?' Her words become even more gentle than they were a moment ago.

I open my eyes while trying to shake my head. The truth is that I can't recall a thing. I don't know what's worse, the fog that's clouding my ability to think straight or the pain that's hammering at the roof of my skull.

'Don't try to move, Cathy.' Doctor Glover frowns at his colleague, probably for not waiting to pose these questions. 'There'll be plenty of time to talk about what happened soon enough. The police will want to speak to you when we give them the green light.'

The police. I swallow, wincing with the pain. Maybe I'm in some sort of trouble. But if I'd done something wrong, surely they'd be here already, watching me, or I'd be handcuffed to the bed. Not that I'm likely to go anywhere. I don't even know yet whether I can still walk.

'Hopefully by the time they arrive,' the nurse picks up from where the doctor left off. 'However you came to be on that train track will have come back, and you'll have something to tell them.'

3

'CAN YOU REMEMBER ANYTHING?' Emma's voice is more urgent than I've ever heard. I stare back at her. She seems to have aged considerably in the week I've been lying in a coma. Surely, my accident can't have stressed her out *this* much? Or perhaps it's just the lighting in this room. But at least the man and the boys haven't come back with her, so she must have put them straight.

'I mean, were you feeling extra depressed that morning?'

I frown at her. *Have I been depressed?* I just don't remember.

'To be honest, you haven't been yourself for a while, hon.'

I point at my throat to remind her I can't talk. She rummages in her bag and pulls out a notepad and a pen. I'd laugh at her in different circumstances. Her bag is always full of necessary items. She was always the go-to girl for plasters when new shoes were rubbing on a shopping trip, or painkillers when we'd overdone it the night before on the happy hour shots. We used to tell everyone we were sisters rather than stepsisters. I was studying journalism, and Emma was studying art at the same university, and because we spent so much time together, we adopted each other's mannerisms and ways of thinking and talking. And we liked the same sorts of clothes and hairstyles. My brother felt pushed out, of course, but Emma was like the sister I'd always wanted.

I try to smile at her, but the movement pulls on my stitches so tightly that my smile probably looks like more of a grimace. Why is it I can remember all of that past stuff in great detail, yet haven't got a clue about how I've ended up in this hospital bed surrounded by the stench of death and disinfectant?

Emma rests the pad on my overbed table, which she wheels towards me. With my good hand, I point at my broken one, hoping she'll get the message that I can't write any more than I can speak.

'Just have a try.' She nudges the notepad closer.

I turn my head one way and then the other, hoping she'll get the message.

'You're going to have to find *some* way of communicating until your voice comes back.'

What if it never does? I want to ask her. What if my ability to speak is hanging in the balance as much as my ability to walk? Or to think straight?

'Tell me what you can remember about that Monday morning.' Her chin juts out with a determination that says, *I'm not going to give up until you at least try.*

I reach forward for the pen with my left hand, feeling like a child again as I painstakingly scrawl a word on the pad. It certainly looks like the writing of a five-year-old.

Nothing.

My pulse races as the man from before fills the doorway, flanked by the two boys. Oh no, he's back again. 'Apparently, they're going to take you for a scan shortly, Cathy. So they can assess if there's any damage now that you've woken up.'

I wish I could tell him that any *damage* of mine has got nothing whatsoever to do with him. *What is he even doing here?*

Surely, Emma will have told him that Brad could arrive at any time now that I'm awake. He won't be happy if there's some weirdo who thinks he knows me hanging around.

'Who says there's *damage*? Cathy understands *me* perfectly.' Emma sounds almost smug as she points at herself.

'She doesn't even seem to *recognise* us.'

'She knows exactly who *I* am.'

'But I'm her bloody husband.' The man's voice is filled with anguish as he lumbers back into the room. 'Come on, Cathy. You're acting like you've never seen me before.'

Husband! No. What an absolute load of rubbish. Why's he lying? I'm already married, for goodness sake. I study him as he stands at the foot of my bed. I wouldn't be attracted to someone like this man in a million years. He's the polar opposite of Brad. He's far shorter and stouter with gingery receding hair and glasses.

'Sit over there, boys.' His tone alters as he gestures to some chairs stacked in the corner. Then he returns his attention to Emma. 'She should be able to remember *me* more than you.' The hurt in his tone as he talks to Emma makes him sound like one of his children. 'We've lived in the same house for the last ten years.'

Now he really *is* talking nonsense. Why isn't Emma putting him straight? My memory can't be that affected by whatever's happened to me, surely? I'd know if I *lived* with him!

'But I want to sit with Mum.' There are tears in the older boy's voice, and for a moment, I feel guilty. If I *was* his mum, I'd pat a space on the bed to make way for him. But since I don't know what the hell's going on, all I can do is lie here, my gaze flickering from one of them to another as they speak.

'I want to sit with Mum too.' I turn my head towards the chubbier and younger boy of the two. Neither of them even looks *anything* like me; they don't look like they're even related to each other. I hate to see the upset expressions on their faces, but I'm powerless to do anything about them.

'What the hell's wrong with you, Cathy? It's me, Daniel. Look, this is my wedding ring.' He points at his knuckle but at least he doesn't try touching me again. Whoever he is, he's making my skin crawl. 'And this is Austyn and Matthew, your sons. Come on, love. Surely you know who we are?'

'We should get the boys out of here, really.' Emma glances over at them before lowering her voice. 'This must be upsetting for them. Do you want me to take them into the family room?'

I glance down at my own wedding finger, expecting to see the ring bestowed on me by Brad so I can prove I'm *his* wife, not this man's, but my finger is bare apart from some chipped pink nail polish. There isn't even an indentation where I wear it. Did I lose my rings in whatever accident I've had? The one where I've supposedly ended up on some tracks? Or did the theatre staff remove my jewellery when I had the craniotomy? Not being able to recall any of this is an absolute nightmare.

The man ignores Emma's question. 'Cathy?' His tone becomes even more pleading. Whoever he is and whatever he wants, I can't cope with this. I just need him to leave.

I look back at him blankly, unsure of what he wants me to do. It's not as if I can kindly explain that I've never seen him before in my life. Meanwhile, the poor boys watch on, both looking teary-eyed. Emma's right, they shouldn't be here – it's not fair on them. I want to help them to feel better, but I can't.

'Why is it you can remember *Emma* but not *me*? I really can't understand it. Look,' – he brushes his hand over his receding hairline, – 'we had a row the last time we spoke – is that it? Is this 'pretending' some kind of *punishment*?'

'The doctor mentioned before how she could have either post-traumatic or retrograde amnesia,' Emma tells him. 'He said he'll know more after the scan and will be able to explain things more fully.'

'She *will* get better, won't she?'

It's none of his business, though what the man's said sounds almost like a rhetorical question – one I wish I could answer myself. But there are no answers – not yet, anyway. Whatever happens from here, I have a nasty feeling that it could be a long road to recovery.

Perhaps this is some kind of elaborate scam the man has cooked up that he's forcing the children, and maybe even Emma, to be involved with. What he thinks he can gain from me, I have no idea. I'm a freelance journalist, so I'm hardly rolling in money. Maybe his own wife is dead or something, and he's having delusional thoughts. Or he could be even more calculated than that and be searching for a gullible woman to take him and his sons on to share the burden.

When that doctor or nurse comes back, I'll write something on the pad to get them to take some action and get him out of here. After all, Emma just seems to be going along with all this. Maybe he's coercing her in some way.

Whoever he is and whatever his motives are, they need to get on with finding out where my *real* husband is. A sob catches in my throat at this realisation. If Brad loved me, surely, he'd have been at my bedside already, holding my hand and willing me to wake up after whatever trauma I've endured. I drag the pad closer to myself and scrawl the word,

Brad.

4

'What's she written? What does it say?' The man cranes his neck over Emma's shoulder.

'Can I see too?' The older boy drops from his chair and lunges across the room. He's dressed better than his dad at least and is wearing jeans, Nike trainers and a hoodie.

'Careful, Austyn, don't trip near any of the machines,' Emma says.

Austyn – I've always liked that name for a boy. She tries to conceal the page before the man can see it, but before she manages to slap her hand over my word, he's already read what I've written.

'Wait in the corridor, both of you.' He doesn't take his eyes off me as he barks out his order to his sons. 'I need to speak to your mother. Do you mind waiting out there with them?' His eyes flit to Emma and then back to me. What on earth is going on? What's he planning to do to me?

Please don't leave me alone with him – I really don't know who he is. There's a lump in my throat the size of a golf ball as I reach for Emma's hand and try to convey my fear by squeezing it as hard as I can. We've looked out for each other since we entered one another's lives in our teens and, right now, I need her to look out for me more than ever.

'Boys – *now*.' With what sounds like a sob, the younger boy follows Austyn to the doorway. Those poor kids. I wish I was in a position to reassure them in some way. The man goes after them. 'I'm sorry I raised my voice – it's just...' His words ebb away. 'I promise I'll just be a few minutes,' he says in a gentler tone. 'Just go over into the family room and don't move.'

If they *were* my children, I would *not* be bringing them to an intensive care unit. But they aren't my children, therefore, I should probably mind my own business. The man heads around to the other side of my bed and lowers himself onto the chair so he and Emma are now facing each other. I wish I could tell him not to get comfortable there – that I just want him to leave. He's far too close to me. I clench my fist beneath my sheet and pray he doesn't try to grab my hand again. Hopefully, the fact that his kids are waiting for him will mean he'll hurry up and get out of here.

'Can you go with the boys?' He's directing his question at Emma.

'They're OK – I can see the door to the family room from where I'm sitting. There's not exactly much damage they can do inside. There's literally only two sofas and a coffee table.'

Thank God she's not leaving me alone with him.

'Look, love.' The man clasps his hands together at the side of my leg. At least he isn't trying to hold my hand again. 'I can't tell you how sorry I am for my part in things last Monday. I've gone over and over it so many times, and if I contributed in any way to what happened that morning, I...' His voice trails off, and he looks at me as if he expects me to reply. Then, when I don't, he carries on with this spiel he's probably rehearsed ten times over. After all, he's had enough time to get his story straight while I've been lying in this bed. As I wait for what he's going to do or say next, his face darkens and suddenly, he looks more angry than hurt. Surely he won't hurt me.

'But you've punished me enough now, Cathy, and this *pretending*,' he spits the word out like it's something nasty, 'this *pretending* not to know us has gone on long enough. You're being heartless and cruel, and those boys out there don't deserve this kind of treatment from you. They've already had to suffer enough of your indifference.'

What the hell's going on here? Why is he saying these things?

'Did you not hear what I told you before?' The man doesn't reply, so Emma carries on talking. 'She might have some kind of amnesia.' Her voice is soft. 'At least wait until she's had another scan and we've heard the results before you get on her case like this.'

'The problem I've got, Cathy, is that you've *never* been satisfied.' The man's face hardens even more as he ignores Emma. He doesn't take his eyes off me as his voice rises. 'Me and those boys of ours.' He points from himself to the doorway and then at me. 'You've *never* been able to count your blessings, Cathy. We've never been quite enough for you, have we?'

I turn my head to Emma as if to implore her to *do something – just get him out of here*. But she seems to be rooted to the spot. It might be a strange thing to notice in the scheme of things, but it looks like she's applied hair extensions to her strawberry-blonde hair. She normally wears it tied back, but I'm sure it wasn't *that* long the last time I saw her. It seems like an odd thing to do – to get your hair done while a family member is lying in a coma.

'You always just want more,' the man continues, 'like *him*, for example.'

Emma looks as confused as I am for a moment. 'Oh, you mean *Brad*?' She raises the notepad on which I've scrawled my husband's name.

'I can't take much more of this today.' The man's voice is so elevated, I'm surprised nobody's been in yet to investigate. After all, we *are* in an intensive care unit. But somewhere over the corridor, an alarm is wailing into the air, so the staff are probably dealing with an emergency. 'I'm going to get Austyn and Matthew home. They need some semblance of normality after how you've treated them today. But mark my words, I'll be back tomorrow and you'd *better* have some answers for me then.'

With that, he turns on his heel and strides from the room. I point at the notepad where I've written Brad's name and wait for Emma to look at me. Through the agony, I wheeze the words, 'Where is he?'

5

'It's only me.' Emma reappears at my bedside. 'Good morning.'

I turn my head toward her. *Is it?*

'Your voice hasn't come back yet?' She offers a sympathetic smile.

I roll my head from side to side against my pillow.

'What about your memory?'

This is the hardest thing – I know there's something wrong with my memory; there's no other explanation. And it's horrendous, almost as if I've woken up in someone else's body.

'Can you really not remember *anything*, hon?' Her eyes are filled with concern.

I shake my head. Then, just as she's about to say something else, a youngish lad arrives in the room.

'I'm Tom, one of the porters. I'm here to take you down for your scan.'

'Can I come?' Emma asks, and I shoot her a look, which I hope she can tell is gratitude. She probably promised Brad that she wouldn't leave my side until he returns. He'll be at home just having a bite to eat, a shower and some sleep. Perhaps he'd just left before I woke from my coma yesterday. They must be long days when you're sitting at someone's bedside in intensive care. Emma will have told him to take his time and have a decent rest.

'You can, but you won't be allowed into the room.'

I squint as the dim light I've become accustomed to is exchanged for the fluorescence of the corridor.

'Your dad will be along soon.' Emma walks alongside my bed as I'm wheeled along the smooth floor.

'Mum? Harry?' Though it's agony, I manage to say the words. I can't understand why my family weren't all at my bedside yesterday. Instead, they've allowed me to wake up to a group of strangers. Thank goodness Emma stuck around.

'I'm not sure.' She focuses on the newly arrived lift. 'So how long have you worked here?' She asks the porter as the lift descends, leaving my belly behind on the third floor. From her avoidance tactics, it seems there could be something Emma doesn't want me to learn. Something about either my mum or my brother. Or even Brad – she isn't telling me much about him either.

～

'My name's Elaine. I'm the radiographer doing your MRI scan today. Before we go in, can I just confirm some details?'

'Cathy can't speak very well at the moment,' Emma explains. 'She's had the tube in for the last week.' She points at her own throat.

'Are you able to nod and shake your head?' The kindness in the woman's face brings tears to my eyes. I feel so confused and really can't get my thoughts in order. 'Just gently?'

I nod.

'Is your full name Catherine Elizabeth Mason?' Then she reels off my date of birth. 'Which makes you forty years old?'

I shake my head.

'Which bit's incorrect?' She glances back into the file she's clutching. 'Your name or your age—'

'It's *all* correct,' Emma says. 'Cathy's just a bit mixed up since she awoke yesterday. The doctor said there might be an issue with amnesia.'

Mason, since when have I been called *Mason*? And why would anyone say I'm forty instead of thirty? Emma knows how old I am – after all, she's the same age. Surely I don't look *that* haggard after my accident? Or is this the thing with my wretched memory? I just can't make head nor tail of things – to use one of my mother's expressions.

I listen helplessly as Emma confirms an address and next of kin I've never heard of. *Daniel Mason*. Then, she confirms my occupation as an associate publisher for Bookish in London. I don't know how she's got that idea. I've barely read books, and I don't really even *like* London. I get excited about visiting, but then am always more pleased to return to the slower pace and the fresh air of Yorkshire. Emma *knows* this – and she also knows I'm a journalist, not an *associate publisher*.

'There's no chance you could be pregnant, is there, Cathy?'

I shake my head, though who knows? *Anything* could have happened in the ten years which might have been erased from my mind.

Emma laughs at the radiographer's question. 'As Cathy always says, she's done her bit for the population.'

I have no idea what she's talking about. It can't be the two boys who were here yesterday – I'd know if I'd given birth to them, surely? I'd have known as soon as I saw their faces.

'You'll have to wait out in the corridor,' the radiographer tells Emma. I want to beg her not to leave me alone. It was hard enough when she went home last night, leaving me with the agony of being unable to piece things together. She feels like the only steady thing I can hold onto right now, while everything else in me is slipping away. Or has already gone. I've no idea who I'm supposed to be – only who I was when I was thirty.

I just want my husband – the person with whom my memories end.

I feel strangely cocooned in the doughnut-shaped scanner as lights and machinery flash and whirr around me. As if nothing and no one can hurt me. But when I get out of here, my new reality will still be waiting. The inability to get out of bed, to think straight or even communicate what I'm thinking or how I'm feeling. But I'm clinging onto how Sister Layton said my voice should fully come back in a day or two. Hopefully, by then, everything will be clearer, and at least I'll be able to start asking questions. And perhaps, when I'm taken back up to the ICU ward, Brad will be waiting for me – since he didn't come yesterday. He's sure to visit today.

Instead of it being Brad waiting for me when I'm returned to my room, it's Dad, and Teresa, my stepmother – Emma's mum. Just like Emma, Teresa and Dad also look to have aged. His hair's thinning and almost grey, and his face is slightly more lined and puffy than I recall. Though I didn't want to believe it at first, I *must* be older than I remember. But *forty*? I can't have simply *lost* ten years of my life.

They both jump to their feet as I'm wheeled back in. 'We've been so worried, haven't we, Bob?' There's something vaguely comforting about Teresa being here as she's wearing a similar outfit to what she wore the very first time we met – a short skirt, woolly tights, an oversized jumper which looks like it might belong to Dad and her still-dark hair tied back with a scrunchie. She couldn't look, act or be any different to how my mother is, which is, no doubt, the appeal as far as Dad's concerned.

'Having the tube down her throat might have left her without a voice,' Emma explains again. 'But she can understand you perfectly.'

'Thank God you're awake.' Dad lowers into the seat beside me and clutches my hand. 'We were terrified you were going to die.'

Now that Dad's here, I just want to be on my own with him, but he and Teresa are very much a double act. She's involved in things more than my own mother – like mine and Brad's wedding preparations, my graduation, and Harry's twenty-first birthday. We get the spiel from Dad, *she's my wife now – I can't come without her.* Hospital visits are clearly the same.

'Why don't the two of us go for a coffee, Mum?' I smile at my stepsister. It's as if Emma can read my mind. 'Cathy's on the mend, so let's me and you go and catch up.'

Teresa shuffles in her seat, and I sense her reluctance. She likes to be a part of things – I get that. But the only people I want here while I'm at my lowest ebb are the people in my immediate family.

Which includes Brad, wherever he may be.

6
___

'I'll tell you what, love.' Teresa slides her purse from her handbag and rises from her seat. 'Why don't *you* go and fetch us *all* a coffee? I need to stay here and support Bob.'

Emma pulls a face and grabs her bag from where she's looped it over one of the chairs. 'Alright, alright, I know when I'm surplus to requirements.'

'It's not that,' Dad replies in his usual peacekeeping tone. 'But it's supposed to just be two to a bed while Cathy's still in ICU. How long have *you* been here today? I imagine you'll be ready for a break?'

'Since first thing,' Emma takes the money Teresa thrusts at her. 'But Daniel and the boys were here at the same time as me *yesterday*. So there were *four* of us in at once then.'

'It might be different when visitors are close family.' Teresa drops her purse back into her bag and edges closer to my bed. 'Like we are.' She smiles. 'So, tell me, what can you remember about what happened last Monday, love?'

'I don't think she can remember a thing.' Emma turns back from the doorway. 'Like I said on the phone, she keeps asking for Brad, and she seems to think she's still thirty.'

'She wishes.' Teresa chuckles as Emma's feet beat their path away from my door. 'Mind you, I wouldn't mind having ten years knocked off me as well.'

'Brad won't be visiting you, I'm afraid.' Dad squeezes my hand in his and, for a moment, I'm small again, with him looking after me when I'm poorly. 'You broke up years ago.'

I shake my head so hard it hurts. *No, no, no. Dad's got this wrong. Brad says we'll be together forever. We've planned out all our adventures, where we'll live, what we'll do, and the places we'll visit.*

'He's engaged to someone else now. And you're married to Daniel,' he continues. 'You live in a fantastic house in Otley with your two lovely boys, and you've worked hard to achieve where you've got to.' Nowhere in that little sentence has Dad mentioned happiness or contentment.

I shake my head again. He presumably means the boys who were here yesterday. They *are* lovely kids, really they are, but I've never seen them in my life. Why won't anyone believe me?

'Can she *really* not remember the last ten years?' Teresa's speaking to Dad as if I'm not even present as she walks from side to side at the foot of my bed. 'Or could she be—?'

'Teresa, actually, you're not being very helpful.' Dad frowns at her. 'Perhaps you should go after Emma.'

I nod in agreement, and she scowls. 'I'm staying right here. I'm part of this family too.' At last, she stops pacing around and sits heavily onto the chair at the other side of my bed.

I point at the notepad still resting on the table, which the nurse has wedged into the corner of the room. Dad follows my gesture and rises to his feet.

'This?' He rests his hand on a jug of water.

I shake my head.

'This?' He points at the sick bowl. I was feeling queasy after being moved about to be washed and changed earlier, but thankfully, that's subsided. Sister Layton said feeling sick is quite normal with the amount of painkillers that are being pumped into my system, so I must try, as soon as possible, to get off this opiate-based medication.

Again, I shake my head.

'This?' He points at the notepad.

I nod.

'But you can't write,' he says. 'Your writing arm's broken.'

I raise my left arm and then point at the table. He wheels it back to where it was earlier – over my bed so I'm able to rest on it while I slowly form the words,

What happened to me?

He and my stepmother exchange glances. It's a telling communication, as if they're uncertain what to say. As I turn my head from Dad back towards Teresa, she's mouthing whatever it is that she doesn't wish for me to hear at Dad.

'We just need to be honest,' he replies.

'OK.' She seems to puff her chest out. 'It was last Monday morning when you were waiting for your train to London,' she begins. I point at Dad – I want *him* to tell me, not her. If this seems cruel, I don't mean for it to be. But he's looking at Teresa, who carries on, either not understanding or simply not caring who I want to tell me the story. 'You were on your way back to work for the week.'

I recall my work being up *here* in Yorkshire as a freelance journalist, so I have no idea what she's talking about. For now, however, I have no choice other than to accept what everyone's telling me. Whether I can remember my life as it was or not, I seem to be someone else these days. Someone's mother, and someone else's wife.

'You were on the platform one minute, waiting for your train to pull in, and then—' her voice falters.

I close my eyes, I hear the roar of a train, its horn, some screaming, the smell of engine oil. I see headlights, then complete blackness.

Have I just had a memory flashback? Or is my imagination simply processing what my stepmother's telling me? It was vivid enough, but I can't be sure.

'Then the next minute, you were sprawled out in front of the train.' Dad completes her sentence. 'You don't know how lucky you are to still be here.' He brushes his eyes with the back of his hand. 'How lucky we are to still have you.'

'But you've no idea what you've put us through.' Teresa plucks a tissue from the bag in her lap and passes it to Dad as she sighs. 'I can't understand why you couldn't have talked – to us, to one of those helplines...'

What does she mean? What happened was an accident, surely?

'A woman came forward to the police and said you'd been crying while you were waiting on the platform. She also said that you didn't seem very *with it*.' Teresa draws air quotes around her final two words. 'Can you remember?'

I shake my head.

'*Did* you jump in front of the train?' Teresa's voice is far too pleasant to have formed the question she's just come out with.

'She fell.' Dad leans forward in his chair.

'Did you *want* to do something bad to yourself, love?'

'She *fell*.' Dad's voice hardens as he stares back at his wife. 'Please Teresa, let me do the talking, eh?' He gives her a pointed look before turning back to me. 'Daniel told us you've been having a few dizzy spells.'

I stare back at him. How am I supposed to have an answer for that when I don't even know Daniel? Even if I could speak, that is.

'And I'm not being funny, love, but I've seen more fat on a chip – I can't believe how much more weight you've lost over the last year.'

Typical Dad, he always calls a spade a spade. *I've seen more fat on a chip.* What he doesn't need to say is how I'm the polar opposite of my mother, who's so clinically obese she can't even leave the house. Unless she's managed to shed some of it during the time that's become such a blank. I've struggled my whole life with being the other way – unable to gain any weight. Whenever I wore shorts as a teenager, Dad's favourite remark was, *I've seen better legs hanging out of a bird's nest.* And while I was still at school, I was known as the *skeleton*. It was awful. People don't realise how it's just as offensive to be ridiculed for being underweight as it is for being overweight.

I'm having no trouble remembering all that – my childhood, my teenage years, and my twenties - but my thirties seem to have been completely erased. However, if I'm no longer married to Brad, maybe it's not such a bad thing that I can't recall us separating. But I don't know how I'll go forward as I really can't imagine a life that he's not a part of.

'Your dad was right – you *have* been fortunate,' Teresa says. If she knew how much pain I'm in and how confused and helpless I feel, she'd know I'm anything *but* fortunate. 'If that train hadn't been slowing – if—'

'Teresa, for God's sake.'

She pulls a face and folds her arms.

'Sorry, love,' Dad says. 'I'm just a bit stressed with it all.' He fixes me with his serious brown eyes and pushes his shirt sleeves up his arms.

I point at the pad again, and he pushes it closer. It takes me a minute or two, but I manage to write the words,

Tell me.

'OK, though we don't know that much, to be honest.' He and Teresa exchange glances again. 'Because the train was slowing to a stop, it only *clipped* you before it managed to come to a stop. Plus, you went forward in its path instead of beneath the train. We've been told if you'd been standing further down the platform as it came in, when it was travelling at a greater speed, it could have been a very different story.'

I reach for the pen again and write,

Mum?

He swipes the pad up from the table and holds it in the air towards Teresa. She suddenly looks as panic-stricken as Dad. 'You're going to have to tell her the truth.'

Tell me *what* truth?

Both of them seem to be frozen to the spot.

'Tell me,' I force the words out, my throat feeling like it's being rubbed from the inside with sandpaper.

'I can't believe I'm having to break this to you, especially as it's been two years since it happened, love.'

I close my eyes again, and there she is, a heap on the kitchen floor – my mother. I rush at her, sitting astride her as panic engulfs me, pummelling at her chest in a vain attempt to restart her heart. My voice whooshes in my ears. 'Mum, Mum!' Harry's there too, rooted to the spot in shock as he watches.

'Your mother had a heart attack. I'm afraid she passed away.'

Tears leak from each of my eyes and slip down the sides of my face, clogging my ears.

Teresa passes me a tissue.

'I'm so sorry, Cathy.' Dad's staring down at the floor. 'This is the thing with this awful amnesia, you're being made to suffer bad news twice.'

A few more moments of silence pass. Neither of them seem to know what to say after that particular bombshell, not even

Teresa, and from what I remember of her, she's *never* at a loss for words.

'Have the police been to talk to you yet?' She eventually asks.

I shake my head and point again at my throat. It's all I seem to have done since I was brought back from my coma – to point at my throat. But people keep firing questions, seeming to forget that I still can't speak.

'The police have been going through the CCTV from the station,' Dad continues. 'They haven't come back to us with anything concrete yet, but at least they're thoroughly investigating what might have happened to you that day.'

He pulls his phone out at his mention of the police. He's probably checking to see if they've been in touch.

'Don't you worry, we'll get you some help.' While Dad's looking at his phone, Teresa touches my hand where the pot ends, sending a jolt of pain up my arm. 'Whatever was going on that made you think—'

'Enough,' Dad snaps. 'Until Cathy can speak for herself—' He stops as Teresa nods towards the doorway, and two police officers peer into the room.

7

'Is it alright if we come in?' asks a female voice from the doorway.

Dad glances at me and then rises from his seat. 'I won't be a second, love.' He rushes to the door, closing it behind him as he ushers the officers back into the corridor.

I point after him and fix Teresa with a look that hopefully conveys the question I'm unable to voice, *what's he doing*?

Teresa's expression is a cross between concerned and baffled. 'Um – he's probably making sure whatever they've come for that they'll go easy on you in the state you're in.'

With the door closed, I can't make out what's being said out there but I'm sure Teresa's right.

'Come on in,' Dad says to the officers as he reopens the door and leads them in.

'We haven't met before, but I'm DI Ruth Turner,' a thin woman with greying roots announces as she moves closer to my bed. 'And this is my colleague, Sergeant Ben Richards.' She points at a good-looking man who looks to be half her age. I'm sharply reminded of the state of myself with my half-shaved head and technicolour bruises, not to mention the NHS-issued nightie I'm wearing. At least now that I'm awake and Dad's here, I can get him to sort some proper things for me for as long as I've got to stay in the hospital.

'It's good to speak to you at last.' The sergeant smiles in my direction. He has a look of Brad, and I bet he wears his dark hair spiky when he's not on duty. A flood of tears wells up inside me. Dad said we're not together anymore. Brad's engaged to someone else.

'You must be—'

'Mr and Mrs Wheeler.' Teresa stands to shake DI Turner's hand. 'Bob and Teresa.'

The detective inspector returns her gesture, obviously taken aback. Most people don't offer police officers a handshake. Instead, they see what I see – that the mere presence of a detective usually means something bad has happened or that someone's in trouble. 'Are you Cathy's parents?'

'Well, I'm her father, but Teresa,' – Dad gestures across my bed at her as he retakes his seat beside me, 'Teresa's my second wife – Cathy's stepmum.'

I glance at Teresa, noticing her face fall at this introduction, as if being my *stepmum* makes her less important.

'OK, well, we've taken the case over from the less senior officers who were initially investigating,' the DI begins, 'and we'll come on to the *why* in just a minute.'

'Do you mind if we sit?' The sergeant nods across the room toward the chairs the boys were sitting on yesterday.

'Go ahead,' Dad says without getting back up. I'm surprised at him. Normally, he'd jump up and carry the chairs over to them, but he just remains in his seat, taking hold of my good hand like before he got up to speak to the officers. It's as if he doesn't want to let me go. I don't want to let him go either, especially now the police have arrived.

They drag the chairs around the edge of the space the machines are occupying and position themselves at the foot of my bed. I've been told the monitors need to remain as they are for another day or two, at least until after the results of my MRI scan. They're talking then of moving me to the high dependency ward.

'Well, firstly, might I echo what Sergeant Richards just said – I'm so pleased to see you awake.' Despite her authoritative voice and her stern appearance, DI Turner's mouth forms a half-smile as she looks at me. 'You certainly look to be in better shape than our colleagues mentioned.'

'If she were a cat,' Teresa laughs. 'I'd say she'd have practically used up her nine lives after what happened last Monday.'

Trust my stepmother to make light of my predicament. I'm all for being positive, but I can't think of *anything* that's all that positive in my life. I'm alive, yes, but my quality of life is hardly looking promising – I still can't speak, I'm not sure who I am, and I don't even know if I can walk. I stare back at the officer as I wait for her to continue.

'Are you up to answering a few questions, Cathy?'

'She's had a tube stuck down her neck for the last week,' says Teresa. 'So, no, she's not up to speaking.'

'When will she be?'

'It will be at least another day or two,' replies Dad.

'Well, as soon as you are, we'll need to ask you some questions,' DI Turner says. 'But in the meantime, can we tell you where we're up to with our investigation?'

'Please do.' Dad shuffles his chair as close as he can to my side as if he's making sure he's ready to support me.

Sister Layton pokes her head into the room with an expression that's stern enough to match *any* police officer's. 'When we told your department that Cathy was awake,' – she looks straight at DI Turner with sharp eyes, – 'what we didn't mean is that you could come marching straight to her bedside. We're in the middle of assessing her injuries.'

'I'm sorry,' DI Turner replies. 'That's not what we were led to believe.'

'She isn't able to answer any questions yet – as I told your department yesterday on the phone.' Her voice is commanding authority, but neither of the officers makes any move to rise from their seats. Nor do I want them to.

'There could have been a miscommunication with our admin staff.'

'Cathy hasn't regained her memory, *or* even her ability to speak.'

Here we go again. People are discussing me as if I'm not even here.

'Our investigation has yielded something that the *family* need to know,' says DI Turner.

'Are we OK just to tell them what we came to say,' asks Sergeant Richards, 'and then we'll come back when Cathy's more able to speak.' The smile he flashes at Sister Layton is probably hard to refuse.

'Very well. Five minutes – no more.'

'Thank you.'

'And just for future reference—' The officers' heads turn back to the door as Sister Layton continues. 'When Cathy's moved down to HDU,' – her voice is clipped, – 'it *is* only supposed to be two visitors to a bed at once.'

Dad, usually an even-tempered people-pleaser, pulls a face after the ward sister as her footsteps fade away along the corridor. 'I'm sure they'd normally make allowances on the visitors rule when it's the *police*,' he says. 'She's probably just having a hard day.'

'So what is it you need to tell us?' Teresa looks from one officer to the other.

'Well, as you already know...' DI Turner seems to be speaking to them, rather than to me. There's only Emma who's been treating me like I'm not a half-wit since I woke up. 'Our colleagues have already spoken to many of Cathy's acquaintances, friends and family, yourselves included, I understand?'

'That's right,' Teresa confirms. Why must it be *her* who does all the talking? She should leave it to Dad.

'And statements were taken from as many eyewitnesses as possible after the incident on the third of March,' she continues.

So they're calling it an *incident* rather than an *accident*. What does that mean? I wish I could remember what happened. Or maybe it's all so bad that my mind is somehow trying to protect me from the reality. The more I try to remember, the more my head hurts.

'From all that, we've been able to build up a general picture of Cathy's life, but until *today*, there's been nothing specific about the moments leading up to her being struck by the London train. Thankfully for us, that has now changed.'

Dad sits up straighter in his seat. I probably would if I could. I was feeling woozy and sleepy before, but what's being discussed here has definitely made me more alert.

'As you'll no doubt have been told already,' Sergeant Richards continues. 'Our colleagues at British Transport Police have been studying CCTV footage in and around the platform, and from all the entrance points to the station.'

'And?' Emma's standing behind the officers now with a tray of cups. I didn't notice her coming back into the room. That ward sister will have a field day now with five visitors around my bed instead of two.

'Can I ask who *you* are?' asks DI Turner, twisting in her seat. 'Are you a relative?'

'She's my daughter,' replies Teresa. 'Emma.'

'So Cathy's stepsister?'

'I'm her friend too,' Emma replies, and I try to smile at her, but it hurts my stitches. I guess it's unusual for stepsisters to get on as well as we do. She rests the cups on my overbed table.

'I won't deny that we've been up against it,' continues DI Turner. 'Not only was it extremely busy at Leeds Station that morning, so much so, that's it's almost impossible to pick out what's happening amidst such a huge crowd of people, but also, it was extremely cold.'

'What difference does that make?'

'It means that many people entering the station and waiting on the platform had their faces partially obscured with hats and scarves. However,' – her voice takes on a sterner edge, – 'from the speed at which Cathy emerged from the crowd towards the railway line, coupled with the position in which she fell in front of the train, we have ascertained some crucial information.'

'Which is?' Emma perches at the side of me on the bed. Sister Layton told her off for doing this yesterday. Apparently, it's 'extremely unhygienic in an intensive care unit,' as well as the risk it poses to me. Though with the several broken bones I have already, I don't think there's much more damage Emma could inflict.

I'm holding my breath as I wait for this so-called crucial information. My memory might have vanished, but somehow, from the moment I woke from my coma yesterday and was informed I'd been injured on the train tracks, I've had a feeling in my bones about what this officer is possibly going to impart. I've also had a sense that things were far from good in my life as I was arriving at the train station last Monday. If my fears are confirmed, there may be little point in trying to get myself better and back on my feet. I might as well give in right now.

'Your daughter...' She's addressing Dad now, but not me. Neither of the officers are looking at me anymore. The only person looking at me is Emma, and I feel the strength of her support.

'Just say it.' Teresa shuffles in her seat.

DI Turner's expression becomes more serious. 'Mr Wheeler, your daughter didn't jump from that platform.'

'See, I told you.' Dad hisses across the bed at Teresa, whose mouth becomes a pout at his words.

'Nor did she fall.'

'So what *did* happen then?' Emma's voice sounds far away as she asks the question I don't think I want to hear the answer to.

If I didn't jump and I didn't fall, there can be only one other explanation.

'As the London-bound train was pulling into Leeds station, I'm sorry to tell you that Cathy,' she looks around our group, but her final gaze rests on me. 'Cathy was *pushed* in front of it.'

'No.' Teresa lets out a gasp of shock. 'Surely not.'

'Whoever was responsible,' DI Turner persists, 'wanted to cause her some serious damage. Whoever was responsible wanted to *kill* her.'

8

AT LEAST EVERY HALF AN HOUR, I've had nurses prodding and poking at me, checking my monitors and shining torches into my eyes. As if that isn't enough to keep me awake, there's the pain I'm in, the unabating pain. Though I've been told I've also got several broken ribs and a fractured collar bone, the pain is mainly confined to my broken arm and my head. But far worse than that is the endless mental torture.

Someone wants me dead.

I'm not even sure I *want* to regain my memory – what if that puts me in even more danger? Once whoever it was finds out that I've remembered what happened that Monday morning, they could try to get to me again – to finish what they started. But why? I can't possibly have been such an awful person that someone wanted me to die.

As the police have suggested, I could have been randomly attacked by some psychopath. The other possibility is that I was pushed by someone who knows my weekly routine to London and it's *this* thought that's sitting on my chest like a dead weight. They could arrive at this hospital at any moment, and I'm not exactly in a position to put up a fight. It could be all over for me in minutes – or even seconds.

I'm exhausted from the effort of trying to unravel my memory. At least when I was in an induced coma, I was able to get some rest. My mind hasn't stopped racing since I've been moved into this three-bed bay in the high-dependency unit, but at least the hush hasn't been quite as deadly as it was in the intensive care unit. I guess that once you've been moved onto this ward, the outlook isn't quite as bleak. I'm in the end bed, there's no one in the middle, and the woman in the bed at the other end seems to be sleeping most of the time.

But I'm fed up with the non-stop buzzers and alarms, hushed voices that aren't really hushed and footsteps squeaking up and down the corridor. Aren't hospital staff supposed to wear *quiet* shoes at night? I just want to sleep – to escape the not-knowing and run away from the never-ending fear.

∼

'Hey.' A gingery head pokes around my curtain. It's the man I now know as Daniel. My so-called husband. In his checked shirt and shapeless jeans, he even dresses old. His outfit isn't unlike something Dad might wear.

I still don't know what happened between me and Brad, but I guess I'll get to piece it all together over the coming hours and days. I've certainly got plenty of thinking time while I'm stuck in this wretched bed. I can't believe Brad and I are no longer together, and the pain of having broken *all four* of my limbs would have been preferable to the pain of missing him.

'How are you feeling?' Daniel edges forward, his shoulders tense, with a couple of photo albums tucked under one arm and a small holdall dangling from the other. If he's brought in some of my things, he really hasn't brought much.

'I've been better.' My voice is partially back, and I've been told there's no reason why it won't completely return. I've only been intubated for just over a week, which is not very long in the scheme of things, so I've been told. I keep wishing I was still out of it – it feels preferable to everything I'm having to face.

'The police came to see me last night.' He takes a seat beside my bed and drops the holdall at his side. It's the first time I've been on my own with him since I woke up, and to say it's uncomfortable is an understatement. He speaks in a hushed voice, no doubt aware of the other woman's presence and not wanting to disturb her.

'Did they tell you what *really* happened to me last week?' The realisation that someone tried to kill me returns like a lightning bolt.

'That you were pushed? Yes, I've been told.'

It's impossible to tell what he's thinking. Maybe he's in shock. Or perhaps it would have been easier for him if whoever pushed me had succeeded – it might be less painful than a wife who doesn't even remember him.

'Can I get you anything, Cathy?' Evidently, he doesn't want to talk about what he's been told. Really, I don't blame him. What can he say? What can *anyone* say?

'Like what?'

'A drink, a magazine, something to eat? I've brought you some things from home.' He points at the holdall. 'Some pyjamas and a change of clothes.'

'That's good. At least I don't have to keep baring my arse every time the staff need to move me.' I pull at the neck of my gown.

'I'm glad your voice is back.'

'Not completely.' I raise a hand to my throat. 'It's still sore.'

There's a palpable expression of relief on Daniel's face as he rises from the chair and rests the photo albums on the table.

'So, you remember me now, I take it? Does this mean you remember the boys?'

I shake my head and give him what I hope is an apologetic look. 'I'm really struggling, to be honest.' I blink rapidly, trying to hold back my tears. 'I feel like I don't even know who I am,' I point at myself, – 'and for now, I'm going to have to rely on what you and the others tell me about the last few years.'

'The boys were so upset the other day.' Daniel evidently can't meet my gaze. 'It's been so hard for them – what's happened to you, your memory problems…'

'I'm sorry,' I croak. 'I honestly thought you had the wrong room when I first woke. It's all these drugs.' I tilt my head toward the machines. There are far fewer than there were when I was in the intensive care unit, but they've kept me on the same level of painkillers as I don't feel ready to reduce my dosage. Then there's my drip and catheter, which I hope they'll be able to get rid of soon.

'It's alright.' But I can see by his face that it isn't.

'Are the boys at school?'

'Austyn and Matthew?' His face relaxes. 'Yes, they wanted to come back and see if you were any better yesterday, but they seem to understand that it's best to give you a few more days to recover.'

'They sound like bright boys.' I *should* already know this. It's horrendous that I've got two sons that I can't even recall giving birth to. I'm glad he's brought these albums – hopefully, they contain photos that will shift something in me.

He smiles. I might not be able to remember Daniel, but he does seem like a nice enough man, if a bit too old. 'Yes, they take after me,' he grins, 'just joking.'

'Well, they wouldn't take after me. My brain feels like mush.'

'Doctor Glover advised me to bring some photos in when he spoke to me the other day.' Daniel opens one of the albums and moves the table closer. 'So, this is our wedding album.' The thin paper dividing the cover from the first page crinkles as he lifts it between his fingers.

'When did we get married?' I hardly dare look at the page. If it *is* me in the photos, all my fears are confirmed. I'm definitely married to someone who's *not* my beloved Brad.

'Eight years ago,' he replies. 'Well, it will be eight years on the nineteenth of August.'

He's clearly different from Brad, who never remembered my birthday, let alone our wedding anniversary. He didn't remember his own birthday most of the time and always left it up to me to organise. *If you can't celebrate the day you were born*, I often said to him, *then who will?* I've *got* to stop thinking about Brad. He's obviously in my past, but I can't seem to help myself. I need to get to the bottom of what happened to break up our marriage, but Daniel probably isn't the best person to ask. I'll speak to Emma when she visits. Now that I'm able to talk.

'We were really happy.' He smooths his hand across the page, and I squint in the dim light to look at what he wants me to see. Sure enough, there I am, wearing some slinky lace number as we both smile into the camera. Daniel looks remarkably younger there than he does today, to say it's only been eight years. He's slimmer, he isn't wearing glasses, and he has a lot more hair. But even then, he still doesn't seem like my type – not like Brad was, the absolute cliche of tall, dark and handsome.

'How did we meet?' I can't imagine how I would have ever been attracted to this man.

'At Ilkley Literature Festival.'

'Really?' That's the last sort of event I could imagine myself attending. As a journalist, I covered news items and had nothing to do with the literary world. I haven't even read since I was a child – before I got too busy taking care of my younger brother when Mum was too drunk. *Mum.* The memory of her wraps itself around me like a shroud. She might have been difficult, but she was still my mother. And she's gone.

'Are you OK?' Daniel jolts me back into the moment.

'I hadn't remembered that my mother had died. Dad told me.'

'Really?' His eyes widen. 'That was two years ago.'

I study the pattern on my curtain. 'So, as you can hopefully imagine, it's come as a shock. *Everything's* coming as a shock. Even my job.' I'd better not mention anything about Brad.

'You're a publisher. I'm a writer.' Daniel points from me to himself.

I still can't get my head around being a publisher. I hope the expertise I must have gained comes back, otherwise, I could find myself out of work. Who knows if I have any sort of a future? Whoever pushed me onto that train track could come after me again, and the next time, they'll no doubt make doubly sure they finish the job. What if the police don't manage to catch them? From what they've told us so far, they don't have much to go on, so finding whoever did this to me doesn't look promising. Nor does having any kind of normal life with my would-be murderer still able to strike at any time.

'You earn the big brass,' Daniel continues. 'While I stay with the boys.'

'So you work from home – writing?' *Home.* I wonder what my home's like. I can't imagine it will be anything like the one I shared with Brad, our newly-built shoebox, that, while being tiny, was all we needed. I spent every spare penny on that house, making it perfect.

'Yeah, I've nearly finished writing my first psychological thriller.'

Which is now the story of my life. A psychological thriller that's verging on horror since I discovered someone wants me dead.

'Samantha's interested in offering me a publishing contract.'

'Samantha?'

'You work together. You were going after the same job.'

The face of a woman flashes into my mind. Long, dark, wavy hair. Killer heels, red dress. 'Manager red.' Her voice echoes in my mind. 'I know I haven't got the job yet, but it's important to look the part.'

'Apparently,' Daniel goes on, 'it would be a conflict of interests for *you* to have me on *your* list. With us being married.'

'That's just as well since I don't remember the first thing about publishing. *Or* psychological thrillers.'

I close my eyes. What the hell will I do if my memory doesn't return? I'll have to start from scratch. Who will I be? What will I do?

The woman in the end bed begins to wail. And I feel like wailing too.

9

Daniel stares at the machine monitoring my heart rate and blood pressure. 'Are you sure I can't get you something to eat or drink?'

I point at the drips attached to my arm. 'I'm being fed and watered, there's no need to fuss.'

'Look, even if you don't recall who I am, I'm still your husband.' He gestures at the wedding album. 'In sickness and in health, supposedly – remember?'

What a stupid thing for him to say. Clearly, I *don't* remember. 'So where are my rings then?' I raise my hand from the bed. I haven't become used to not wearing Brad's rings since I awoke. We didn't have much money when we got engaged so the ring, which was always too big for my skinny ring finger, was a small blue topaz with a few tiny diamonds in its halo. It had been in the sale but I adored it. Then, my more tightly fitting wedding band held it in place after we got married.

'You keep losing weight.' Daniel touches my finger where I should be wearing them. 'They're in your jewellery box on our bedroom windowsill, so you don't lose them.'

I close my eyes. *A wooden box – a tiny replica wardrobe fills my* mind. The south-facing window overlooks a sunny field where several dog owners are gathered. I'm not one of these people – they don't speak to me if ever I'm walking among them.

'Oh, right.' I can't imagine sharing a bedroom with this man, but evidently, I do.

'Really, you should have had your rings adjusted, which was yet another bone of contention.' He sighs.

'So there were a few? Bones of contention, I mean?'

'Do you honestly need reminding?' His arched eyebrow over the frame of his glasses suggests he's wondering if my amnesia is all an elaborate act.

'I get the occasional tiny flashback – but that's it. I've had a glimpse of the train and, just then, I thought I could see my jewellery box. Do we overlook a field?'

'That's right – to the back of the house.' For a moment, he looks thoughtful. 'Well, *flashes* of memory are a *positive* sign, aren't they?'

'After what I've found out about having been pushed, I'm really scared of what I'll remember.' I might be confiding in Daniel, but this doesn't mean I'm comfortable in his company.

'Have you heard anything back about your scan results?' He closes the wedding album and slides it back inside its sleeve.

'They came back yesterday.' I adjust my plastered arm with my good one, wincing at the stab of pain.

'And?' He sits forward in his chair.

'It's one of the things the doctor first suspected – *post-traumatic amnesia*. He explained a few things about it, but I was struggling to absorb what he was saying.'

'It's OK – I can read up on it.'

'One thing I *can* recall him saying was that my memory could be impaired for days, weeks, months or even years. Sometimes it lasts forever.'

*Like Brad and I should have d*one, I think with a jolt of misery. But nothing's forever, as Mum used to say, especially after she and Dad divorced. I wish she was still here - well, the version of her before hitting the bottle and an unhealthy diet took her prisoner.

'Do you recall the two of us rowing the morning before you set off?'

I shake my head, then lean back onto the soft pillow. 'Not in front of Austyn and Matthew, I hope?' The names of my sons sound weird in my mouth, almost like a foreign language.

'No, they were still sleeping – which I guess is normal at quarter past six in the morning.'

'I'm sorry – I really can't remember. Why were we arguing?' Great, so not only am I married to a man who isn't Brad, but it's not even a happy marriage. If my memory doesn't return, I can't imagine being able to stay. How can I share a home and a bed with a man I feel absolutely nothing towards, other than repulsion?

'It was more of the usual, I'm sorry to say.' He hangs his head.

'Which is?'

'OK – I'm just going to be honest.' He takes a deep breath. 'It was the knowing that you'd rather be at your fancy-pants job in London with your ex working at his swanky job across the street – instead of being in what you called, I quote, *mind-blowing drudgery*.' He draws air quotes. 'At home with me and the boys.'

'Is that what I said? I'm sorry. But when you say *ex*, presumably you mean Brad?'

Daniel's face darkens. 'I honestly can't believe you're able to remember *him* but not your two bloody sons.' He reaches for the other photo album and drops it on top of the wedding album. 'Look, they're *our* boys – y*our* boys.'

I look down at the first photograph. It's me, alright, pink and happy, cradling a newborn baby in a delivery room. It's more how I'd expect myself to look. More me than the horrific vision I saw when I persuaded Sister Layton to bring a mirror into my room yesterday. I look *terrible*.

'Keep looking.'

I turn the page, and a more professional shot fills my vision. I've had my unruly dark curls straightened and am wearing heavy makeup. I do recognise the dress. It's one I bagged from Emma for a night out when I was younger – she must have let me keep it. In the photo, I'm flanked by younger versions of Austyn and Matthew, each boy clinging to either arm as though they're scared I'll leave. A sheen of tears clouds my eyes. They should have been far more important to me than my job.

'Am I a good mother?'

Daniel looks away, answering my question without saying a word.

'Tell me the truth.'

'As I've told you, until I'm blue in the face, they need you more than *anyone* else in your life does, including *him*?'

'You mean Brad?'

'Who else?'

'So Brad's still in my life – is that what you're saying?'

'Let's not go there.' His eyes fix themselves on the shiny white floor. 'If you can't remember what was going on, then let's not cause ourselves the aggro of opening it all back up again, eh? Not right now.'

'But I need to work things out.' Panic rises at Daniel's reluctance to be open with me. He evidently knows so much but seems to be prepared to tell me so little. 'How can I carry on with my life if I don't even know who I'm supposed to be...' My voice trails off. '*Whatever* that might have looked like.'

'You're back with us *now*, aren't you?' His tone softens. 'Look, maybe some good *can* come out of all this.'

'How on earth do you work that out?'

10

'Come in, mate.' Daniel's voice is loud in the mid-afternoon lull. I've been drifting in and out of sleep, which is less tedious than pretending to be Daniel's wife, particularly when he can't, or won't, help me get to the bottom of who I was before I was pushed. He must know of people in my life who might have wanted me out of the way, enough for them to risk their conscience and even their liberty.

'My dad rang to say she's awake.' It's my brother's voice.

Harry and I are facing each other in what could be his hallway, and he's shouting into my face. Really shouting. Venom, spittle, the works. But I'm struggling to make out his words.

Then, as suddenly as the roar of his voice has filled my ears, it's all quiet again, apart from the soft snoring of the woman at the other side of the room.

I keep my eyes tightly shut. If I pretend to be asleep, I might hear something from one or both of them that could be useful – something which will actually help me, instead of the watered-down answers to the questions I've asked so far.

'Yeah, on Monday. I'd have thought you'd have been in earlier.'

'Are you sure?' His voice becomes closer, and the whiff of aftershave I catch evokes something. I'm certain it's the same one which Brad used to wear. 'She looks just the same as she did when I was here at the weekend.'

At least Harry's already visited. I know how much he hates hospitals from the times we had to visit Mum over the years. My brother *sounds* just the same as I remember, but he probably doesn't look the same. No one does after ten years. I'm dying to open my eyes to find out if he's changed much, but I'm best just lying here and listening.

'She's still very tired,' Daniel replies. 'The cocktail of painkillers she's on isn't helping.'

Neither is the heat, I would say, if I wasn't pretending to be asleep. It seems to be a few degrees warmer in here than it was in the intensive care unit.

'Is it true that she's lost her memory?' There's a creak of a chair as Harry sits.

'Mostly. Years of it. She thinks she's still thirty.'

'She wishes,' Harry laughs. 'Anyway, it's probably just as well.'

'What do you mean?'

'Only that she hasn't exactly been the jolliest person to be around recently, has she? Before all this, I mean.'

Now we're talking. This is where I could make some discoveries.

'To be fair,' Daniel's voice is hesitant, 'the version of Cathy that's woken up is far nicer than the one who landed in front of that train.'

'Well, that's good then – isn't it?' Harry's voice is light and airy, like they're discussing a football result instead of his sister's too-close brush with death.

'She seems to want me around more today.'

'That sounds like a huge step forward.'

Blimey, if Daniel prefers me when I can't even remember who he is, then our marriage must have been pretty terrible.

'I'm trying to look at it all positively,' he continues. 'It could be like some sort of re-set.'

'If you say so.' Harry's voice is filled with scepticism. 'If you can get over how she feels about *Brad*.'

'At least I won't have *that* to worry about anymore,' Daniel says. 'Nor can I imagine her returning to her job.'

'How come?'

'She thinks she's still a freelance journalist – hasn't your dad mentioned anything?'

'So much for her hot-shot director job.' Harry says with a trace of amusement.

It's an effort to keep my eyes closed when really, I'd like to open them and tell him what I think. Talk about kicking a dog when it's down. However, I'm going to keep listening to see what else they might say while they think I'm asleep. I've looked after Harry all his life, and if it wasn't for me being there for him throughout the times Mum wasn't able to be, he'd have probably ended up in a children's home.

'Her success at work has been all Dad ever drones on about,' Harry continues. 'He's constantly singing her praises – it's the story of my life. Hopefully, they'll just give the promotion to that Samantha and be done with it.'

'You've heard about her, have you?' I can imagine Daniel raising an eyebrow here.

'Just a few times.' Harry laughs. 'Has she been in to visit Cathy? She's well fit, that one.'

'Briefly.' Daniel slurps a drink, and I suddenly find myself craving a cup of tea. Since I awoke, I've been fed and hydrated through the drip and the occasional sip of water. At times, I wonder why they're even bothering, and it's a fight to fend off feelings that I'd be better off dead. Maybe it would be preferable to waiting for my would-be murderer to come back and finish things up. 'It was during Cathy's first couple of days here.'

'Shame it wasn't when I was here. Did she stay long?'

'No, only for a few minutes. She was dropping off a get-well card from the publishers.'

'Like that was going to do Cathy any good.' My brother laughs again. 'She must have said *something*.'

'The usual.'

'Perhaps *she'll* get the blame for shoving her in front of that train since they were going for the same job,' Harry says. 'It's certainly one way of getting your opponent out of the running.'

'Samantha's a far cry from someone who'd do a thing like that.' Daniel's voice takes on a defensive edge. 'Besides, if we're going to play the blame game, *you'd* be a more likely candidate.'

'What's that supposed to mean?'

'I gather the two of *you* were arguing the night before this happened?' Daniel's words drift around the room as though he's pacing the floor. 'And it's interesting how this is only the second time you've shown your face since she was brought in.'

'There didn't seem to be much point being constantly here while she was lying in a coma,' Harry replies. 'She wouldn't have even known.'

'She's still your sister.'

'It's not as if there's been much love lost between us over the last couple of years. No matter what's happened, I can't forget some of the things she's said.'

I can't lie here any longer listening to them talk about me as if I'm not here. I need answers – straight answers. 'Such as?' I blink my eyes open, clearly making them both jump with my voice. 'I'm not in a coma anymore – I can hear you now. Every bloody word.'

Harry, eight years my junior, looks completely different to the gawky lad from my memories. His hair is no longer as blonde, and even though he's teamed a hoodie with his jeans, it's obvious beneath its kangaroo pouch that he's developed a sizeable paunch. I have no idea who the boy I used to know inside out has become. By the sounds of it, perhaps Harry won't even want me to know. It seems he doesn't like me very much, and I've no idea how I'm supposed to feel about him in return. What could we have fallen out over to make him so hostile?

The woman in the other bed sounds upset.

'Poor woman,' I say.

'What's wrong with her?'

'I don't know, but she's out of it most of the time and then really confused when she isn't. Even more confused than me.' I force a smile.

'Are you seriously telling me you don't remember our last conversation?' Harry shakes his head. 'Or is this a sick game? Treating everyone in your life like crap then pretending you don't remember how badly you've affected them. You're lucky I'm even here.'

I glance towards Daniel, who's pulled back the curtain and is gazing out of the window as if he doesn't want to be involved in our conversation. From where I'm lying, there doesn't appear to be much of a view to be gazing out at. Just brick walls and rooftops.

'You lie there in your blissful ignorance.' The irritation in Harry's voice sharpens. 'It doesn't matter what you've said or done, we're all here to pander to you.'

'Emma's been completely fine,' I reply. 'At least she doesn't have an agenda. She just wants me to get better.'

'Saint Emma,' Harry retorts. 'I'm supposed to be your flesh and blood, yet you've always thought ten times more of her. You wouldn't have given *her* a fraction of the shit you gave me the last time we spoke.'

'What are you talking about?' My chest tightens as tears

pool in my eyes. I can't take this. My head's banging, every inch of me hurts, and the void inside me feels like it will never be filled.

And someone's loitering in the doorway.

11

'I DO HOPE you're not upsetting my patient.' A young woman with fair hair in tight French plaits paces into the room. She's wearing a dark tunic and leggings, so she must work here. However, she's dressed differently from the nursing staff. 'I'm Zoe. I'm going to get you back on your feet,' she explains. 'I'm your physio.' She turns her attention to Harry and then Daniel. 'Perhaps you gents would like to take yourselves off for a coffee while Cathy and I get acquainted.'

'Thank you,' I say as they obediently file from the room. I like her already. 'I wish I had as much control over who visits me.'

'You have, and you don't have to see anyone you don't want to.' She tilts the blinds on my windows. 'You're here to get better – not to listen to what I caught as I was on my way in.'

'To be honest, there are only two of my visitors I even *want* to visit.' The smile I attempt hurts my head as the skin tightens over my stitches.

'We can certainly talk more about that,' she laughs. 'Not that I'll be working with you in a psychological capacity as such, but it's all interlinked with your physical improvements. It's important that you only have people around you who speed up your recovery rather than upsetting you.'

'What's the saying,' I reply. 'God gave us our family—.'

'Thank God we can choose our friends.' She perches at the edge of my bed. 'Anyway, on a more positive note, having read your notes, it looks like you're doing amazingly well.'

'How do you work that one out?' I glance down at my broken self, the self that hasn't even tried to stand or walk yet. How can anyone say I'm *doing amazingly well*?

'Well, you're out of ICU for a kick-off,' she begins. 'You're going to be out of HDU over the next couple of days, *and* you're *talking*.' She smiles. 'To be perfectly honest, Cathy, what you've endured could have resulted in *serious* brain damage.' Her voice falters. 'Or far worse. But you don't need me to tell you that.' Her tone rises again. 'In any case, I'm here to help you focus on the bright side.'

'But I can't even recall anything over the last ten years. It's all a complete blur. I don't even know who I am.' The tears I've been holding back finally spill from my eyes. 'It's like I'm stuck back then – but of course, everything's changed.'

I want to talk about Brad, but I'll just go to pieces if I start. I don't know how much I'll have already grieved for our marriage when we split up, but how I'm feeling now is like it only happened yesterday. It's the same with my mum – but somehow, the pain of no longer being with Brad is more acute than losing Mum. Brad *loved* me; Mum just needed me.

'We're hopeful everything's going to come back.' Zoe squeezes my good arm. 'I see it all the time. Just be patient and don't try to force things.'

'Do you know if my memory will suddenly return all in one go, or will it carry on as it has been?' I rub at my throat. I've been advised to talk minimally and have probably talked far more today than I'm supposed to. 'I've been getting dribs and drabs of flashbacks, but nothing I can reliably piece together.'

'It's not my area of expertise,' she replies, 'but I imagine it could be either. But what I *am* here for,' her voice becomes more authoritative, 'is to get you moving.'

'I just want to get that thing off me.' I point at my catheter bag.

'Positivity is what will get you there faster. And lots of determination, so today we're going to get you sitting up at the edge of your bed with your feet on the floor, and we're going to try a few exercises to get some movement in those legs.' She pushes my curtain back.

The smile I return to her is as weak as I feel. Right now, I don't have any positivity or determination. I just want to lie here and wallow in the state I've found myself in. Is there even any point in fighting back to fitness? I can't shake the feeling that whoever pushed me in front of that train is going to come back and finish the job.

But at least I'm here, safe in hospital. I've been told the doors to all the wards are locked. Whoever wants to hurt me can't get anywhere near.

At least, I hope they can't.

12

'So what if the house is in your name?' Daniel slams the dishwasher door. 'It's the boys' home.'

'Meaning?' I stride across the kitchen.

He moves before I reach him, and he heads towards the fridge. 'There isn't a court in the land that would force me to leave this house. Not when I'm their main carer.'

'We'll soon see about that. I paid for it, remember?'

'Do your worst, Cathy. You can't lord this one over me anymore.' He wrenches a beer from the fridge. 'Besides, without me, you wouldn't even have a career. Who'd look after our kids twenty-four-seven?'

'I'd sort something out. Anyway, I've supported your career.' I point at him. 'You wouldn't have the freedom to write your book if my money didn't enable it.' I slam myself onto a chair at the table.

'Your money. We're supposed to be married, aren't we?' He raises the bottle to his lips. 'We're supposed to share.'

'We both know you only stay with me for the house and the money.' My voice echoes around the kitchen. I can't believe we're arguing. I haven't even checked to see whether the boys have fallen asleep.

'Well, it's not for the affection and the sex.' He roars with false laughter, which raises my hackles even more.

'You shouldn't have messed up your credit so badly, should you? I've never known a grown man so inept at managing money.'

He slams his bottle on the counter. 'Your brother's no better, so don't give me that crap.'

'I'm just letting you know what's coming, that's all – a letter from my solicitor. You can't say you haven't been warned.'

***

'How's the patient today?' I'm jolted from my sleep in the new room I've been moved to.

I squint through the early afternoon sunshine to where my stepsister is peering from the door.

'Oh, bloody hell, I'm glad it's only you.' My voice is as shaky as my body.

'Well, I'll take that as a welcome.' Emma laughs. 'Are you OK?'

'I was just having a funny dream,' I reply. 'I was having a row with Daniel.'

'No change there then.' She arrives at the chair beside me. 'We've all kind of gathered that you haven't been getting on too well.' She peers at me more curiously. 'Was it just a dream, or do you think things could be coming back to you?'

At least I can just be myself with Emma – whoever *myself* is since I awoke.

'I'm not sure – but it was vivid.'

'What was happening?'

I take a breath before replying, the voices of nurses at their station filling the silence. Then, as I'm about to describe my dream, I can't find the words. I scrunch my eyes together, but all I see are coloured flashing lights and shapes. 'Do you know?' I tell her. 'I don't think I can remember it.'

'Oh well, perhaps it wasn't worth remembering. Maybe it'll come back to you later.' She reaches for my hand. 'Anyway, you never answered my question.'

'What question?'

'I asked you how you are? I hope your memory isn't so bad that you can't remember what I said less than a minute ago.' She laughs again. I wish I could laugh back, but finding the joy in *anything* feels a long way out of reach. Whenever I've seen someone smiling since I woke up – a visitor or one of the medical staff, I think, *what could there possibly be to smile about?* It's like I'm in a deep, black hole, and it's a very lonely place.

Emma looks so 'together' in herself. While I'm lying here, still attached to this wretched catheter and still unable to get out of bed, she looks cosy in her thick jumper, denim skirt, woolly tights and boots. I glance down at my fleecy pyjamas. At least I'm out of that hospital gown.

'They've told me I'm doing well,' I reply, 'but it doesn't feel like that way. It all feels pretty hopeless, to be honest.'

'I can't imagine what you must be going through.'

'I don't know what to do.' I close my eyes, not wanting to see the sympathy etched across her face. 'To be honest, I'm *terrified* of my memory flooding back and the truth about what happened hitting me.'

'What do you mean?'

'I'm scared of *knowing* who pushed me in front of that train for certain – and of finding out *why*. When I remember, perhaps that will give them a good enough reason to finish what they started? They'd want to stop me from being able to take action.'

'Maybe it's just as well if you don't remember. What's happened to you is the stuff of nightmares, and you're probably better off not knowing.' Emma points at my box of grapes. 'May I?'

'You don't have to ask.'

She plucks one from the box and pops it into her mouth. 'What is it with grapes and hospitals?'

'Daniel said the boys wanted to buy me flowers, but flowers are no longer allowed – it's something to do with allergies. So I got grapes instead.'

'Daniel's been in again?'

'A couple of times.' I sigh as a vision of Brad with his kind eyes and lopsided grin fills my mind. I'd give anything for it to have been *him* who'd *visited a couple of times*. 'Every time he arrives, I just wish he was Brad. I have no feelings whatsoever for Daniel.'

'Ouch,' she replies. 'It must be rough. What about Austyn and Matthew? Have they been back?'

'He's bringing them later. I can *act* like I'm their mother, but I've had so little to do with *any* kids that being around them won't come naturally, especially in an environment like *this*.'

'So how are you going to handle things?' She fiddles with the edge of her ponytail and looks distracted as if she's waiting to change the subject.

'Zoe said there's a chance that my maternal instinct will just naturally kick in when I'm around them.'

'Who's Zoe?'

'She's my physio – she's been fab. If it wasn't for her, you and Dad, I'd have given up completely by now.'

'Speaking of maternal instinct – do you want to hear some good news?' She tilts her head to the side as she waits for my answer.

'I could certainly do with some.'

Her face takes on a coy expression as she reaches into her bag. 'There you go, Auntie Cathy?'

It takes me a moment to compute as I stare at the white blobs and lines on the picture she's handed me. 'Oh my goodness, is this what I think it is?' I raise my eyes from the picture to her face, which breaks into a smile. 'Well, this is amazing news – congratulations.' But even now, I still have to force enthusiasm into my words. This is how low I've sunk.

'Thank you.'

'I'd hug you if I could, of course I would, but I've only got one arm. How far along are you?'

'Only twelve weeks, but far enough along to start telling people.'

'I'm not just *people*.'

The smile fades from her face. 'If I'm honest, Cathy, you seem a little underwhelmed. I thought you'd be more excited.'

'I am, of course, I am. It's just – look, ignore me, I'm just down at the moment. I really will try and pull myself out of it.'

Will I, or are these just words?

'We'll celebrate properly when I get home.' I force the cheeriest smile I can muster. 'Hopefully, I'll be up to organising a baby shower.'

This wretched fall, well, push, has even snatched *this* moment away. I should be over the moon for Emma, but I'm finding it so difficult to genuinely celebrate.

'Can you remember both of your baby showers?'

I shake my head. 'I'm just praying the feelings of *being* Austyn and Matthew's mum come flooding back.'

'You do *know* you're their mum?'

'Of course I do – Daniel brought some photo albums in – so I've seen photos in the delivery room. They couldn't have been fabricated.' I force a laugh.

'It must be so hard for you right now.' She glances around the side room. 'But at least you've been moved to a proper ward. It's much better for you *here* than the other two wards, and at least it means you're improving.'

'I just hope I hold onto this room until I'm discharged. At least I'm getting a bit more sleep.'

'Has the doctor or physio said anything about you being discharged?'

'I need to be able to manage better,' I reply. 'Zoe's coming back tomorrow, and she reckons she'll have me walking. Once I've shown I can get myself around and take care of myself, they'll probably let me go home. Apparently, I need to be able to get myself up and down a flight of stairs.'

'Even if your memory hasn't come back?'

'Apparently so. Honestly, Emma, it all stops when I'm about thirty.'

'So you still remember everything from before then, but *nothing* about now?' She pushes a strand of strawberry blonde hair behind her ears. Instinctively, I try to do the same, but my fingers rest on my stitches. I can't believe half of my hair has been shaved away. Some might say it's saved my life, so I should be grateful, but I just can't feel that way.

'Not a thing. And I'm really scared of bringing it all back, to be honest. I'm not going to like what I find out, am I?'

Emma pauses. 'Do you want me to be honest – just to lessen the angst if your memory comes back?'

'It's about time *someone* was. I've gathered that it wasn't hearts and flowers with Daniel, and there were clearly issues between my brother and me.'

'Well, you know me – and you know I'm coming from a place of kindness.'

'Just spit it out.' I sigh.

'Look, Cathy, there's no way of sugarcoating this, but you were at loggerheads with nearly *everyone* before your accident.'

'It wasn't an accident.'

Tears prick my eyes. I don't want to be at loggerheads with *anyone*. God only knows who I became in my thirties, but it doesn't sound as though I'd like myself.

'So what did I do to deserve it? If anyone deserves to be pushed in front of a train.'

'All I know is that you'd become really work-focused – it seemed to be all that mattered. Well, not just work – also...'

'Brad?'

She nods.

'Is that why he hasn't visited me?'

She gives me a strange look. 'You split up nine or so years ago.'

'Does he even know about my accident? Has anyone told him? Is your Joel still his boss?' I fire the questions faster than she can possibly answer them.

'Well, erm, yes. He's worked at the company for as long as I can remember.'

'So he's bound to have heard about me being in this state by now. I can't understand why he hasn't visited.'

'I don't know. I can't say—'

'Look, can you ask him to visit me?'

She frowns.

'Please, Emma. Seeing him might jog my memory. The doctor has told me to keep talking to *everyone*. That's the best chance I have at fully regaining the last ten years.'

'How would Daniel react if Brad was to suddenly show up? Have you thought of that?'

'He doesn't have to know, especially if Brad calls in around school time when Daniel will be collecting the boys. Look, Emma,' – I try to sit up some more, – 'There's no one else I can ask to get in touch with Brad. I'd ask my dad, but I can't imagine he'd want to get involved to *that* extent. In any case, he'd probably just say what you've said – *what about Daniel?*'

'OK, OK – I can ask him but, of course, there's no guarantee he'll want to come in, so don't get your hopes up.'

I relax my head back against the pillow. While I'm desperate to see Brad, part of me is scared to death. To be honest, I don't know what road I should be heading down.

Maybe I should just run for the hills and live for the rest of my days as a recluse.

I'd be safer that way from whoever wants me dead, and at least I wouldn't have to play at being mum and wife to children and a man I don't even remember.

13

I'm losing track of how many days I've been awake. With only mealtimes to demarcate time, I don't even know what day it is. Not that I'm really eating. Just enough for them to begin reducing my drip. I've no appetite, and it's not as if I'm expending any energy.

Night has once again turned into day. I blink in the emerging dawn before closing my eyes. I don't want to be awake – I don't want to face another day of not knowing who I am. But sleep doesn't come to my rescue. Instead, as always, all I see is Brad's face.

'You're back a day early.' I click the lounge door behind me and step towards him as he comes through the door into the hallway. But instead of the grin that has never failed to melt me, his face is hard with anger.

Maybe I've misread his mood, or it's someone else's fault he's upset. But, no, he's statue-still as he continues to glare. *'Well, this is a surprise,'* I say.

'More like a shock, you mean?' He looks beyond me to the closed door of our lounge. 'Who've you got in there?'

'It's no one. Just a friend.' I cross the distance between us.

'That's not no one, is it? What friend?' He shifts to the side.

'It's to do with work – we're working on a piece together.' I turn and reach to hug him, but he dodges out of my reach.

'I know you're up to something,' he snaps. 'Which is why I'm back.' He never usually raises his voice.

'I'm not up to anything – honestly.'

'How am I supposed to build my career to give us the life we've promised ourselves when I can't even trust you while I'm working away?' He repeatedly jabs his finger in the direction of the lounge door as he speaks.

'You can trust me. I love you,' I protest.

'So why have I heard the same thing from three different people, Cathy?'

'What people? What are they saying?'

'About what you're getting up to when I'm away.' His voice rises some more.

'I'm not getting up to anything – I swear.'

'I'm waiting for an introduction.' He heads towards the lounge. 'So are we going to call your friend out here or what?'

'Good morning. How are you feeling today?' Zoe's smiling face appears in the doorway. My breath comes thick and fast after my imagined encounter with Brad. Have I remembered something? Or was I just dreaming? Our altercation felt as real as the nose on my face, and now that I've awoken, I'm overwhelmed with a sense of regret. It's as if I've done something wrong – something I'm not even aware of.

'Cathy?' Zoe's heading towards me.

'Sorry.' I force a smile. 'I just had a weird dream, that's all.' I'm still baffled by it. What have I done?

'OK. Well, if you'd like a minute before we get started,' – she waves a strange-looking walking stick in the air, – 'that's perfectly OK. Or would you like to talk about things?'

'Like what?'

'Your dream.' She rests the stick on the floor. 'Your brain will be processing all sorts of stuff right now, trying to make sense of things, trying to recover from the trauma.'

'Yeah, it was weird, it was like—'

'What?' She sits on the seat beside my bed.

A similar foggy feeling to what I had yesterday envelops me. 'Do you know,' – I close my eyes, – 'I don't think I can even remember it.'

'Did the doc mention speaking to a therapist?'

'Yeah, he's put in a referral somewhere, but warned me I'll be waiting a while.' I don't add that I might not have a 'while' available. Not when someone wants me dead.

'That sounds about right. You could go private?'

'It sounds like I could – I mean from what I can gather, I've got a good job and enough money. I'll ask my dad to look into it.'

She looks puzzled. 'Won't you ask your husband?'

I shake my head. 'To be honest, I don't think things were too good between us before all this. It sounds as if we're hanging by a thread. He's probably only coming here because he feels as though he should.'

'Has he told you that?'

I nod. 'And I really can't imagine how I'm going to suddenly have feelings for him, whether or not my memory returns.'

'It's a really difficult situation.' Her face is etched with sympathy.

'To be honest,' I gesture to the stick at her side. 'It doesn't feel like there's any point in doing *any* of this. I'll probably be dead soon.'

'You could look at things another way, Cathy.' She sits forward in her seat.

'What do you mean?'

'Obviously, it's going be hard *if and when* the actual moment of being pushed comes back to you. But if you were to remember, there's a good chance the maniac who did this to you could be locked up for many years.'

'The doctor said it may *never* come back to me. I can't remember how he worded it, but it was something about how my brain may not have stored the event as a memory.'

'Yes, I've heard of that. The mind can do funny things to protect a person.'

'I'm sorry. I know I'm hard to deal with right now. Maybe you should move on to your next patient.'

'Rubbish.' She gets to her feet. 'I'm not taking no for an answer. I'm getting you up and walking today even if it's the last thing I do.'

'It *really* might be the last thing I do.'

She's still smiling as she reaches for the stick. Much as I like my physio, she's so pretty that she makes me feel like Quasimodo. I haven't looked in a mirror since that day in ICU, but my battered face and shaved head are more than etched in my mind's eye.

'I don't feel up to it today.'

'You're really having a Debbie Downer sort of a day, aren't you?' She perches on the edge of my bed beside my leg, still clutching her stick.

'Every day is that sort of a day.'

I brush a tear away. I can't bear feeling like this, and I can't even say that I want my life back, or I can, but it's not the life I was supposedly living with Daniel. It's the one where I was happily married to Brad and had everything to look forward to.

'Look, Cathy, you're still young, you've no underlying health issues, so there's no reason why we can't fight this fight together and get you properly back on your feet.'

'But it's not *your* fight, is it?' The tears are coming faster now.

'No, but it's my job.' Her voice is gentle as she tugs a tissue from the box on my table and passes it to me. 'And I'm here to help and support you.'

'I'm sorry, I don't mean to lay this all on you. I don't *want* to feel like this.'

'Well come on then.' She stands from my bed. 'You've got a lovely family and an important job waiting for you when you get out of this hospital. So let's get moving.'

'But it's a life I don't even *want*.' I turn my head away. The lump in my throat is so huge, I can hardly speak. 'If the police don't catch whoever did this to me, I'm going—.'

'You must remember what I said the other day about staying positive?' Zoe fixes me with her gaze. 'How it will make or break what happens from here?'

'That's easy for you to say. You're not the one that's lying here with a shaved head, a load of broken bones and no clue of who you're even supposed to be.'

'That's true.' Zoe seems to be choosing her words with care. 'But since you mention it, do you know what I'd do if I were where you are? Shall I tell you?'

I stay quiet as I have a feeling that she's going to tell me whether I want her to or not.

14

'I'D BE *FIGHTING* to regain my memory and my physical health,' Zoe says. 'I'd stop at *nothing* to get myself better, which is exactly what *you* should be doing.'

'But look at the state of me. How the hell am I supposed to do that?'

She takes a deep breath. 'Well, you've got me for a start. But *you've* got to do some work.'

'But how?'

'Well, firstly, you need to keep practicing *everything* I ask of you, all of which we'll run through in a few moments. All the movement and exercises.'

'But that won't catch who put me here, will it?' I lean back on my pillows and stare at the tiles on the ceiling.

'Then,' she persists, 'you need to pick the brains of *everyone* in your life about the gaps in your memory. You find out about your relationships and your feelings towards each other. You take voice recordings so you don't miss a thing, you journal,' – she gestures at the notepad I was writing the single words on before my voice returned. 'You should also start writing down any dreams you're having the *moment* you wake up, or you could even try hypnotherapy if we can get the all-clear for you to go down that road,' – Zoe checks off the items on her fingers as if she's reeling off a shopping list, – 'And just as important as everything I've already mentioned, you must scrutinise your online activity – that should be *very* telling.'

'But how can I journal when I can't even write?' I point at my notepad. 'And I can't get at my phone either – the police have it. My messages and calls are still being checked.'

'That should help you when the police come back with it. They'll hopefully have printouts of your messages and call logs.'

'I'm scared of what I'm going to find out about myself. And some of the rows I was having with people. I'm hearing dribs and drabs, but it's like everyone is wary of telling me the truth.'

'How long did the police say it would take?' Despite me throwing an obstacle in front of each of her suggestions, Zoe's tone is still airy and optimistic.

'At least a couple of weeks. But they also said that my phone's in a bit of a state after my fall, well, my, er – you see – I don't even know what to call what happened, my *accident*, my *attempted murder*, my—'

'Call it whatever fires you up enough to take action,' Zoe replies as she adjusts her ponytail. 'Anyway, staying on the subject of technology, you must get access to your emails, your social media, any files you've been working on, as much stuff as you can – as soon as you can. Get your employers on board. You must have been using a laptop. Or a tablet.'

'It's good advice, I know it is.'

'Then *act* on it.' Zoe sounds like Emma, as I remember her from when we were younger. It's probably why I feel so comfortable working with her. We'd be friends in different circumstances.

'OK, I'll ask Daniel to bring me what he can find at home.' Inwardly, I bristle at the prospect of having to ask him for help, but it's not as if I have much choice. 'Then I'll have to work out what I'm doing. I imagine a few things will have changed on phones and laptops in the last ten years.'

She laughs. 'You probably won't know TikTok, or one or two other platforms, but Facebook and Instagram are more or less as they were. And emails haven't changed.'

'So you really think I should be fighting harder?' I sit up as much as my ribs will allow.

'I *really* do. If you don't fight harder for yourself, who will?' She shrugs.

I can't deny I'm feeling more fired up since Zoe arrived this morning. My thinking has been so foggy that it hasn't even dawned on me that my online activity might yield some clues. Not just images I might have posted, but also the responses of other people. It'll be slow progress doing everything with only my left and less dominant hand, but it's not like I've got anything better to do while I'm lying in this wretched bed.

'I'd help you go through it all, Cathy, but I've got a caseload as long as my arm.' She holds out a milky and slender forearm as if to prove her point. 'But you must have others you can call on? People who can perhaps make notes while you scroll through it all?'

'There's my dad, but he's usually with his *wife*.' My voice dips as I say the word. I've always understood why Dad preferred Teresa to Mum, especially in the housebound and obese state Mum ended up in, but that doesn't mean I want to be around her every time I'm in Dad's company.

'I take it you don't like her very much?'

'On the surface, we get along OK, but I *know* she sees me as a rival for my dad's attention – especially where my stepsister's concerned.'

'What do you mean?' Zoe tilts her head to the side as she listens.

'I've always had a sense that Teresa would like me to vanish into thin air – then Dad might pretend Emma, that's my stepsister, is his daughter instead.'

A younger version of Teresa rises in my mind. The one that was always super-nice in my presence but never looked me in the eye when she was speaking to me.

'How do you get on with your stepsister?'

'Strangely, like a house on fire. We always have.'

'You've got a brother as well, haven't you?'

'Yeah.' I close my eyes. It hurts me to think of Harry after what he said. 'We used to be close, but now, I'm not so sure.'

'Families, eh?'

'Well, I don't really class my stepmum as family. Perhaps I should – maybe I'm the one who's been causing the problems.' I point at myself.

'I'll let you into a secret, shall I?' Zoe leans closer. 'I'm also not so keen on my stepmum. There's a reason they cast them as villains in fairytales.'

I can't help but laugh. I think it's the first time I've laughed since I woke up.

'Now there's a fabulous sound.' Zoe nudges my good arm. 'Right, I'd better get on with what I'm supposed to be doing with you before that ward sister comes in and tells me off.' She laughs again. 'Let me at those legs. Honestly, with what happened, it's a miracle there were no broken bones in them.'

Her words tug me back to my reality. Whoever pushed me wanted far more than broken limbs.

After some wiggling, bending and stretching of everything I've got that still works, she says, 'Right, let's get you to the edge of the bed. Lean forward, and I'll help you to get there.'

As I follow her instruction, she plucks a pillow from behind me. 'I'll hold this against your ribs while you shuffle yourself – to keep them still. That's it. Slowly, gently.'

'Don't you think this is too much, too soon?'

We both turn towards the voice at the doorway. It's Daniel, with Austyn and Matthew. I smile at them. 'Hi, boys, I won't be too long.'

'She remembers us now.' I hear one say to the other in an excited voice.

'If you wouldn't all mind hanging on there for a few more minutes, we've got a little more to do here.' Zoe ignores Daniel's negativity as I perch at the edge of the bed.

'It hurts.' I'm almost breathless with the pain in my ribs. I point at them.

'See, I told you it would be too much.'

'I'm told broken ribs can be as painful as childbirth.' Again, Zoe doesn't acknowledge Daniel's comment. 'Not that I'd know.'

Not that I know either, but I can't very well say this with the three of them standing at the door. It would have been better if Zoe had sent them completely away while she's still here. 'How long will my ribs take to heal?'

'Again, you've got off fairly lightly,' she replies. 'In that you've only fractured three of them. They usually take about six weeks to get better. I can get your painkillers increased?'

I shake my head. 'I'm on enough of that stuff as it is. I need to clear my thinking, don't I? Not to keep fogging it up.'

'That's my girl. When we're done here, I'll bring some ice packs. You're doing great, Cathy. Right, get a hold of this quad cane, and I'll keep hold of your arm as you pull yourself up.'

'Now, this is *definitely* too soon.'

As we continue to ignore the negativity emanating from the door, a sudden wave of determination washes over me. I want to let my boys see me trying to get better. I want them to know I'm working as hard as I can to get home.

I Don't Like Mondays

I'm shaking from the inside out as I stand at the frame. But it's wonderful to feel the chill of the floor beneath my bare feet.

'How do you feel?'

'It's a relief to be out of that bed.' My voice is shaky, too, but I've done it. 'And now I've come this far, I'm damn-well going to walk.'

'Just let me move a couple of these monitors and drips so I can wheel them with you.' Zoe begins gathering wires and tubes.

I continue to stand, my legs feeling stronger with every breath. It's just my ribs and light-headedness that are causing the problems.

'Go on, Mum.' One of the boys is clapping.

'Yeah, go on.'

Daniel stays quiet.

'You're going to move that cane forward, then step towards it.'

I do as Zoe says.

'Now again. And again.' It's her turn to clap her hands together. 'Excellent – we've got you walking.' She wheels everything along once more. 'That should hopefully allay any fears of nerve damage. Excuse me.' The boys and Daniel step to the side as Zoe squeezes past me and curls her head around the door. 'Sister, you need to come and see this.'

By the time the ward sister has moved from behind the nurse's station, I'm already at the door.

'Well done you.' She looks happy to be looking me in the eyes rather than down at me in my bed for a change. 'There's nothing wrong with those legs. The doctor will be delighted when I let him know.'

'OK, that's enough for now,' Zoe says. 'But I'll be back, you can count on it.'

'Not today, surely,' Daniel says. 'I think that's enough until tomorrow.'

I'm starting to believe he doesn't want me to come home, but I don't say anything in front of the boys. It will keep.

'Remember, *positivity*, Cathy. Today is only the start. And I'm sure your husband will be just as positive too.' She shoots a look in Daniel's direction as though silently daring him to be anything else.

15

'She was a tad overbearing.' Daniel rests two envelopes onto my table – probably get well cards. I'm sitting in an easy chair. Zoe said it would be good for me to have a short time out of bed.

'Actually, she's been amazing – she's really dragged me out of the doldrums.'

'You certainly seem happier than you have been for the last few days.' He gives me a strange look. 'But should you be sitting in that chair *already*?'

'They'll want me to go home.' I gesture to the door, 'Rather than hogging a bed someone else might have a greater need for.'

'Can you come home *today*, Mum?' Asks one of the boys. I'm not sure if it's Austyn or Matthew. If I'm to be completely honest, I quite like the sound of the word *Mum*.

It's as if something's shifted in me in Zoe's presence. Her advice was spot on. I'm going to do everything in my power, not only to get 'back to myself,' but to be the mum these boys deserve. It's up to *me* to ensure that whoever tried to take me away from my sons forever is caught and locked up.

'It might be a while until she comes home,' Daniel replies. The boy's face falls.

'Positivity.' Zoe's shrill voice rings out as she strides back into the room, waving an ice pack in each hand. 'It's a bit gloomy in here, and I don't just mean what's being said.' She snaps the overhead light on. 'There, that's better.' She passes the ice packs to my good side, one at a time. 'Actually, if Cathy carries on like this, she'll be good to go within the next two or three days.'

'But what about her memory loss?'

'That doesn't mean she can't be at home, recuperating. It's a scientific fact that patients recover far more quickly at home than they do in a hospital bed. Or chair.' She smiles.

'Thanks.' I press one of the ice packs to my ribs through my pyjamas, flinching not only with the pain, but also with the sudden chill against my body. 'And thanks for everything you said. You've no idea how much you've helped.'

'It's all part of the service. Anyway.' She nods towards the ice. 'Keep those held to your ribs for about five minutes, and they should start to feel less sore.' She turns to Daniel. 'And seriously, Mr Mason. I can't emphasise the importance of remaining upbeat around Cathy. She's been through a terrible ordeal, which is going to take some serious overcoming. If you want her home as fast as possible, she needs all your support.'

'We want her home right now, don't we, Matthew?' The oldest of the boys perches on the edge of my bed. At least, who is who has now been confirmed.

I smile at him. 'I'm looking forward to being back home too.' I've no idea what 'home' is like, or where it even is, but since spending time with Zoe, I'm suddenly looking forward to discovering. The only fly in the ointment is Daniel. What living with *him* will look like, remains to be seen.

'We'll give you another ten minutes in the chair, Cathy, then one of us will be in to help you back into bed. Are you still comfortable?'

I nestle back into the cushion at the small of my back. 'Yes, I'm fine.'

'Fabulous – right, I need to get to my next patient.'

'Do you remember us now, Mum?' Matthew's face is filled with hope. They're lovely boys, and no matter what I might have been through, they need me to be present and attentive. Besides, from the vibes and occasional comments I'm picking up, there's a good chance that I've put Austyn and Matthew through more than enough over the years. I've probably got a lot of making up to do with them. 'And is your hair going to grow?' He points at my head.

'I hope so.' I force a laugh. I can't imagine either of them would want me at their school gates yet, not the way I'm looking.

'I've brought you some chocolate.' Austyn reaches into a carrier bag at Daniel's feet and places a box of Maltesers on the table.

'And I've drawn you a picture.' Matthew also delves into the bag and rests a painting on the top of the Maltesers. 'It's me, you, Austyn and Dad outside our house. I drew it at school.'

'What's that in my hand?' It's interesting how there's a gap between where he's positioned me in relation to the three of *them*. To work that one out doesn't take a psychologist.

'It's your suitcase.' He wrinkles his freckled nose, and his voice falls. 'For when you go to London.'

My chest tightens as tears pool in my eyes. *Is this really how he sees me?*

'Will you still have to go to London *now*?' Austyn's face bears a similar expression of hope to how Matthew's did when they first arrived. Now that I'm giving them my full attention, I can see they *do* look like each other; in fact, both of them remind me of Harry when he was a child. I wish my brother would come back in to see me. If the two of us could be left alone to talk, I'm sure we could sort out whatever it is I've done to upset him. People always say that Harry and I are alike, so I guess the boys *must* look like me too. Hopefully, I'll be able to see it soon.

'We don't know about that yet.' Daniel hitches his trousers and lowers himself into the chair at the other side of my bed. 'Your mum's got a lot of getting better to do.'

'I'd have thought you'd have wanted me back to my job as soon as possible.' I laugh for the second time today, and it feels good. I'm fighting back. I've gone from despair to determination. 'To help your book get published faster, I mean.'

'Like I mentioned already, one of your colleagues is handling it all – there's nothing you'd be able to do.' His gaze is fixed on the floor as he replies. 'You probably won't remember when she called in here – you were out of it.'

'*Samantha,* you mean? I heard you and Harry talking about her.'

Daniel looks even more uncomfortable as he shuffles in his seat.

'So I asked Emma if I'd ever mentioned her.'

'And?' He gives me his raised eyebrow look, the one I've learned means that he's really interested in whatever's about to be said.

'All she could tell me is that Samantha's on a par with me as a publishing associate, and a couple of years younger. We've been going after the same promotion. I didn't know what she was getting at when she mentioned some rivalry. Have I ever talked to *you* about it?'

'Bits and pieces.' A flush crosses Daniel's face, so I continue watching him. Might Samantha and I be rivals over *more* than she and I wanting the same promotion? Not that I care. She can take *Daniel* off my hands if she wants him, but *not* the boys.

Thankfully, something's stirred in me towards them – probably because I *know* since seeing those photo albums that Austyn and Matthew *are* my sons. I carried them, I nurtured them, and they're a part of me. But as far as Daniel goes, I don't feel a thing towards him and can't imagine ever doing so. He seems to have closed up on the subject of Samantha. But I haven't. However, it will keep.

'I need you to do me a favour.' I tell Daniel as the boys tuck into the Maltesers.

'What?'

'Can you bring any tablets and laptops I have at home, along with any passwords? I'd use my phone, but obviously it's with the police.'

'I don't have access to your passwords.' His face darkens. 'You've always kept them to yourself – why, anyway? What's all this about?'

'Zoe reckons looking at my messages and social media will help my memory.'

'I might have known *Zoe* would be behind this.'

'Like I said before, she's really helped me.'

'You'd have had your laptop with you that morning – you were as surgically attached to it as you were to your phone.' A flicker of something I can't put my finger on crosses his face.

'So I'll need to ask the police about it – is that what you're saying?'

'I would have thought so.' Daniel looks down at the floor as though he's considering what to say next. Then he raises his eyes back to meet mine. 'Surely by going on social media, all you'll come across is a ream of meaningless words, posted by people you don't even remember.'

'It can't do any harm to try.' I can't believe he's being so negative. 'I'm bound to still be friends with people I was friends with from ten years ago, people who I *will* remember.'

'I wouldn't count on it,' he mutters.

'What's that supposed to mean?'

'Nothing, love. I'm sorry.' He pulls an apologetic face.

'Do you want some, Mum?' Austyn thrusts the box of Maltesers in front of me, so I take one.

'I just honestly think you're trying to rush things, Cathy,' Daniel says. 'You're supposed to be resting.'

'Says who? You've just seen how Zoe's got me walking again, and *she's* the medical professional. Believe me, over the next couple of days, I'll be ready to be discharged.' I pop the Malteser into my mouth.

As the wonderful taste of chocolate dissolves onto my tongue, Daniel stares at me as if he can't understand the change I've undergone. I can hardly believe it myself. Until half an hour ago, I was a weeping, wallowing mess, but now I'm not going to stop until I've helped to nail the bastard who did this to me. And if I die trying, then so be it.

'What's the company called that I work for again?'

He gives me a funny look. 'Bookish in London. Why do you ask?'

'I'm going to get in touch. They can tell me what I've been working on, what contacts I have, and hopefully other stuff about myself that I'm unable to recall.'

He frowns. 'I think you're going too fast.'

'I don't care what you think. Have you got your phone?'

Daniel taps his pocket. 'No, I must have left it in the car.'

Judging by the look on his face, he's probably lying, and somehow, I'll get to the bottom of why. He's gone really cagey all of a sudden – it seems to be since I've started to turn a corner in my recovery. Perhaps he prefers me helpless and out of action in a hospital bed. Whatever it is, I'm struggling to put my finger on it.

'Will you be taking us to school when you come home, Mum?'

'Yeah, you never take us,' adds Matthew through a mouthful of Maltesers.

'Don't talk with your mouth full,' I tell him, realising with a stab of misery, how much like my own mother I sound.

Have I been so career-focused that I've completely missed my children growing from babies into the lovely boys they've become? Just because I hadn't got around to having children with Brad never meant I didn't want them. But I'd always imagined myself as a hands-on sort of a mum, one that would have fun with my children. I'd do everything my mum wasn't able to do with me.

'You work away through the week.' Daniel's tone is snappy - possibly in response to what must be a downcast expression on my face as I'm considering what the boys have just said. 'What do you expect them to say?' I don't know what's got into him today. He's far more abrasive than he's been so far. I'm not the only person to have experienced a shift.

'No matter what happens, things are going to change.' I look from Austyn to Matthew, my new biggest reasons for getting to the truth. Instead of clearing off down to London and leaving them with their dad all the time, I'm going to be around. If my job's as demanding as it sounds like it could be, I bet I've had no energy for them at the weekends, either. The poor kids – I'll have to sort something out.

'You risk setting yourself back if you're not careful.'

'How do you mean, *if I'm not careful?*' I stare at the stranger who I still can't reconcile as my husband.

'I mean if you go rushing headlong into social media, ringing your work and all that. You've had major head trauma, and we still don't know if you've wiped your memory out completely. Honestly, Cathy, you need to give yourself time to recover. At best, you'll only be able to decipher whatever you find in tiny snippets. And at worst—'

'So you're my psychologist now, are you?' I don't mean to

snap back at Daniel, especially in front of the children, but I can't help it. He probably holds the largest pieces of the puzzle in helping me put back together the person I was, and whatever led up to me being on that train track, and I need his help, not *this*.

I *really* need his help.

16

'YEAH, I wasn't surprised when I heard she'd missed the train this morning.' The voice echoes from the kitchen, shrill above the hiss of the boiling kettle. 'I bumped into her on Saturday night on my way back from the theatre.' Her voice is light and airy, almost suggesting we might be friends. 'I probably shouldn't be telling you this, but you've got a right to know about her being so drunk.'

'What's that got to do with her catching a train this morning?' The other voice sounds puzzled.

'Well, she's always joking how it takes several days to get over a drinking binge – anyway, I just hope she's not in too much of a state.' Cups are clattering about as they speak. 'It seems to be happening often from what I can gather. I was worried when I didn't see her at the station this morning.'

'I'm sure she'll be fine.'

'I think the pressure of needing this promotion might be getting to her.' She's not letting up. 'Her marriage is apparently in trouble so she might be facing single parenthood in the foreseeable future.'

'Really? I haven't heard.' The fridge door bangs. 'Should we even be considering signing him up with our company if they're going to separate? It could all get very awkward.'

'I'll make sure it doesn't. Don't worry.'

'Gosh, poor Cathy – I had no idea.'

'She'll be asking for flexible working, I should imagine. She'll have to be at home more with her kids.'

'Do you know all this for a fact?' There's a stirring sound, but not as much as my colleague seems to be stirring things behind my back. I should get myself in there, but I need to hear what else she has to impart.

'I don't know if I should say anything about the other stuff – I don't want to get Cathy into trouble.'

'Well, this is in confidence – strictly between me and you. If we can do anything to help her, we should be doing it.'

'Breakfast time.' A woman's voice wakes me with a jolt. She's clad in a stripy uniform and apron as she pushes her jangling trolley into my room.

It's on the tip of my tongue to ask for just a slice of toast, but I'm suddenly reminded of the promise I made to myself. I'm going to fight, and I'm going to get better. And whatever *that* was, whatever I was dreaming about, obviously it's my brain trying to make some sense. I'm not even sure who the people I was dreaming about were. Zoe was right. I need to start writing things down the moment I wake, but it's difficult with only my left hand.

'Well?' The woman has an impatient air.

'I'll have two slices of toast, please.' I point to the rack. 'And an orange, and also some of that muesli, please.'

'Jam? Marmalade? Butter? Tea? Coffee?' She's clearly bored with repeating the same spiel to patient after patient. I feel sorry for her. I don't think I could do her job. Or my job. Or any job, for that matter. The dream I just had was taking place in the workplace. By someone out to get me, but that's as much as I can recall.

I Don't Like Mondays

As the woman sorts out my breakfast, I scrunch my eyes together, trying to bring the dream back to mind. No, it's no good; it's gone. I glance around for the writing pad. I'll make sure it's right beside me next time I fall asleep.

I pluck a packet of butter from the bowl she offers and point at the teapot. 'Tea, please, no sugar. Also, can you tell me what day it is? And the date?' Not that it's going to make much difference. It's not as if these dreams I keep getting are time-stamped.

'It's Monday 17th March, it's five past nine and you're at the Leeds General Infirmary, Ward Twenty One.'

So that's more than I asked for, but I smile sweetly as she slops the stewed tea into my cup. The colour of it alone is enough for me to get my act together as fast as possible and get myself home. If I had a phone, I'd be asking Emma to bring me a decent brew when she arrives at visiting time.

∼

'Good morning, Cathy.' Zoe appears at my door with the quad cane. 'You're certainly looking much brighter this morning, which is wonderful.'

'It's all down to *you*.' I smile. 'Although I didn't get a lot of sleep last night for overthinking.'

'Sleep's important for your recovery.' She brings the cane closer. 'So try and limit your thinking to during the day. Also, as I said, you need to keep talking to your visitors. That's probably better than turning everything over and over in your mind. You'll be less confused if you can just get it out – talking will help you process things.'

'I'm hoping my Dad will come in today so we can get the ball rolling with a psychologist appointment.'

'While you're still here,' – Zoe waves her arm around the room that's become my place of confinement, – 'you can always make use of me while we're doing your physio – I might not have all the answers, but I've got a sympathetic ear.' She sits at the side of me, her hand still resting on the cane. 'Blimey, what on earth's that?' She peers into my cup.

'Tea, supposedly.' I laugh. 'Which is why the cup's still full.'

'I'll see if I can find you a decent cuppa after we've had you out of bed.' She pulls a face.

'That would be great.'

'Oh, I see they've taken you off the catheter.'

'Yeah, they've been wheeling me to the loo.'

'Well, we'll have you walking to it after today, so I'll leave this with you.' She raises the cane and taps it back to the floor.

'I'm determined to.'

'That's the spirit.'

'Also, I don't know if I've been dreaming, or if things are starting to come back.'

'Really?' She presses the pillow to my ribs in the same way she did yesterday.

'And I've been told a few things too – but they're not very good.'

'Such as?'

'Emma's told me I was at loggerheads with people, Daniel's told me that *I shouldn't count* on still having friends from ten years ago, whatever *that's* supposed to mean, and even my brother seems really off with me for some reason. He's only visited *once* since I woke up.'

'What about the dreams? Shuffle yourself forward – just like you did yesterday.'

'I can't remember much about them, but I know they haven't been pleasant. I'm waking agitated and depressed.' I wince as the pain in my ribs rears its ugly head again.

'Have the police been back?' She moves the cane so it's within my reach.

'They're supposed to be coming today,' I reply. 'They

wanted to come on Friday, but Sister Layton asked them to give me over the weekend to recover some more.'

'You've certainly made a ton of progress.' She pats the top of my hand. 'And hopefully, they've been hard at work trying to catch whoever did this.'

'They're supposed to be going through the CCTV and speaking to more witnesses.' I reach for the handle of the cane. 'But I'm just one in a long line of cases.'

'That's it, up you come.' She holds out her arms like a mother might do with a newly walking toddler. 'What do you mean?'

'They're not going to be working night and day just on what happened to *me*.' I move the cane forward and step to it. 'They've got other crimes to solve.'

'Wow, go you. You're doing brilliantly.' Zoe claps her hands as I keep going forward. 'It sounds like you need to get Emma to elaborate on exactly *who* you might have wronged, in what way, and how they retaliated. She obviously knows you well enough to be able to shed some light on things.'

'There's also Samantha, the rival I've got at work for the same promotion.' I pause and lean onto the cane. 'I can't remember her, but there are clearly problems. Then my ex-husband's fiancée might have an axe to grind.'

'It must be tough, Cathy,' Zoe says. 'But you're doing—' She stops, and we look at each other as the sound of a sudden commotion echoes from the corridor.

'I mean it. Let me in there.' A woman's high-pitched voice reverberates through the ward.

Zoe grabs one of the light plastic chairs and tucks it behind me. 'Sit down for a moment, Cathy. I'm not sure what's happening.'

'You can't go in there.' There's a scuffling noise, sounding like someone's being held from further movement. 'Seriously, you have to leave.'

Another voice is on a radio, asking for security to attend Ward Twenty One as a matter of urgency.

'It's all *her* fault, and she's going to pay.' The woman's screeching like a maniac.

'I'll be back in a minute.' Zoe rushes to the door. 'Let me see what's happening.'

'She's taken everything from me. *Everything.*' Is the woman referring to *me*? They can't be. I haven't *taken* anything from anyone, as far as I know. Have I?

'If you could just go back out into the main corridor, I'll get someone to speak to you.'

'I only want to speak to *her*.'

Zoe suddenly appears at my door again and closes it behind her.

'What the hell's going on out there?'

She looks flustered. 'It's a relative with a grievance, that's all. It's nothing for you to worry about.'

'Well, *she's* got plenty to worry about by the sounds of it. This hasn't got anything to do with *me*, has it?'

'No, of course not – why would it?' Zoe shakes her head, but for the first time since she's started working with me, she seems insincere.

'Why have you closed the door?' I shuffle against the hard plastic of my chair. 'Is it so I don't hear any more of what she's saying?'

'All the other patients' doors are being closed.' She remains with her back to it. 'Just until security arrives. They'll be here any minute.'

'You *must* know what's wrong?'

'I'm sorry – I really don't.' She pushes herself off the door and comes further into the room. 'But one of my colleagues will help her. Someone will take her off the ward and calm her down.'

17

Visiting is from one until eight o'clock, so I'm pleased when at one o'clock on the dot, Emma bursts into my room.

'Wow, you're eating.' She points at my plate.

'The only thing is that chewing hurts my stitches.' I put the segment of orange I was about to eat back on the plate and point at my head.

'You could always eat soup.'

'I wouldn't fancy having to use a spoon with only my left hand. I'd have it all over the place. Anyway, how are *you*?' I tap my belly. 'One thing I haven't forgotten is my job-to-be as an auntie.'

'I'm glad to hear it.'

'Come and sit down.' I point at the easy chair I've been periodically sitting in. It's comfier than the plastic things meant for visitors. 'Are you going to find out if it's a boy or a girl?'

'That doesn't happen until the twenty-week scan. Besides, Joel doesn't want to know. Period.' Something in her voice suggests that Emma's husband *really* doesn't want to know.

'What do you mean?'

'Oh, nothing.' She sighs.

'Come on, out with it.'

'It's just that he's never at home.' Pain flickers in her gaze. 'I keep worrying that I'll end up as a single parent. It's keeping me awake, if I'm honest.'

'You'll always have me to help you.'

'I've brought you some magazines.' She lays them on the table, evidently not wanting to discuss her marital problems. 'I don't know if you're up to reading yet, but they'll help to pass the time.' She slides her coat off and hangs it on the back of the chair. 'I imagine the days are pretty long in here now you're on the mend.'

'I'll give them a go later – thanks.'

She gives me a curious look. 'You seem a lot brighter today.'

'I'm working on it.'

'I've been concerned about you, if the truth be known,' she says.

'It's all been a hell of a lot to process. Not being able to remember things has been seriously dragging me down. Anyway, enough of that – thanks for coming in. I'd have gone stir crazy on my own all afternoon.'

'You don't have to thank me.'

'I expect you've got better things you could be doing with a Monday afternoon.' I gesture at the sunny day beyond the window.

'It's still freezing out there – it's far warmer in here. And wow again – you even know what day it is.'

'I asked someone.'

'Well, that's cheating.' She grins.

'I meant what I said before – I *am* grateful. You've been my most consistent visitor.'

'Your dad's coming in later this afternoon,' she says. 'When they finish up at school.'

'So he'll be with your mum?' It's an effort to keep my voice light. I'm not sure what I was like before all this happened, but

I'm trying not to say anything against my stepmother in front of Emma. After all, Teresa's her mum.

'I'm not sure. Maybe.'

It's a stupid question, as Teresa rarely lets my dad out of her sight. At least when I'm back at home, I'll have more control over who visits. 'Have you got your phone?'

'Of course. I'm never far from my phone.' She pats her handbag. 'Why?'

'It's just that Daniel reckons *both* my phone and computer were with me – you know – on the day I—' My voice trails off. 'He also says that he knows none of my passwords to get into anything.'

'And you want to try on my phone?' Emma looks puzzled. 'Is that what you mean? Surely that'll only work if you haven't set up two-factor authentification to get into your accounts.'

'The other problem is that I haven't a clue what any passwords might be.'

'We could try the different combinations of things like your birthday or the kids' birthdays.'

'I don't even know them.' I stare at the drawing Matthew left for me yesterday. Fancy not even knowing my own children's dates of birth. It's shameful.

'I do.'

'I keep forgetting you're their auntie.' I smile. 'Well, step-auntie.'

'Let me check all this with your doctor first.' She signals toward the door with a jerk of her head. 'You might not be up to all that social media stuff yet.'

'Don't you start, Emma.' I roll my eyes. 'I've had enough of Daniel trying to hold me back.'

'I'm sure he's only trying to protect you.'

'I don't *need* protecting. Anyway, looking at messages was my physio's suggestion, so I'm sure it will be alright.'

'If you say so. I'd still like to make sure, though. You're doing so well, and I don't want to set you back.'

'How can it? Besides, I've promised the boys I'm going to get better. Not only that, I've also promised myself I'm going to be the mum it sounds like they've never known.'

'Well, this is a turn up for the books. A few days ago, you were asking me to tell them they'd got the wrong room.' Though she smiles, she still looks concerned.

'It was Daniel I didn't want around.' I watch for her reaction and sense she's trying to keep her thoughts in check. Over what, I'm not sure. 'Look, I might not remember the boys or recall being their mother, but I *know* I love them.' I smile. 'They're mine – I can tell they are.'

'Well, that's all well and good, but—'

'And guess what? Zoe's had me walking.' I'm not going to allow Emma, Daniel or anyone else to dampen what little optimism I have. 'Finally, I'm managing to get myself to the loo and back. And they're sitting me in the chair several times a day.'

'That's so quick. I thought it would be a while longer before they'd be getting you out of bed.'

'But why? It's not as if I broke my legs. The only adverse effect of walking is that it crucifies my ribs. Oh, and it also makes me feel lightheaded.' My head swoons at the recollection.

'So there's no nerve damage to your spine?'

'Nope.' I smile. 'I know how lucky I've been. I mean, what are the odds of being hit by a train, no matter how slow it's going, and living to tell the tale.'

'I guess so.'

'Apart from the effects of the painkillers, I'm feeling much better. I'm going to ask for my dose to be lowered.'

'Is that wise?'

'Absolutely.'

'Perhaps you should be eating proper meals instead of just

an orange. You need to build yourself up – that's been your trouble for a long time.'

I point to the drip to my left. 'They've been decreasing that and have told me to get as much food as I can manage down me whenever the meal trolley comes. Honestly, Emma, I'm fighting. And somehow, I'll win.'

'Well you're certainly sounding a damn sight better than the last time I spoke to you. Depressed doesn't even begin to cover it.'

'I'm sorry. I must have been hard work. What was it Zoe, my physio called me?' I pause for a moment. 'Oh yes, a Debbie Downer. That's not how I want to be known.'

'When are the police coming back?'

'Today, supposedly.' I glance at the clock. I'm sick of watching its hands crawl around and around, and I can't wait until I don't have to look at it or listen to the thing morbidly ticking its way through each minute and hour of the night. 'At least, that's what they told the ward staff.'

'Daniel said something about them waiting until you were stronger before speaking to you again. But you seem stronger to me, so you might as well get it over with.'

'There's nothing more I can tell the police, but they'll hopefully have more they want to tell me.'

Emma stays ominously quiet.

'If you know something, you need to tell me – please, Emma.'

She shakes her head. 'I don't know a thing – I'm sorry.'

'I just bloody hope they've gone through that CCTV with a fine tooth comb.'

'They will have done.' She unravels her plait, allowing her hair to fall around her shoulders.

'The thought of the person who did this to me still being out there is horrendous. I'm trying my hardest to stay upbeat, but the fact that they haven't been caught is like a huge black cloud.'

'I bet it is.' She reaches over and rubs the top of my hand.

'And it's not the only thing that's a black cloud. Did you speak to Brad like you promised?'

I'm desperate to see my ex-husband. I want to watch his reaction at seeing me. If there's nothing there from him, at least I can accept that we were right to split up and that it's all truly over.

Emma looks uncomfortable.

'Did you even *ask* him about visiting?'

'Look, I'm really sorry, Cathy, but—?'

'You said he still works for Joel's company?'

'Well yes, but the thing is—'

'So you should have been able to get hold of him?'

I've seen that look on Emma's face before. It was there when we were in our twenties, and one of my exes had made a pass at her. She was mortified, even if it wasn't *her* fault. 'I'm sorry, but no, I haven't seen him.'

'Have you even *tried*?'

I must look crushed as her tone changes. 'Look, Cathy, I think you should be just focusing on yourself for now.'

'If Brad only knew I might have died that day, and if he knew *someone* had done it to me on purpose, he'd be *straight* in here to see me. He loved me once. Surely–'

'I know it's hard, but it's been nine years since you parted company, Cathy.' Her forehead creases into a frown.

'Tell me why we split – it's the only way I'll believe we did.' The faces of my sons swim into my mind. I wish I'd had them with Brad instead of with Daniel.

'Me and you lost touch for a few months around that time.' She gestures from herself and then to me. 'So I don't know what happened – you never confided in me about what was going on with you.'

Judging by the look on her face, I'm certain she knows more than she's letting on, but I understand she's probably trying to protect me until I've improved more.

'*Please* get in touch with him for me, Emma?' My gaze doesn't leave her face. 'Tell him I only want ten minutes. I was his wife once – surely he can spare me ten minutes.'

'I don't see why you need to speak to him so badly,' she replies. 'Or is there something you're not telling me?'

'Like *what*? I barely remember who I even am, so what on earth would I have to tell you?'

'Look.' Emma takes a deep breath and leans towards me. 'I'm going to be honest about how you were with Brad – before, you know...' She looks even more uncomfortable.

'Before someone tried to murder me,' I finish her sentence. 'Well, I'll thank you for that – that's all I need, just for you to be honest.'

'You were almost, for want of a better word – look I'm just going to come out and say it.' She's colouring up. 'You were almost *stalking* him, Cathy.'

'Brad?' The way I screech his name hurts my head. '*Stalking* him? Give over.'

'It was after you'd heard he'd got engaged – you were completely psycho. Ultimately, you hadn't wanted him, but you hadn't wanted anyone else to have him either. Honestly, it was like something from Oprah Winfrey.'

'That's not true – I *did* want him, and I would *never* have *stalked* him.' I raise my hand to my shaved head. 'Not Brad – not *anyone,* for that matter. I'm not like that.'

'Unfortunately, you just can't say what you were like.' Emma's voice has fallen and is more gentle again. 'Look, I'm trying to be truthful. You need to focus on your current husband, not your ex – he's gone.' Her face is as downcast as her voice. 'He's not yours anymore.'

I lean back against my pillows. Dad will know what

happened to break up my first marriage. And what, if anything, might have happened since. He'll tell me the truth.

Or Harry, perhaps. He and Brad always got on like a house on fire. A little too well at times when they started drinking. Surely he'll tell me if he knows something. I'll get a message through Dad to him. We can also air whatever problem we had before all this happened.

'Do you want to know what I think?'

Probably not, but I wait to hear what my stepsister has to say next.

'I think that until you're fully better, you should stay clear of things like texts and social media.' Her voice is sharper than her face, which, thankfully, is etched with sympathy.

I'm going to get no further with Emma. So, getting my hands on a phone and some more answers now rests on the shoulders of Dad and Harry.

One thing I do know is that there's *no way* I'm going to let things lie.

18

'Yoo-hoo.' Teresa sticks her head into my room. For a moment, she appears to be alone, so I'm relieved when Dad strides up behind her. I can't imagine Teresa and I could sustain much of a conversation. 'Room for two?'

If it wasn't for the Catholic school where Dad's a headteacher and Teresa's the school secretary, perhaps they'd never have met. But if it hadn't been her, it would have been another woman. Mum once said Dad only stayed with us for so long because he'd have been hauled up in front of the school's board of governors and the diocese for his 'indiscretions.' He'd have wrecked his reputation, hence his career, if word had got out of their affair. Particularly as the state Mum was in was common knowledge.

'Come in,' I tell her. Not that she would usually wait for an invitation.

'Emma's been telling us how you're getting on. Pretty well, eh?'

'I'm just getting bored.'

'Sorry we haven't been in for a day or two, love.' Dad's face twists into an apology. 'Teresa's been full of cold.'

'Hence why I'm not coming too close.' She tugs a chair back against the wall. 'I'll keep my germs at this side of the room.'

'Couldn't you have come in on your own, Dad?'

What's Dad's problem? Is Teresa controlling him, or is he just too wrapped up with her to do anything or go anywhere by himself? Surely, they both know that the last place Teresa should be taking her germs is into a hospital.

'We're here now, aren't we?' He gives me a look which seems to say, *Button it.*

'We had to wait for your dad to finish up at school,' Teresa goes on. 'I've been off work today.'

'But you must be feeling better now, yeah?' I bloody hope she is. The last thing I want is a stinking cold. Not on top of everything else.

'Much better – thanks for asking.' She smiles across the room.

'Have you got your phone with you, Dad?'

He taps his shirt pocket. 'Yes – why?'

'I want to ring the publishing company. See if they can shed any light on things.'

'O-K-?' He sounds hesitant. 'What sort of light?'

'Well, I was in London every Monday to Friday,' I reply. 'They probably know me better than my own family.'

'That, I very much doubt.' He smiles.

'Well, I want to try. Can you search for their number?'

Teresa already has her phone out of her bag. 'What's the name of the company?'

'Bookish in London,' Dad replies.

She types it into her phone. 'Do you want it now?'

'Yes, please.' I turn to Dad. 'Can I borrow your phone?'

'Of course you can. Read it out to me, Tee.'

I hate it when he calls her Tee – his pet name for her. Somehow, it's always made me feel lonely and left out. This is probably ridiculous when I'm supposedly forty years of age and a mother of two sons.

He types the number in and passes me his phone. 'I take it you want to ring them straightaway?'

'I might as well. But you speak to them first, Dad.' Suddenly, I feel a crisis of confidence enveloping me. 'Would you mind getting whoever my boss is on the phone? I don't even know his or her name.' I feel certain it's a woman, but the more I try to remember, the more it evades me.

'Will do.' He takes the phone back and raises it to his ear. 'Ah, yes, hello. My name's Bob Wheeler, I'm Cathy Mason's dad – she works for your company.'

I can hear a woman's voice at the other end, but can't make out what she's saying.

'Yes, she's currently off work following an accident, and I was wondering if we could speak to Cathy's line manager. I've got Cathy with me now.'

She says something else.

'That's right – Cathy Mason. She's an Associate Publisher.' He moves the phone away from his ear. 'Is that right?' He mouths the words.

I shrug. 'Apparently.'

'OK, thanks for your help.' He thrusts the phone in my direction. 'She's putting us through. Your manager's name is Bonnie.'

'Right – thanks.' I take the phone from him.

I hold it to my ear, trying to catch my breath as some irritating piped music plays. If I was still plugged into my heart monitor, I'm certain it would be shooting up to its maximum reading. 'Hello?'

'Bonnie speaking – Cathy – it's so good to hear your voice. We've all been so worried!'

'Erm, thanks.' I won't tell her that I haven't actually got a clue who she is. 'I appreciate that.'

'How are you doing?'

'Well, I'm still in hospital, but I'm improving faster than they thought I might. Physically, anyway.'

'We certainly didn't expect to hear from you just yet. When Samantha dropped in, she said— Well, it doesn't matter, how can I help?'

'I'm ringing to ask a favour.'

'Of course – anything we can do.'

'You must have heard I've been struggling with amnesia after my, erm, fall.'

'Yes, and we've all been thinking of you.'

'And I've been wondering if there's any of my tech at work that I might be able to get access to.'

'Tech? What do you mean?'

'A work laptop, for example? Or my phone? Anything that will jog my memory. If I could look at my emails and that sort of thing, it might help me to remember who I was and what I was doing before what happened.'

She's so quiet for a moment that I wonder if she's still on the line.

'Hello?'

'Didn't your husband mention the conversation he's had about you?'

'Daniel? No. What about?'

'Well, he discussed the extent of your injuries and the impact they've had.'

'It's my memory mainly – which is why I'm asking for your help. Hang on, what else did he say?'

'He told, well, he told Samantha, that it's unlikely you'll be returning to work. He told her that even if you do, it could be a while. She said she'd have to let me know, as your line manager. We're a business after all, and we need to keep things running smoothly.'

'Hang on – what are you trying to tell me?' My voice is

snappy, but I don't care. It sounds like I'm being fired. I agree it's unlikely I'd be returning, but that's supposed to be *my* choice, not *hers*. And it's certainly isn't *Daniel's*.

How *dare* he go talking to my colleagues without consulting me? Dad and Teresa are both frowning, clearly itching to know what Bonnie just said.

'Obviously, we're sorry to lose you, Cathy, but we understand that your health and your family has to take priority.'

Her words hit me like a thunderclap. 'Wait – is that it? Is that what you're telling me? So I suppose you've given the job I was going for to Samantha?'

'We interviewed for the position at the end of last week,' her voice is hesitant, 'just like we'd planned. Samantha was the best candidate on the day.'

'Better than me?'

'Honestly Cathy, you were a serious contender for the position. If what happened to you *hadn't* have happened, we'd have had a very difficult choice between the two of you.'

'Have you filled *my* job too?' I've tried to be positive over the last day or two, but it's all been squashed. The deep, dark void in my centre is widening. Not going back to work is a decision which should have been mine and mine alone. Wait until I see Daniel.

'Not yet, but, Cathy – it doesn't sound as if you'd be able to perform your job to your full ability anyway.'

'Who says? Who even knows? My memory could completely return at any time.'

'Why don't you focus on getting yourself better? We're paying you for the next three months, and you've also accrued a decent amount of holiday pay.'

'It's not the money I'm bothered about, it's—'

'All I can say is if and when you're ready, if you're interested in working for Bookish again, we could maybe look at whether we could create a position where you could be doing a little editing, maybe working from home in the first instance.'

A little editing from home. Probably at a fraction of what I was earning before. 'Was it editing I've been doing?'

'Amongst other things, yes. Look, we'd have kept your job open a little longer, but without a timescale, we just can't.'

I wipe a tear that's slipped down my cheek. Dad and Teresa exchange glances. 'Are you OK?' Dad mouths.

'I'm sorry, Cathy, really I am, but on behalf of Bookish, I'd like to thank you for all you've done and to say—'

'Hang on. Before you go, what can you tell me about who I was before all this?'

'You mean before your accident?' She sounds puzzled. 'In what way?'

'In every way.'

'I don't understand. I'm not sure what you want to know.'

'Was I good at my job, for example? Did I have many friends at work? What did I do with my lunchtimes – with my evenings when I was in London? *What do you know about me?*'

19

'You were great at your job.' The voice of my now former line manager relaxes as though she's relieved to have landed on safer ground. 'And yes, you did have friends.'

'But not Samantha?'

She doesn't reply. Very telling.

'I want to know about Samantha. Her name's cropping up too often for me not to ask.'

'In what respect?'

'I want to know about these *differences*.'

She hesitates. 'Clearly, I must adhere to the boundaries of confidentiality here, but yes – you *did* have some differences. However, you both remained professional in your dealings at work.'

'What sort of dealings?'

'Obviously, you were going after the same promotion, but there were one or two other rivalries I was never able to put my finger on. However, on the whole, you both kept things amicable. If anything, Samantha was sometimes concerned about you.'

'What do you mean, *concerned*?'

'There was nothing on record – just a couple of things she dropped into conversation.'

'If someone's been saying things about me at my place of work, surely I've got the right to be made aware.'

'Right, OK, but I'm only going to tell you all this in case it might help.'

'Go on.'

Dad and Teresa are waiting with bated breath. I should have put this call on speakerphone to save me from repeating it all.

'Samantha mentioned your drinking a time or two – she told me it had reached problematic levels. Plus the marital troubles she said you were having.'

'She's right about the marriage but *not* the drinking – no way. However, if we weren't even friends, how would Samantha have known any of this? She sounds like the last person I'd confide in.'

'I really can't get into this any further, Cathy – I'm sorry. But like I mentioned, our door is always open, and I hope you get better very soon.' She's speaking fast as if she can't wait to get me off the phone. 'I'll have to go – I've got another call coming through, but you take care. I'll see that your money's paid into your account over the next few days.'

'OK, but just—' I lower the phone from my ear. She's already gone.

'Well, that was an eye opener.' I shake my head as I pass the phone back to Dad. 'It seems that because of Daniel thinking he's in charge of me, I'm now out of a job.'

'They're a business, Cathy,' Dad says. 'No business would keep your job open indefinitely.'

'That bloody work colleague of mine has a lot to answer for, too.'

'Daniel's probably just told them how it is.' Teresa pipes up from the other side of the room.

'What's that supposed to mean?'

'That there's no guarantee your memory will come back, or if it does, when that will be.'

'Yes, I'm well aware of that, Teresa. Thanks for your optimism.'

'I know it must be tough,' Dad says, 'but that job did take over your life. At least you'll be able to spend lots of time with the boys when you're discharged.'

'What about this drinking problem she mentioned? While I've been here, I haven't so much as thought about drink.'

'If you had a problem.' Dad looks puzzled. 'You've kept it well hidden.'

'I honestly don't know what to think. I don't even know who's telling me the truth.'

Perhaps, as Zoe suggested, social media should be my next port of call. If I *have* a drinking problem, it could be more evident there.

'Are we still friends on Facebook, Dad?'

'Unless you've fallen out with me.' He grins.

'Would you mind me having a look at my page through your account?' I nod towards the phone in his hand.

'Your phone is still with the police, I take it?'

'Yeah, but even when they're done with it, I'll still need to get a new one. I've been told it's well beyond repair.'

'We can sort that for you, can't we Tee?'

She nods from the corner.

'Or is Daniel already on with it?'

'Chance would be a fine thing,' I snort. 'When I mentioned I needed one, his reply was *I should be resting*. Like I'm made out of glass.'

'He's got a point, Cathy.' Dad's quiet brown eyes, which my brother and I inherited, are filled with concern. 'You really *should* be resting. You're doing quite enough work already with the physio from what Daniel's told us.'

'Please, Dad – I'm well aware of what I can and can't cope with.'

'Alright, alright.' He holds the palms of his hands towards me in mock surrender.

'So *can* I have a look at your Facebook page, Dad? Please?'

'Will you be able to see much?'

'If I can get onto *your* profile, I'll at least be able to see my photos and posts. Oh, and do you have any texts from me?'

He presses on his screen. 'I generally wipe them every month or so, but here you go, you can fill your boots with what's there.' He passes me his phone. 'I've left the message screen open for you.'

I look from Dad to Teresa. 'If you'd just excuse me for a moment.' They don't say a word in reply but just sit, watching. I can almost read what must be going through their heads. *What does she think this is going to achieve?*

'It just might help me to piece things together,' I explain. 'Honestly, I know what I'm doing.'

I scroll down to a recent text conversation between me and Dad. 'What date was my accident?'

'The third of March – it was a Monday morning.'

That sounds about right. The final lot of messages between the two of us is time-stamped with the evening of the second of March.

> Good luck for tomorrow, love. Knock em dead. 🔥

> It's only a pre-interview presentation. But it's still important, and all feeds into the selection process. xx

> We have the pre-interview process for our teacher candidates, and they definitely carry weight. How many of you are going for the promotion? xx

> There's me, that Samantha, you know, the one who keeps ratting on me, and two others. Though I have it on good authority that I'm the favourite! xx

> Of course you are! That's my girl. And ignore that Samantha. She's only jealous.

There's her name again – bloody Samantha. So I knew about her *ratting* on me. It must have been a memory flashback rather than a dream I had. By the sounds of it, she had an absolute nerve calling into the hospital when I was in a coma. I can't imagine she'll return now that I'm awake, but I hope she does. I'd love to have it out with her.

At least Dad's been involved in the minutiae of my life. Messaging with him is probably the only time I have his undivided attention, that's if his wife doesn't monitor his messages.

I scroll down. Our next lot of texting is from two days earlier – the twenty-eighth of February. And I now see from the very first message why my brother's been giving me such a wide berth.

20

Just to warn you that Harry's after a loan, Dad – and a large one. He was pretty unpleasant when I turned him down flat, and I've got a feeling that he won't leave it there. xx

> He's already been on to me, love. I had to say no. We're just not in a position to help him right now, not with all the stuff we're having done to the house. Who's got a spare hundred grand? 😶

He says it's cash flow until his house sells, but I don't believe a word. I think he's in some kind of trouble. Just be warned that he might approach Teresa. He said something about how he should have gone straight to her instead of to you. That was when he was still reasonably talkative – before he lost it! 😶

> Are you OK? You shouldn't have to put up with your brother being nasty. xx

It's all I've known lately. Anyway, I gave as good as I got. Plus, he got a few home truths. xx

I Don't Like Mondays

> Fun and games, eh? Don't worry, it'll all blow over soon enough. xx

'I'm not sure why Harry bothered visiting the other day.' I look up from the phone.

'Is that an opinion or a question, love?' Dad's voice is low and even.

'Well, I've obviously upset him.' I tug my blanket further up myself as a chill creeps over me, and I shiver.

'We've all upset him, love – it wasn't just you.'

'Is how he's being just because I've refused to lend him money?'

'To be honest, there seems to be more to it,' Teresa replies. 'Daniel heard you arguing that weekend, but he wasn't sure what it was all about.'

'Harry just can't cope with the word *no*,' Dad says, patting the top of my hand. 'Nor can he accept criticism, not from *anyone*. He was like it as a kid, and it looks like nothing's changed.'

'He could hardly bear to look at me.' His bitter face floods my mind. I don't want to see it – I'd prefer to recall the face of the brother I *used* to know. The one who I could trust and whose company I enjoyed.

'Let it go, love. You've got enough on your plate.'

'Shall we grab a cuppa, Bob?' Teresa looks bored. I fight the urge to tell her she should have stayed at home – Dad wouldn't be happy.

'If you're buying.' Dad grins.

'Can you bring *me* some tea, please? And some chocolate?'

'That's my girl,' Dad says, and I'm warmed by his words. 'I'm so glad you're improving. We certainly couldn't foresee this a fortnight ago. Chocolate is a very good sign.'

I point at the empty box of Maltesers in the bin. 'The boys brought me these and then proceeded to eat them themselves.'

'That's the sort of thing *you'd* have done as a kid.' He gets to his feet, still smiling.

'It's great to hear Cathy talking about the boys like she knows them again, isn't it, Bob?'

I hate it when people talk about me in the third person – especially when they're in the same room. It's been a similar story several times when they think I'm sleeping, and they've stood muttering with one another, either just out of earshot in the corner or right outside my door.

'I'll leave you with my phone,' Dad says. 'We won't be long.'

'Is leaving your phone such a good idea?' Teresa's voice echoes back into the room as they set off along the corridor. 'What if—' However, I don't catch any more of what she's saying as the click of their heels fades away from the door.

I tap into some of Dad's other messages. There's a recent conversation between him and Daniel, all communicating things like visiting times so as not to have everybody here at once. Scrolling back through their exchanges, they were both pretty angst-ridden a couple of weeks ago. Dad loves me, that's for sure. Even Daniel's acting like he loves me from the tone of his messages. But when he was here yesterday, he was *very* different. I'll ask Dad about it when he gets back. They're clearly in touch, so perhaps *he* knows why Daniel was so off when he was here with the boys.

There's a ton of vitriol from Harry to Dad. I skim down the screen. Much of the conversation is one-sided, and Dad hasn't even replied to most of the messages. He's always been like that and would rather leave the other person to fester than get involved in any argument. *Leave the other person with the gift* is one of his mantras.

> I've always been a disappointment to you.

> You couldn't wait to leave our family.

> I bet if Cathy was asking for your help, you wouldn't hesitate, would you, Bob?

This is another of Harry's tactics, thinking that calling him *Bob* instead of *Dad* will upset him.

> You've never done anything for me, and all this is proof that you probably never will.

If Harry had just been asking for a loan of a few thousand, I'm sure Dad would have helped, but a hundred grand is too big an ask — family member or not.

Dad's iPhone is slimmer but with a much bigger and better screen than the last iPhone I recall of my own; however, the functionality is pretty much as I remember. I click out of the messages app and press onto the Facebook app, searching for Cathy Stratford before remembering with a heavy heart that I'm Cathy Mason now. What I'd give to still be Cathy Stratford. I bet Brad would have been here, at my bedside, almost twenty-four-seven.

I stare at my profile picture. I look like Mum before she fell into ill health. I always hated my unruly dark curls when I was young, but now that half of them have been shaved away, I'd give anything to have them back.

I scroll through the *about me* section. *Married, Publisher, Mum, from Yorkshire* – nothing riveting there. There are a few groups I belong to, mainly bookish ones, and several authors I follow, maybe people I represented before Bookish let me go, but that's it. I can't believe I'm out of a job. Surely, they can't do what they've done on Daniel and Samantha's say-so. It might be worth taking some action.

Or maybe I don't have the energy or the inclination.

The last thing I posted was a photo of myself on the train, on the Friday before the accident. I'm all dressed up, glamorous even, which isn't how I remember myself. Especially not when I'm just at work. A night out maybe, but not work.

The next one was posted the day before. I'm in a swanky bar, dressed up to the nines – and the caption says, *On the verge of many good things. It's time to make it all happen.* I scroll through the comments.

Daniel Mason You seem to forget the two good things you've got at home.

Bob Wheeler I'll always be proud of you.

Samantha Corben Don't count your chickens.

Sue Mansford You go, girl.

Mel Connors Watch your back.

Watch your back? What? I click on Mel Connor's name, but Dad's not friends with her, so I can't message her directly. Her profile seems to be all locked up, so I can't even see her header photo. I need to find out who she is and what she knows about me to post a comment like that – just as soon as I can get back onto my own profile. I'll have to take Dad up on his offer to get me a phone. But getting back online without any passwords is going to be a challenge, as Emma's already pointed out.

It was a couple of weeks prior when I posted before that – a picture of me at my desk with the caption, *I've got the best job in the world, and London is my happy place.*

There's a load of yays and agreements from women who must be my colleagues, and then Mel Connor's commented again with, *You need to watch yourself.* She *must* be something to do with my work as her comments aren't anywhere on the photos I've posted of the boys or on any of our rare family days out. They all seemed to be focused on the photos posted from London.

Her comments are few and far between, but there's another on a photo of me on the train with a glass of something in my hand. She's written *plenty to celebrate but not for you*. Talk about cryptic. And then again on a rooftop photo I posted in October. Her words, *Don't lose your balance* send a chill up my spine.

Who the hell is she, and what have I done to upset her? Maybe she's one of the contenders for the job I was going after? But if that was the case, surely Bonnie would have mentioned her during that phone call?

I wonder if Dad's still Facebook friends with Brad. Unless it was a massively acrimonious separation nine years ago, there should be no reason for them not to be. As I type *Brad Stratford* into the search bar of Dad's friends list, I'm very aware of how curiosity killed the cat.

And when I read the first post on Brad's profile page, I realise I should never have looked.

21

The post is dated today. Monday 17th March. There he is, my gorgeous Brad, his dark hair now flecked with grey but still with his unruly spikes and lopsided grin. Underneath this photo are nearly eighty comments already, the first few all offering a similar sentiment.

Sorry for your loss. Brad will be missed.
OMG – I just can't believe it. Am absolutely gutted. RIP Brad.
Thoughts with all Brad's family. Such a senseless waste of life.

And on and on and on. But I can't read any more. Oh. My. God. So this is why Brad hasn't visited. And why everyone's been so cagey whenever I've mentioned his name. He's dead. The love of my life is bloody dead.

How did he die? How the hell did he die? I scroll down the comments, but tears are blurring my vision. He can't have gone forever – there has to be some mistake. I lean back against my pillows, choking on the ferocity of my sobs. It was bad enough when I knew I'd lost him through divorce, but *this* – well, it's more than I can bear. I bring the phone closer to my face, trying to read through my tears. I *have* to know what happened.

'Hey – what's going on?' Dad flies back into the room with Teresa hot on his heels. They place their cups and drop several bars of chocolate onto my table before arriving at either side of my bed.

'It's Brad.' I drop the phone onto my bed. 'He's bloody dead.'

Neither of them says anything, but their faces say it all. Dad reaches for the phone and drops it back into his pocket. 'You said you were looking at *our* messages. And at your *own* Facebook page – not Brad's.'

'To be honest, I'm shocked it's been announced so soon,' says Teresa. 'Not when—'

'You both *knew*. So why the hell didn't you tell me? I've been going on about him to anyone who'd listen since I woke up and all the time…' My voice trails off.

Dad sinks to the chair beside me. 'We've only just found out ourselves that he's died. Earlier today. We were waiting for the all-clear from your doctor to make sure you were strong enough to handle the news.'

Out in the corridor, all is ordinary. The incessant doorbell, the voices, the clatter of trolleys. I don't know how life *can* continue. My Brad is dead, and I wasn't even there at his side, holding his hand.

'And we needed to check with the police,' Teresa adds. 'To use their words, it's an ongoing investigation.'

'What have the police got to do with Brad?' I tug a tissue from the box to dab at my face, but the tears won't stop. It's like they'll never stop coming. To have discovered I lost my husband through divorce nine years ago has been terrible. Since I awoke from the coma, it's been like losing him all over again. And now, it's final – there's no way of getting him back like I was wishing for. I've lost him forever.

Somehow, I *expected* the news of my mother's death. After all, she had no quality of life. I loved her, of course I did, but she leaned so heavily on me that her death in a lot of ways would have been a relief.

'Like you, Brad's been lying in a coma.' Dad's words cut into my thoughts, his eyes full of sorrow.

'But *unlike* you,' Teresa continues. 'Brad never regained consciousness.'

'Hang on, has he been in *here*?' I stab my finger into the bed sheet. 'In this same hospital?'

'He was *also* in Intensive Care,' she replies. 'Yes.'

'On the same ward?' To think, my darling husband, well, the man who I thought was my husband, has been only *meters* away from me, and I haven't even known. If I could have been at his bedside, maybe I could have changed things. Perhaps he could have pulled through with me rooting for him. I blow my nose and try to steady my breathing, but still, the tears keep falling.

'There are three ICU wards,' Dad explains. 'Brad was on one of the others.'

'They were never going to put you on the same ward.' I don't like Teresa's tone. I want to know what she's getting at.

'Why? And what do you mean he never regained consciousness? From what, exactly? What the hell happened to him?'

They look at each other again, like they have some secret code I'll never be able to break. 'We need to wait for the police before we tell Cathy anything else, Bob,' Teresa says. 'They're coming in today, aren't they? We should leave this to them.'

'When did Brad die?' I try to swallow my sobs. '*How* did he die? Please tell me – come on, Dad – I've got the right to know. I don't want to wait for the police. I want to hear it from *you*.'

'You'll know *everything* soon enough,' he replies. 'But Teresa's right – all this has to be handled properly. We'd be way out of our depth trying to explain it all.'

'I'm not some delicate little flower.'

'And you *haven't* got the right to know.' Teresa's voice might be gentle, but it carries an edge of sharpness. 'After all, you're not Brad's wife anymore.'

'What the hell's going on?'

We all turn to the voice at the door. Oh no – this is the last person I want to see.

22

I DON'T WANT Daniel here, especially if he's in the same frame of mind as last time. Dad passes me a tissue, and I dab at my tears.

'What's the matter? Why are you crying?' Daniel's voice is loaded with accusation.

'Cathy's just found out about Brad,' Teresa explains. 'Clearly, with her memory not being as it should be, it's hitting her hard.'

'Would you both mind leaving us alone for a few minutes?' Daniel looks from her to Dad as he ventures further into the room. His expression is difficult to gauge.

'Perhaps we should stay,' Dad begins. 'She's very upset, and I don't think—'

'No, he's right, Bob.' Teresa catches his arm as he rises from where he's been sitting on my bed. 'We should leave them alone and come back later. We'll get a phone sorted out for her, like we promised.'

Dad beckons Daniel back to the door. 'Go gently,' I just about catch him saying. 'Don't take her being upset about Brad personally – you must remember that she's had a terrible head injury.'

Daniel doesn't reply; rather, he spins on his heel and marches back towards my bed as Dad and Teresa's footsteps beat their path along the corridor. They left me here with Daniel too easily. I didn't want them to go, but they didn't give me a chance to protest.

'How did you find out about Stratford?' His jaw is set in a firm, hard line as he leans over me.

'Why are you like *this*?' I shrink back. 'The man's *dead*, for God's sake.' Fresh tears bubble up at what I'm saying. It feels like I'll never stop crying.

'I want to know how you found out.' He tugs a chair towards himself with a scrape and lands heavily onto it.

'From Facebook — Dad left me his phone. I was supposed to be looking at something else.'

'Why the hell...' – Daniel's voice rises – 'do you think I've been trying to keep you away from the internet?'

'I had a right to know.'

'It's me and the boys that are supposed to matter to you now, not *him*.'

'My head's just a jumble, that's all. I keep dreaming about things. I keep remembering all sorts, but I can't be clear about what's real and what I might be imagining. You wouldn't want to be in my head right now.'

I wipe at my cheeks with the tissue, which is wet through. I can't reach the box, but I'm not asking Daniel.

I try to slow my breathing. If I'm going to find anything out, I need to pull myself together. 'Tell me what happened to Brad, Daniel. Please. I want to hear it from *you*, not from the police. Dad and Teresa wouldn't tell me anything.'

'I'm pig sick of hearing about the man.' Daniel shakes his head. 'He's been a thorn in my side for years. I've never been able to measure up to him, have I?'

'I don't remember.'

'How do I know you're not lying about your memory loss?' He leans back in his seat. 'We both know how good you are at lying.'

'What's happened to my ex-husband has just come as a shock, that's all.'

'I can't do this anymore.' His lip curls with what could be dislike. For himself, for me, for our situation, who knows?

'What do you mean?'

'I've had enough of the endless drama, the constant loneliness, the being forced to live as a single parent.' He drives his finger into the side of my mattress as he lists each item.

I could defend myself. I could confront him over him resigning on behalf of me from my job without even consulting me. But all that's paled into insignificance in the wake of Brad's death.

'Everyone keeps telling me I should cut my losses, take what I'm entitled to and get the hell out of this so-called marriage,' he continues.

'What you're *entitled* to? Why, what *are* you entitled to?' I wish I could remember more. Is he talking about money, our house, the kids – what?

'You'll find out soon enough. And if you try to fight me, you'll wish you hadn't.'

'Why are you turning on me like this, Daniel?' I study his face. 'I thought you wanted me to get better? The boys—'

'I thought I could do this, but there's no way. The boys are better off without you. And I *definitely* am. I've already made an appointment with a solicitor.'

'What the hell are you talking about?'

'All you care about is *him*.' Daniel slaps his palm against his forehead. 'Him, him, him.'

'Just stop it, will you?'

He moves his chair as close as he can and bends his head

right into my face. He's so close I can smell the sourness of his breath. 'I've had enough of it all, and I'm not going to end up the same way *he* did.'

'I haven't got a clue what you're talking about.' I shuffle to the other side of the bed. How many times have we hissed into one another's faces like this, snarling names and trading insults? I wonder if we ever did it in front of Austyn and Matthew. I bloody hope not.

'Your precious *ex*-husband.' He hisses as he pushes his chair back with a scrape and stands from it. 'I'll tell you what happened, shall I?'

'I wish *someone* would.' Tears are running down my face faster than I can wipe them away.

'Do you want me to say exactly *why* he's dead?'

'Just tell me.'

'Because...' He jabs his finger into my pillow. 'Are you honestly still keeping up this act that you can't remember?'

'It's – not – an – act.' I sob between each word.

'I'll tell you why he's lying in a fridge in that mortuary, shall I?'

My eyes don't leave his face. It's like he's enjoying this moment of power. Him knowing something that I don't.

'He's where he is because *you* put him there.'

23

For a moment, we just stare into each other's faces.

'You're lying,' I whisper. 'His death has *nothing* to do with me. I loved him.'

'You *killed* him.'

For a moment, I wonder if Daniel's going to slap me.

'I can't be around you a moment longer.' He storms to the door. 'I'm going to collect my sons from my mother's.'

'Please, you can't leave me like this. I need to know what happened – what I'm supposed to have done.'

He turns back but I can tell by his face that I'll get nothing else from him today. 'You can rot after how you've treated us. I loved you, Cathy. I'd have given anything for you to love me back. But I no longer care.'

I stare after him as he strides from the room, too numb to even continue crying. How can he say that I killed Brad? I wouldn't have done that – not in a million years. And if I did, why aren't I under police guard or in handcuffs, instead of being a normal patient in a normal hospital ward with staff being kind to me and with visitors allowed in to see me?

I close my eyes. I wish Zoe was coming back today, but

I Don't Like Mondays

we've already had our physio session. Or Emma. I need to talk to someone.

I glance around for my call bell, but it's out of my reach on top of the cabinet. And the quad cane is right over at the other side of the room. As soon as one of the staff comes in with my meds or to do my observations, I'll ask them to contact the police. They were supposed to be coming today, but it's after five already. I need to know what's going on, and I need to know *tonight*.

I close my eyes, willing myself to escape back into sleep until someone comes, but at the same time, I'm frightened of where sleep could lead me. The last time I dreamed about Brad, we were having a horrendous argument. I want to relive a *happy* memory with him. We *were* happy. There's no way on this earth I could be responsible for his death.

∽

My door gently clicks into the frame, and I open my eyes. 'Who are you?'

A ponytailed woman darts to the blind at the left of the door, then she slips to the right, silently twisting the rods until each of them is closed. She isn't dressed in scrubs or any kind of hospital uniform. She's wearing leggings, jumper and trainers so neither can she be anything to do with police. Maybe she's some kind of volunteer visitor. If that's the case, I'll be sending her packing.

'We don't want anyone disturbing us, do we?' Finally, she speaks.

'Tell me who you are.' I shrink back into my pillows. This isn't a social call. I can tell from the look on her face and the tone of her voice that she *isn't* a volunteer visitor either. Nor is it simply a friend I don't recognise. Oh my God, she looks like the woman who posted the random comments on Facebook – Mel

Connors. 'Stay over there.' I point at her. 'Don't come any closer.'

'You don't get to tell me what to do.'

'I've no idea who you even are.' My heart's thumping. Here I am, lying powerless in this bed with some woman who clearly has a vendetta. I could be in trouble.

'Don't give me that crap – you know *exactly* who I am.'

I can't take any more today. First, the news about Brad, then Daniel being awful to me, and now *this*. I'm going to take Zoe's advice and pay for some therapy. I have to remember everything – I *need* to remember.

I glance at the woman's hand from which a single solitaire glistens and instinctively go to twist my own ring, finding only a bare finger. Hers is a far cry from the engagement ring I once knew. The ring Brad gave me. She notices me looking, and her face hardens some more. *No!* Could she be…? Is it…?

'You couldn't leave him alone, could you? You weren't happy until you'd hounded him to his death?'

'*Brad?*'

'Don't even say his name.'

'But I don't know anything. I wasn't even there when he died. Why are people saying it was *my* fault?'

'Because it *was* your fault.' A sliver of silver in her other hand catches the light from my overhead lamp. But this time, it's not a ring I spot. It's the point of a syringe. 'And now I'm going to make you pay for what you've taken from me.'

I shuffle to the right-hand side of my bed, looking up at my call bell. I have to get to it – I have to get her out of here.

'No one's coming.' She edges closer. 'Because of you, my fiancé's lying in the morgue. *You* ended his life.'

'Please – I don't remember a thing. Just tell me what I'm supposed to have done.'

'You *know* what you've done.' Her voice is a snarl as she

emphasises the word, know. 'If it wasn't for *you*, he'd have never been hit by that train.'

'I don't know what you're talking about. It was *me* on the train track, not Brad.'

'It should have been *you* who died,' she sobs, 'not him.' She brings the syringe in front of her chest, and her eyes narrow. Unless someone comes to my aid within the next minute, hers could be the last face I see, depending what she's got in that thing.

'Please – let's just talk about this.' I sit up and swing my legs around to the side. 'I don't even know what happened. I didn't mean for anyone to die. Surely I'm not worth doing time for murder over.'

She raises the syringe to the height of her head and grits her teeth. If I don't do something quickly, she looks like she's going to aim at my eyes.

Since I awoke from my coma, I've often thought I wanted to die. But a fight I wasn't aware I had is rising within me, and suddenly, I want to live. I want to be me, and whoever *me* was, I'm going to be better. Far, far better. With a father like Daniel, those boys need me to live. They need me to become the mother I should have been all along. I lean back, ready to stand. I'm going to get to that bell without my quad cane.

But she yanks me back by my shoulder.

'Help,' I scream, which is what I should have done in the first place. 'Somebody.' I hold my breath and brace myself for the stab of the needle's puncture. Whatever's inside it, it's mixed with pure hatred. I'll never have the chance to find out the truth, whether I *was* 'stalking' Brad and whether I *was* responsible for his death. Mel Connors is going to end it all here and now, and I'm powerless to stop her.

With a screech, she plunges the needle downwards, but I lurch forward, throwing myself to the ground beside the bed, numb with agony as I land on my broken arm.

'Help me please,' I shriek as I try to get up from the floor. My head swoons with the exertion.

She's already on her way around the front of my bed. I'm on the floor, she's on her feet and even if she doesn't manage to stab me with that needle, a kick to somewhere that's already broken has the potential to cause me just as much damage. 'Help me, someone,' I shout again, but the pain has weakened my voice. I try to shuffle backwards and away from her – but there's only the wall behind me. She's got me cornered, and I'll only be able to kick out for so long before she manages to stab me.

The door bursts open. 'What's going on?' A male voice booms from the doorway. I freeze as our eyes connect, and then he looks at the woman. 'Against that wall – now.' He points at it, his gaze hardening with his voice.

I'm paralysed by pain as her foot slams into my head. I can't breathe; I can't move. I just crash back against the wall.

'Help me.' As I force my eyes to open by a slit, the shapes of several people are clustered around her. She's being pinned to the wall by three people dressed in scrubs. But the pain's too intense, and I can't keep my eyes open to watch.

'Get security,' a voice yells.

'I've just called 999.' This time, the voice is more distant.

Meanwhile, someone's screaming.

'You're safe. It's OK. You're safe.' Someone's crouching over me. 'Let's get you onto the bed and check you over.'

I can't keep my eyes open. My head's going to explode. The screaming is even louder.

'Try and calm down.'

The screaming, I then realise, is coming from me.

24

'This will just make you sleepy for an hour or so,' a kindly voice cuts into my darkness. 'But it will take away some of that pain.'

The nurse's movement around my bed and the clicking of whatever she's inserting into my cannula is soothing. I want to sleep, I want to be warm and in the dark. I want to be as far away as possible from my reality.

'I'll be out there if you need me.' But her voice already sounds miles away. 'Just at the nurse's station. I'll send your friend back in to sit with you while you rest.'

I can't do anything else as I drift towards the welcome oblivion she's created. Maybe wherever it is that they're sending me, Brad will be there, waiting.

'Meeting someone?'

I glance up to where a woman is looming over me. She's about my age and wearing an extremely hostile expression. 'Yes, I am, actually.'

'Well, he's not coming.' Perhaps this is some random way of her getting me to move so she can have this table.

I curl my fingers around my wine glass. 'What are you talking about?'

'He's sent me instead.'

I continue to stare at her, waiting for an explanation.

'I'm Brad's fiancée.'

'You're what?'

'He's told me what's been going on.'

I feel sick. I'm not bothered that she's confronting me. What I am bothered about is that Brad's sent her here.

She slides into the booth and sits facing me. 'I'll make this crystal clear, shall I?' In the looks department, she's no one I need to worry about. Except she's got Brad's sparkly ring on her finger, and I haven't.

'I've got nothing to say. Just leave me alone, or I'll tell the staff I'm being harassed.'

'Well, you'd know all about that, wouldn't you?'

'I'm not harrassing anybody. If Brad and I have met up from time to time, it's been because he's wanted to.'

'He's chatted to you on the train, or when he's 'bumped into you,' – she draws inverted commas with her fingers, – 'because he's nice. Too nice for his own good. But I'm not. Not when someone's trying to muscle in on my fiancé. So you can take this as a warning.'

'Is that a threat?' In her skinny jeans and trainers and with a mousy ponytail dangling into her hood, she doesn't look like she could fight her way out of a wet paper bag. 'I don't make threats, I make promises. Just stay away from him, do you hear me?'

'If Brad tells me to, then I will. But I'm not reacting to anything you say.' I look her straight in the eye. Even her eyes are mousy. What the hell does he see in her? Why won't he just try again with me?

'He's sent me here, you stupid cow. He doesn't know how to handle you anymore. You turn up at his gym, when he's out with his workmates, when he's at his digs. I bet you only took the job down here so you could stalk him, didn't you?'

'I'm not stalking him.'

'What would you call it then? Look, love, you had your chance with him, and you blew it. Now, you're trying to do to your current husband what you did to Brad.' Her lip curls as she stares at me like I'm a bad smell that's wafted in. 'Well, he knows what you're up to as well.'

My stomach somersaults. 'What do you mean?'

'I've messaged him – he has a right to know.'

I want to slap the smug grin from her face, but I won't descend to her level. 'How dare—'

'Women like you give the rest of us a bad name.'

'Please, look – alright. Just go away, will you? You're going too far with all this.'

'No, lady. You've gone too far.' She picks up my glass. 'And if there's any more of this stalking, you'll know exactly what too far means.' I gasp as she throws my nearly-full glass of red wine into my face, spluttering as she slides back out of the booth and strides toward the exit.

'Hey, hey, hey. It's alright, Cathy. I'm here, it's Emma. Everything's going to be alright – she can't hurt you now.'

'She wanted to kill me. She had a syringe. She—'

'She's been arrested. Was it her you were dreaming about just now?'

I try to force my eyes open, but the light flooding in through the doorway forces them closed again. My head's still throbbing after she booted it.

'You were right. I *was* chasing after Brad. And Mel Connors was well within her rights to warn me off. But I wouldn't– I didn't—' I can't get my words out.

Emma doesn't say a word. She's looking at the floor.

'I'm sorry for wanting him back so badly – for getting so jealous when I found out he was getting married. But that's my only crime.'

'Daniel told me what he said to you earlier. That you killed Brad. Which is why I've hung around until you've woken up. You need to hear the truth about it all.'

Thank goodness it's *Emma* who's at my bedside when I've awoke and not Daniel. If I'm about to hear more bad news or negativity about myself, I'd rather hear it from Emma. 'The truth about *what*?'

She rises from her chair and paces across to the window. She looks out into the darkness before returning to my bedside. But she doesn't sit again. She remains standing, looking jumpier than I've ever seen.

25

'We'll talk about what happened earlier with that Mel Connors first,' Emma says. 'Brad's fiancée.'

The two words are like a knife to my heart, *Brad's fiancée*. That was me, then I was his wife – and always his soulmate. We were *never* supposed to part.

'And that will lead into what Daniel said to you earlier today.'

'Visiting's nearly over.' The ward sister pokes her head into my room.

'Can we have a little longer?' Emma turns towards the door. 'Cathy's only just woken up.'

'Really, she needs to carry on resting,' the nurse replies.

'I promise I'm OK,' I assure her. Emma's on the cusp of telling me something it sounds like I need to hear, information that might speed up my recovery if I can only make sense of it.

'You need calm and space to recover,' the nurse insists. 'Or do you want to set yourself back to where you started?'

'I'll keep myself calm, I promise. How long have I been sleeping?'

'Just for a couple of hours.'

'I'm OK, I really am.'

'The police are wanting to talk to you as well,' she continues. 'But I've asked them to return in the morning. So you have the chance to get over what happened earlier and to prepare yourself for the questions they'll be wanting to ask.'

'So can I have until half past?' Emma asks with an expression I remember from when we were teenagers. A look that could sell ice to Eskimos.

'Just twenty minutes,' she replies. 'After that, Cathy *really* must be allowed to rest.'

'Thank you.' She turns back to me.

'I'm just at the nurse's station if you need me, Cathy.'

'Thanks.' I look back at Emma. 'Did my dad come back while I was sleeping?'

A cloud enters her eyes. I'm sensing that she envies the relationship I have with my dad, which I suppose is natural given that she and her own father don't have much to do with each other from what Dad told me. But at least she's still got her mum. Mine might have only died fairly recently, but she was lost to me many years ago. 'No, they've just asked me to keep them posted.'

'Not until you've kept *me* posted.' I pull myself onto one elbow. 'Is that woman going to be charged?'

'Of course,' she replies. 'She booted you in the head.'

'If I hadn't chucked myself from the bed to the floor.' I close my eyes. 'If that porter hadn't come in when he did, she could have stabbed me with whatever was in that syringe.'

'Mum reckons she'll be treated leniently,' Emma says. 'Being that she's grieving.'

'If every grieving woman went around stabbing someone with a syringe and booting them—' I begin.

'She was due to marry Brad in eight weeks.'

The reality of their forthcoming wedding drops into the pit of my stomach, as heavy as a rock. So they'd have been marrying in May. That was *our* month. That's when *we* got engaged – *and* married. I've always loved May, the month of my birthday, a month filled with blossom, birdsong and the promise of summer. But she's even taken that away.

'Brad died rescuing *you* from the track that morning,' Emma continues. 'He was hit by a train arriving from the opposite direction. It was going faster than the train that hit you.'

A gasp escapes as I clasp my hand to my mouth. 'He was trying to *save* me? He was there at the same time?'

'Just like you, he commutes Monday to Friday. Well, he did.'

I close my eyes.

The throng of people huddles together on the station platform like a herd of sheep. A tannoy repeatedly cuts into their buzz. The cloying scent of perfume and aftershave mingles with the smell of engine oil. Brad's walking away, with his hand in the air as if dismissing me. And someone else is watching.

Then, as quickly as this image enters my mind, it vanishes.

'As I mentioned before, you were *really* going after him, turning up at his work, at the places he went to after work, and even to where he was staying.'

'I was just dreaming about it. That's what woke me up with such a start.' I stare at the window, at the darkness beyond. Brad's face emerges on the other side of the glass. Instinctively, I raise my arm, but he turns away and disappears.

A sickly jealous feeling is swirling around in the pit of my belly. Clearly, this feeling is what I've been living with. 'I couldn't accept that he was getting remarried, could I?'

'That's the understatement of the century. Both Daniel, when he found out about it, and Mel, Brad's fiancée, were going insane.'

'But why? I mean, if I was remarried with two kids of my own – why was I carrying on like that?'

'Because Brad was still so nice to you. He felt a sense of duty and hated seeing you upset. He even met you a couple of times in London, trying to let you down gently. But you kept reading more into things than was there.'

'How do you know all this?'

'Daniel told me. He's gutted, you know.' She smooths a stray hair from her face. 'He was trying to get beyond his own feelings when you were in your coma and be here for you, but he's struggling. Especially after your reaction to the news of Brad's death.'

'I loved Brad so much, so why did we split? That's what I can't understand.'

She fiddles with the lip of her paper cup. 'You weren't having a full-blown affair, but things were developing with someone else while Brad was working away.'

'Why didn't you tell me this before – when I asked you?'

'I was told not to.'

'Who was I having this not-quite-full-blown-affair with?'

She shifts her focus from her cup to me. 'Daniel.'

'No way – I'd have never–'

'But you did. You were still working as a journalist, and Brad was down in London helping Joel set up the London office.'

'I must have been completely nuts.'

'That's what we all thought at the time, but there you go. You were bored and lonely during the week when Brad was away.'

'I still can't believe I'd have chosen Daniel over Brad.'

'Neither could we. Although in the end, Brad decided for you.'

'How do you mean?'

'He couldn't trust you anymore, so that was it for him. Somehow, you'd had your head turned by this more, as he portrayed himself back then, sophisticated older man.'

'Sophisticated? Daniel? You've got to be joking.'

'He was offering you something that Brad *wasn't* back then.' She scrunches her paper cup in her hand.

'But he doesn't even have a career, does he? Daniel, I mean? From what I can gather, it's my salary that supports *him*.'

'It wasn't always that way. His business went under during the pandemic. That's when he started writing.'

A vision of Daniel at our kitchen table with his head in his hands slips into my mind. Then slips out again.

'Bits and pieces are *beginning* to come back to me.'

'Are they?' The look on her face suggests she's sceptical. 'How do you mean?'

'Through dreams mainly, but I'm having the odd flashback even when I'm awake. Just then, when you were speaking, for example – snippets of things keep appearing in my head.'

'That's good. Or maybe not so, in your case. Like you've said yourself, sometimes it's better not to remember.'

I wouldn't have liked myself much as I was before my fall – a dissatisfied, materialistic, career-obsessed stalker from everything I've been told. My priorities were all wrong, and there's no way I ever want to return to being that person.

'So let me get this straight,' – I prod my fingers into my sheet as I speak, – 'when Daniel insisted *I killed Brad*, and when his so-called fiancée—'

'She *is* his fiancée. Well was…' Her voice trails off.

'When she attacked me earlier,' I continue. 'Was it because it was *me* he attempted to rescue?'

'Well, kind of.'

'So that's not *my* fault then, surely?

'That's what the police are still trying to get to the bottom of,' Emma replies.

'I'm sure they'll have some more answers when they speak to me tomorrow.'

'Do you want me to be here? You shouldn't have to deal with them alone.' She shakes her hair behind her back.

'If you're allowed to be – I guess it depends whether they come within visiting hours.'

'That's it now.' The ward sister pokes her head around the door. 'It's nearly twenty minutes beyond visiting time. The doctor will shoot me if I let you have any longer.'

'Thank you for letting me stay.' Emma smiles at her before turning back to me. 'Try to rest,' she says. 'I'll see you tomorrow.'

26

'Hey Brad,' I call out to my former husband, hoping he'll hear me above the platform's din. But he continues looking in the opposite direction.

I push through the crowd, determined to get to him before the train arrives.

I want to apologise for any upset I've caused. I still can't believe his fiancée found out we were meeting and turned up at the pub.

I'm within touching distance of him when an arm rests on his shoulder. It bears the flower motif of his fiancée's jacket, the same one she wore when she warned me off in the pub. Hers is the last face I want to set eyes on. Bloody hell. She never used to travel with him, and I've no idea why she'd suddenly need to. She must be so paranoid that she can't even let him out of her sight.

I slide my phone from my pocket and lower my gaze as I turn to face the other way. Has she spotted me? God, I hope not. I just want to speak to Brad – and don't want to cause any more trouble. Mainly for myself.

But as I shuffle through the swarm of people all waiting for the 7:02 to King's Cross, I sense her eyes boring into me. I can only hope *she didn't see me approaching Brad and didn't hear me calling his name...*

Sensing a figure looming over my bed, I wake with a start. Thank goodness. It's only Zoe. But I'm not used to seeing her looking so serious.

'Hey – I'm only checking in. Thankfully, you look better than I expected. Are you OK?'

'Yeah. I was just having another of my funny dreams, that's all.' I shuffle up on my pillows as best I can with my broken arm. 'This seems to be how a lot of my memories are coming back.'

'I've just heard about yesterday.' Zoe nods towards the door, perhaps referring to whoever's told her at the nurse's station. 'I can't believe the woman managed to get in here. But then, she'll have known the ropes of the hospital after being here for a couple of weeks. She's probably entered the ward when someone was leaving. There's a sign on the door now, so it won't happen again.'

'Thank God someone out there realised what was going on. I was this close.' I hold out my thumb and forefinger. 'To her stabbing that syringe into me. Did she get whatever was in it from *here*?'

'To be honest, I don't know what was in it. I'm sure the police will be able to tell you more.'

I glance up at the clock – 9.20 am. 'Is she still in custody? They'll have had her for around sixteen hours. Surely she'll have been charged.'

'I'm not sure, but I know the police are on their way here to speak to you. They double-checked with the ward sister that you're feeling up to it a short time ago.'

'Can–' I begin. 'Oh, it doesn't matter.'

'What were you going to say?' She steps closer to my bed.

'I was going to ask whether my stepsister could be contacted to sit with me when the police arrive, but it doesn't matter. I'm a big girl – I can handle it.'

'We can get in touch with her if you *want*.' She tilts her head back at the door.

'I reckon I've put my family through the mill enough.' I force a smile. 'Besides, getting in touch with her might delay things, and to be honest, I want to get this meeting with the police over and done with.'

'Good for you.' Zoe smiles. 'You're tougher than you know.'

'I'm just hoping they'll have more answers about what happened at the train station.'

'Has much else come back?' She perches on the bed at my side.

'I'm not sure, to be honest. I'm struggling to make sense of what's real and what's in my imagination. Particularly when people are giving me their own takes on things. I don't know what is an actual memory or what is me just processing another person's recollection.'

Zoe looks thoughtful. In another circumstance, I'm certain the two of us would be friends. She cares – she genuinely seems to care about me. But then it's her job to – it's not as if we have a proper friendship. I don't know the first thing about her.

'Do you want me to come back for some more walking practice after they've been? We could go further this time.'

'Yeah, that would be good.'

'Are you sure you're feeling up to it?'

'It's like you said – the quicker I can take care of myself, the faster I can be at home.' I don't add that I'm unsure of where home might be. After Daniel's outburst yesterday, I might be better staying with Dad if Teresa's OK with that. There's also the boys to consider, but they're another matter entirely. I'm not up to looking after them yet, but hopefully, it won't be long.

'I see you're off your drip. Are you managing to eat OK?'

'I've had toast, cereal *and* fruit this morning before I dropped back off to sleep.'

'That's brilliant.' Her face breaks into a smile, which displays a row of perfect white teeth. 'You keep fighting.'

'I am trying, but it's hard after what came to light yesterday. My ex being dead, then the attack...' My words fade.

'It must feel like a huge setback, but we'll get you there. We'll have you back with those little boys of yours in no time.'

'Has anyone told my husband what happened?' My words have a tentative edge to them, and it doesn't feel right to refer to Daniel as my *husband. Besides, do I want him to know?*

'I'm not sure, but I can check in the notes if you want. I would imagine he's been informed. After all, he's your next of kin.'

I like that idea even less. 'If you'd be able to check, please. He left under rather a cloud the last time we spoke, and he was talking about seeing a solicitor.' I rest my head back onto my pillows.

'Oh dear.' She clasps her hands together and shakes her head. 'That kind of talk isn't going to get you better any faster.'

'I really do want to get out of here.' Moisture gathers in my eyes. 'I don't feel safe.'

'I promise you are.' Zoe rises back to her feet. 'Mel Connors won't be getting anywhere near you again.'

∼

'Are we OK to come in?' The detective I recall from a few days ago hovers near my door. 'You remember us, don't you? I'm DI Turner, and this is—'

'Sergeant Ben Richards.' The good-looking officer, the one who reminds me of Brad, steps into view at her side. The heat of tears once again stabs at the back of my eyes. If only we'd never split up. But it's all my fault. I still can't get my head around it, but it's definitely all my fault.

'Yes, it's fine. Come in.'

'It's good to see you on a normal ward.' She points to the chairs at either side of my bed. 'May we?'

'Help yourselves.' I sit myself up straighter.

'Is there any news on when you might be discharged?' DI Turner sits on my left and Sergeant Richards on my right. They've arrived earlier than I thought.

'Hopefully in the next couple of days. They want to keep me under observation after what happened yesterday.'

'Yes – well – firstly, Mel Connors was charged late last night and released on police bail.' There's a hint of an apology in the DI's voice.

'Released?' Dread crawls up my spine. 'So she could return here to have another go? Why didn't anyone let me know she'd been released?' It's probably a good thing they didn't. If I'd have known about this last night, I'd have got even *less* sleep.

'Her bail conditions forbid her from coming within a hundred metres of this hospital, your home, or you, wherever else you might be staying,' adds Sergeant Richards, his monotone suggesting this is a line he verbalises regularly. 'They also forbid her from making any contact.'

'You say she's been charged? What with?'

'Grievous bodily harm *and intent* to cause grievous bodily harm – this relates to the kick you sustained to your head and the syringe she threatened you with.'

'Surely she should have been charged with intent to *kill* me.'

'I hear what you're saying, but it's the decision of the Crown Prosecution Service. And she *does* have extenuating circumstances.'

'What was in the syringe?'

'Nothing. A nurse's trolley had been momentarily left unattended, and she'd just grabbed it.'

'So what if she comes back to finish what she started?' I look from one officer to the other.

'She's not allowed anywhere near you, like I said.' DI Turner speaks slowly, as if clarifying something to a confused elderly person.

'Like that's going to stop her.' I can't believe she's been released. Unless they were to put a constant guard on the door to this ward, she could wheedle her way back in here at any time.

'She's blaming you for the death of her fiancé after he tried to save you, misguidedly so, but it's this anger that fuelled her attack.'

'So it's all true?' I brush away a tear. 'He died rescuing *me*.'

'As we've shown your family, we have footage of the brief moments between you being pushed, then Mr Stratford jumping to your rescue,' says DI Turner. 'But we'll spare you having to look at it.'

A tear leaks from my other eye. At least I don't have to watch that. I couldn't bear seeing a video of the exact moment the love of my life died. Who could?

'But what we would like to show you are some stills taken in the minutes leading to you being pushed,' continues Sergeant Richards. 'They contain people who were closest to you on the platform. As mentioned before, it was such a cold Monday and many faces are obscured with hats and scarves, but perhaps you'll still see something that could offer a further lead.'

I glance towards the window where the early spring sunshine is making its way around the building. I want to be back out there again. I want to find myself. I need to live. So as I tentatively cast my eyes towards the first still that's been laid across my table, all I want to see is something that will nail the bastard who put me here.

But DI Turner is right. It *is* just an ocean of hats and scarves.

I shiver as a chill washes over me, feeling almost as if I could be back among them all.

I stare at it, shaking my head. 'No, I don't recognise anyone.'

'What about this one?'

I lower my gaze again, scanning from left to right. Then I see it, a distinctive motif on the sleeve of a jacket, just like the one I saw in my dream. 'It's her – it's Mel.' I drive my finger onto the image. 'She's there, only three people behind me.'

'Are you sure it's her?'

'It's that flower motif on her jacket.' I point.

'But how can you remember?' The officers look at each other.

'Because bits are starting to come back to me. It's her – it's Mel Connors. And you've let her out on police bail.'

27

'MEL CONNORS HASN'T YET ADMITTED to being at the station that morning,' says Sergeant Richards.

It's on the tip of my tongue to tell him that it's their job to have found this out for themselves, but being hostile won't do me any favours. Not when I need them to keep me safe.

'Before we bring Miss Connors back in for questioning, we'd just like to show you the other two stills, to make sure there's no one else you recognise.'

I lean forward. 'That's Brad.' I trace my finger over the picture. I'd know his face anywhere. He has the same stubbly chin he had in his late twenties. Tears fill my eyes. I've got to stop thinking of him in the present tense. He's no longer here, and he wasn't even mine anymore. 'She looks familiar. I stare at a woman with dark hair that cascades around her shoulders, wearing boots and a long coat. She's at the back of the crowd, turning around and looking straight at the camera.

'That's Samantha Corben – you work together.'

'So I keep hearing,' I reply. 'I take it you've spoken to her – if she was there that morning, I mean?'

'Yes – we've taken a full statement. But as with all the

passengers we've spoken to, she only witnessed the moment at which you were pushed out of the crowd. And everyone witnessed your former husband jumping after you.'

'Samantha witnessed that too?'

Sergeant Richards nods.

'From what I've heard about her,' I say. 'She isn't to be trusted. She sounds pretty underhand.'

'What do you mean?'

'I've found out she was stabbing me in the back at work – mainly to make sure she got the promotion we were both going after. If it wasn't for Mel Connors being a suspect, I'd have said Samantha was the next most likely candidate for shoving me off that platform.'

'What was going on between you and your former husband before the incident?' asks DI Turner. 'We've heard several different versions of events, all seeming to point to the same thing – that you might have been *overly* interested in him.'

'Which has seemingly inflamed Mel Connors,' adds Sergeant Richards.

I hang my head. 'I'm remembering bits and pieces, and yes, I know I was jealous of them. It seems I'd have done anything to win him back.'

'Even though you're married yourself and with children.'

'All I can say is that this new me, the one who's woken up in this hospital, wouldn't carry on like I was doing before.' I look her straight in the eye. 'If anything good has come from all this, it is that it's changed me.'

'The ward sister told us on the phone about your memory,' says DI Turner. 'How it's coming back in fits and starts. So if you remember something after we leave, you must get in touch with us straight away.'

'So, is this a murder enquiry now? With Brad being...' My words fade away.

'Whoever did this to you will find themselves being charged with attempted murder,' he says.

'And you're going to arrest Mel Connors *now*,'

'That's our next port of call.'

～

'I'm sorry I'm so late.' Emma rushes in. 'I wanted to be with you while the police were here, but I got held up.'

'They've been and gone.'

'And?'

'They were on their way to rearrest Mel Connors. She was at the train station that morning and literally feet away from me in the seconds before I was pushed.'

'So they'd already let her go after what she did *yesterday*. I can't believe it.' She rests a packet of biscuits and a bottle of juice on my table.

'Yes – on police bail. Let's just hope they get to her before she can think of coming back here to have another go.'

'Bloody hell. I'm sorry I wasn't here when they told you.' She sits beside me, looking pale. I'm unsure if that's because of the stress she's been under, or whether it's pregnancy-related.

'It's fine.' I tug the sheet higher up my chest. 'You've been here every day since I woke up. What does Joel make of you never being at home?'

'It's like I mentioned the other day, he's never at home anyway.' She slides her jacket down her arms.

'You seem flustered – have you had a busy morning?'

'I have been rushing around, yes.' Her shoulders sag.

'You should be taking it easy in your condition.' I point at her belly. I don't want to talk about the fall, the police, *or* Mel Connors, I want to talk about something positive for a change. 'When's your next check-up with the midwife? If Joel's not able to go in with you, perhaps I could?'

'Oh, right – yes. Well, we'll see how you are by then, shall we?'

I sweep my gaze over the whitewashed walls which are closing in on me. 'I can't bloody wait to get out of here.'

'I bet you can't.' She seems subdued – probably because of Joel.

'So where have you been this morning?'

'Oh, I just had an appointment with the midwife.'

'Was everything alright?' I hope the memories of my pregnancies come back to me soon. I hate not being able to recall such an important time.

'Yeah – I found out at my first appointment that I've got rhesus-negative blood. I'm in a fifteen per cent minority, apparently. Most people are O or A positive.'

'Is that a problem?'

'And then my mum rang when I was on my way here,' she replies, sidestepping my question.

I want to tell her she's lucky she can still speak to her mum, but I stay quiet. I was *never* able to speak to mine – our relationship just consisted of her guilt-tripping me into supporting her. It was a one-way street with little to nothing coming back the other way.

'Mum and me agreed it was time to tell you something.'

'Oh?'

'Bob doesn't want you to know yet, but I think you've got the right – and so does my mum.' A flush is creeping up Emma's neck. It seems I'm about to discover why she's so subdued.

'Go on.'

'When I found out about having what they call *monkey blood* about four weeks ago, I mentioned it to my mum.'

'Right?' I haven't got a clue what she's getting at.

'Just to see if being Rhesus negative had meant anything when she was pregnant with me – if it had caused her any problems as apparently your body can produce antibodies that fight subsequent pregnancies as if they're a foreign body.'

'And?' I want to tell her that if I'd wanted a biology lesson, I'd have asked for one.

'She said she didn't have a clue what blood type she was, but she was acting cagey, do you know what I mean?' There's something in Emma's face I don't like – it's almost a sense of one-upmanship.

I've been sitting for so long, my backside's numb, so I shuffle on my bed to get comfier. I have no idea why Emma's or Teresa's blood types should be anything I need to know about, but maybe she's just getting something off her chest.

'My mum was acting as if she had a secret. So much so that I decided to get in touch with my dad.'

'Right?'

'It was the first time I've seen him for ages. Not that it matters.'

'You went to see him about your blood type?'

'Yeah, and he's A positive. He said he recalled my mum being the same when she was having me – A positive. So I've been busy Googling, as you do.'

'And what have you found out?' I wonder if she's about to break some bad news to me about the baby. I do hope not – that would be terrible.

'Firstly, I found out that blood tests on babies are usually only done if the *mother* is Rhesus negative – which would explain why I've only just found out about my blood type and didn't know when I was younger.'

'And what else?'

'I've also found out that while there are *anomalies*,' she draws air quotes around the word, 'we normally inherit our blood types from our parents.'

'So what are you getting at?'

She gives me a look that seems to say, *are you stupid or what?*

Do I have to spell it out for you? 'That one, or even both of my parents can't be my parents after all.'

'Are you saying you could have been adopted?'

'Nope – I know Mum's my mum. I've seen photos of when I was in the delivery room with her – so no, it's who my father is that I've been questioning.'

'You're saying that *my* dad might not have been the first time your mum had an affair?'

I remember how I felt as a teenager when I found out about Teresa. It blew my world apart. Dad said he'd waited until we were old enough before leaving Mum and moving out, but in many ways, it was harder – especially because after he left, it was down to *me* to support Harry and Mum. It wasn't fair to dump all that responsibility onto a teenager – but they did, anyway.

'Exactly,' she replies. 'So I went back round to Mum's to have it out with her.'

'When was this?'

'A few weeks ago.'

'Well, you've got a right to know who your father is.'

'I'm just here to do your obs,' calls a cheery voice from the door. 'I won't keep you a moment.' The nurse who's been coming in for the last couple of days since I was unhooked from all the machines wheels her monitor into the room, taps on a few keys and then perches on the chair at the opposite side of the bed to Emma. 'I don't need to ask you which arm you'll be presenting for your blood pressure.' She smiles at the pot on my right arm.

'Does it say on the screen what my blood type is?' I ask as the band tightens around my arm. 'Just out of interest.'

She glances across at it. 'Rhesus negative,' she replies before returning to the blood pressure monitor. 'That's all fine.' She rips the velcro on my arm cuff open. 'Your stats are exactly where they should be. 'You'll be a candidate for discharge in no time.' She enters my results into her system and wheels the screen back towards the door.

Emma and I stare at each other.

'You already know what I'm going to tell you, don't you?'

'I think so.' My voice is small.

'Bob was there when I went to see Mum. I could tell straightaway what they'd been keeping from me. It turns out that they'd known each other well before they claimed they had.'

'But me and you are nearly the same age. Our mums would have been pregnant at the same time.'

'Exactly – and all this time, I've been treated like some kind of dirty secret.' Her face hardens.

Oh. My. God. Emma's my bloody half sister! 'Did I know about any of this *before* my accident?'

'No – your dad, well he's *my* dad as well now, said he needed time to get his head around everything before he told anyone else. It didn't do me any favours that he wouldn't acknowledge me publicly, I can tell you.'

I don't believe this. I really don't believe this. 'I don't know what to say.'

'Then you ended up in here, and he said we'd wait until you were better before telling you. I didn't want to wait, but he said he could only deal with one thing at a time.' Emma's face is a cross between hurt and anger.

'It's just a shame he couldn't deal with one woman at a time.' Wait till I see him. Wait until I bloody see him.

'I do understand it must be a shock for this to come out of the blue.'

'He was cheating on my Mum for at least *eighteen* years before he finally left her.'

'The two of them are claiming that they *tried* to stay away from each other.' She shakes her head.

'They did a right good job of that, didn't they?' I let out a long sigh.

'They agreed they'd make their respective marriages work. From where I'm standing, it sounds like it was all to protect his precious reputation and good standing in his job. That was more important than acknowledging *me*.' Her jaw hardens.

'My poor mother. All those years, she put up with him living a dual life. Perhaps it's little wonder she turned to food and drink to numb her pain. She often used to say that eating and drinking were her only pleasures in life – that they'd never let her down like *people* did.'

The air's heavy with our respective thoughts until Emma suddenly leans forward in her chair. 'It might not sound like it, Cathy, but now I've got used to the idea, I'm *glad* things have turned out this way.'

'How do you mean?'

'My dad couldn't have kept me any more at arms' length if he'd tried. Bob will be far more of a dad to me, after all, he's got a lot of lost time to make up for. So yes, I *am* glad.'

I stare back. I just can't take it in. And I can't feel *glad*. Not yet, anyway. Maybe that could come in time.

'If you and Daniel don't manage to sort things out, why don't you stay with me?' She reaches for my hand. 'After all, you're not just my friend now – you're my sister.'

28

'READY FOR A STROLL?' Zoe rests on the quad cane in front of me.

'I guess so.'

'How's it going?' She supports me to shuffle to the edge of the bed, and I lower each of my pyjama-clad legs to the floor, wincing as my bare feet connect with the cold tiles.

'Don't ask.' I reach for the quad cane. 'Will I be allowed to take this home with me when I leave?'

'Of course – it seems to be helping.'

'I don't think I'll need it for long, but it keeps me more stable with the wooziness.'

But it can't protect me from Mel Connors unless I use it to whack her around the head.

Zoe walks slightly ahead of me, her blonde bun wobbling. 'If you keep on like this,' she says, 'you should be home soon.' She presses the button to let us off the ward. 'Let's go further today.'

'The doctor said it would have been tomorrow if it wasn't for yesterday's attack.'

The glare of the fluorescent lights in the lift area makes my eyes ache. Out here, life marches on. It's easy to forget this while I'm stuck in the confines of my tiny side room. A room that's beginning to feel like a holding cell.

'You're very quiet today,' Zoe remarks, 'but getting faster on that cane.'

'I still feel wobbly,' I reply. 'I'm spaced out – as if I'm not really here.' I probably shouldn't be telling her any of this. It might mean they keep me in for longer.

'That's to be expected. You're recovering from a serious head injury, and you've been laid on your back for over two weeks. Which is why you've got the cane to hang onto.'

∽

The last of the afternoon crawls by. When I was in intensive care, I had little concept of time, but now, with the sun moving around and setting in front of my hospital window as the endless hours tick by, I know I can't lie here for much longer. Things need dealing with – the boys, my marriage, and what's going to happen. And I need to know whether they've caught up with Mel Connors – and whether this time, they're going to charge and detain her properly.

∽

'I understand you've been told.' Dad looks uncomfortable as he walks in just as I'm starting my dinner. It's probably obvious from the expression on my face that I'm far from happy.

'Things just get better all the time.' I gaze at my plate, my appetite suddenly vanishing.

'It all comes at once, doesn't it?' He shakes his head as he hitches his trousers to sit.

I swallow my mashed potato. 'What does?'

'Family drama. Ours, especially.'

'It's far, far more than that, Dad.' My tone is snappy, but I don't care. 'I've got a half sister who I didn't have a clue about.'

'I'm sorry. What else can I say, love?'

'You must have suspected *something* back then.' I rest my cutlery on my plate. 'If you were sleeping with Teresa forty years ago, then lo and behold, out pops a baby, you *must* have known.'

'We did suspect, of course we did, but we were both married to other people.' He rubs at the stubble on his chin that he used to chin-pie me with when I was growing up. The memory of this almost drowns me in a wave of melancholy. Whether it's selfish or not, I've grown up believing I'm Dad's only daughter. Sharing him will be hard, even with Emma. 'Teresa and I made what was a very tough decision to stop seeing each other. Don't let me stop you from eating your dinner, love.'

'I'm not hungry.' I glare at him. 'I thought you'd only got together when I was eighteen. It seems like I don't know you any better than I know myself.'

'It was easier that way.' He brings his chair even closer to my bed with a scrape. 'I'm sorry. I might be your father, but I'm not above making mistakes.'

'You're supposed to be the head of a Catholic school. You're supposed to be a Catholic.' A vision of the altar at our local church enters my mind. 'You rammed your religion down our throats often enough when we were kids.'

'That's precisely why we *did* keep it all under wraps. Things were very different when you and Emma were born. I'd have never got to the place I've reached in my job if our affair had become common knowledge. Cathy, please eat your dinner. I'm sorry I've arrived when you're eating.'

I ignore him. 'I just can't believe I've got a half-sister, literally only a few months younger than me. Does Harry know?'

'Not yet, and I'd prefer to keep it that way, at least until I get my own head around everything. I asked Emma to hold off telling *you* she's my daughter. At least until you were out of here.'

'Your *daughter*.' I repeat his words before pointing at myself. '*I'm* supposed to be your daughter.' That she's suddenly become my half-sister is twisting at my insides. I don't want to feel like this, but I can't help it.

'It doesn't change *anything* between me and you,' he says. 'I'll still be the same dad you've always had.'

'I just can't cope with much more.' I wipe the tears which are spilling from my eyes. 'I've been pushed from a station platform, then I wake with no memory, my husband and sons virtual strangers. Then I find out about Brad...' My voice fades into an uneasy hush.

'I know, love, and I'm so proud of how you're coping.'

'Next Brad's crazy fiancée comes in, trying to finish me off. Have you heard they were rearresting her? It turns out it's *her* who pushed me in front of that train.'

'Emma told me.'

'And now my stepsister has become my half-sister. Meanwhile, I'm stuck in this bed, with a shaved head and umpteen broken bones.' I'm almost breathless as I reel it all off. 'So if you expect me to be throwing a party, Dad, think again. Oh yeah, and to top it all off, Daniel's planning to speak to a solicitor.'

'I know things are pretty tough right now, but I'd have thought he'd have stood by you. Now more than ever.'

'It sounds like he wants to take me for all I've got while I'm down and out like this. Namely the house and the boys.'

'That house is in *your* name.' My voice might have risen an octave or two higher, but Dad's is, as always, low and calm. 'And Daniel's credit history is probably as dreadful as Harry's. He won't have a leg to stand on.'

'That won't make any difference to any divorce settlement he'll be entitled to. He'll automatically be granted half of any assets. We're married, aren't we – in name at least.'

'Oh, love.' Dad reaches for my hand.

'But I couldn't feel less married to him if I tried.'

'Things will improve when your memory returns.' Dad squeezes my hand. 'The two of you loved each other once, hell, you even broke up your first marriages for each other. I always said you were making a mistake, but would you listen?'

'I love how you've managed to turn the tables from your own indiscretions here, Dad.' I can't help but smile at him.

I'm gutted with how things have turned out – that I've got to share him with Emma, but I love my dad, and it's hard to stay mad at him. Plus, there are worse half sisters I could have ended up with. At least Emma and I get along.

'We'll get you out of hospital, we'll all pull together and somehow, we'll muddle through.'

'Where am I going to live when I get out of hospital? I can't exactly go *home*.'

'Once your memory—'

'Nothing will change, Dad. I could *never* love Daniel – I don't even *like* the man. The thought of living in the same house as him and sleeping in the same bed turns my stomach.'

'What about Austyn and Matthew?'

'I'll do whatever it takes to be a full-time mum. But how that's going to look largely depends on Daniel. It also depends on me making more of a recovery.'

I follow Dad's gaze to the door where DI Turner is standing. This room has become like Piccadilly Circus over the last couple of days.

'Sorry to bother you again.' She ventures in. 'But I'm here with some news.'

'I'm alright to listen in, aren't I?' Dad gets to his feet.

'Of course you are.' I scowl at him. 'You're my dad, aren't you? Or at least I hope you are.'

DI Turner looks puzzled as she approaches the bed, but if

she senses the atmosphere in here, she doesn't say anything. 'We've had to release Mel Connors without charge.'

'Without charge?' Dad echoes.

'Obviously, the charges still stand for what happened here, in the hospital, but as far as pushing your daughter in front of the train, it couldn't have been her.'

'Oh?'

'We've had some more time-stamped images sent through from our tech department. Images that put Mel Connors a carriage length away from you at the exact moment you were pushed. We're still looking for someone else, Cathy.'

29

'I'm Doctor Finch – you asked to see me.' He swaps places with the nurse who's left my painkillers in what looks like a bun case.

'Yes, I'd like my daughter at home where I can keep an eye on her,' Dad says. He looks tired, really tired.

'So I gather from the ward sister, but really, we feel that at least another twenty-four hours of observation is in your daughter's best interests.' He moves to the front of my bed. 'Especially after yesterday's trauma.'

'Which should *never* have happened – not in a *hospital*.'

'You have our word that we're addressing our security policy to minimise any further breaches on *any* of our wards.'

'Look, I hear what you're saying, but I really feel Cathy would be safer at home.' Dad paces to the window. 'Mel Connors has been released on bail, and I'm worried she'll come back.'

'She won't get in here.'

'It's not just that, but whoever put my daughter in here in the first place is still out there.' He gestures into the dusk beyond the window. 'I want her where I can keep an eye on her.'

'My dad's right,' I tell Doctor Finch. 'I do want to be discharged.'

He pauses what he's filling in on his screen and peers at me over the top of his glasses. 'You'd be going against medical advice, Cathy.'

'We'll get her everything she needs at home – physio, counselling, *everything*.' Dad ticks off the items on his fingers.

'It's going to take more than counselling to unravel my head.'

'Very well, if you're *really* sure you can cope at home.' The doctor moves his attention from me to Dad. 'And that you can cope looking after her, I'll issue the discharge paperwork.'

'I'll take some time off work,' Dad says. 'For as long as necessary.'

'Really?' I don't know what he's been like over the last few years, but he rarely took time off work when I was younger. But this was probably so he could be around my stepmother. The thought of her suddenly hits me.

'Don't you need to check with Teresa that it's alright for me to stay?'

'We have a spare room. Besides, I don't need to check with *anyone* – you're my daughter. You need looking after, and you need a place to stay.'

Things might be awful, but his words warm me. Then I remember that I have to share him with Emma from now on. The two of us are very different – what if she's the daughter he always secretly wanted? She's prettier, smarter, and funnier. And I can't get away from the fact that he left me once. Yes, I might have been a teenager, but I still felt abandoned.

'It might take a couple of hours to get Cathy's meds and the discharge admin completed.' Doctor Finch checks his watch.

'No problem.' Dad smiles. 'She's been in here for long enough – I'm sure a couple more hours won't kill her.'

'Unfortunate turn of phrase, Dad.' I roll my eyes.

As the doctor leaves, Dad retakes his seat. 'It will all be OK, love. All that matters is getting you right, then you can get back to your boys.'

'Are *you* close to Austyn and Matthew? It's so frustrating that I can't remember any of this stuff.'

'Not as close as I'd like to be. I'd love to be a more involved Grandad – it's just my job that gets in the way.'

'You're going to have another grandchild soon.' I think of Emma's pasty face and the baby, my niece or nephew, that's growing inside her.

'Let's just focus on *you* for now, shall we?' He opens and closes the doors to the cabinet next to my bed. 'Is this all the belongings you've got here?'

'It's all Daniel brought in,' I reply. 'A couple of pairs of PJs and one change of clothes. The police still have my wheelie case and my handbag.'

'We need to arrange to get them back.'

'If they're anything like my phone, they might not be in a fit state.'

'We're going to need some of your things from the house,' Dad replies. 'So as soon as the doctor's sorted your meds, we'll call round there. You're going to have to go sooner or later, so we may as well get it over with.'

∼

'It's like waiting to be hung, drawn and quartered.' Dad fiddles with the edge of his scarf. 'How long can it possibly take them to put some pills in a bottle?'

'They're busy,' I reply. 'I'm one of *how* many patients?'

'You're used to this place.' Dad blinks in the glare of the overhead light. 'But I've always detested hospitals.'

'How was Teresa when you phoned? Is she alright about me staying?'

'How can she not be? Yes, she's absolutely fine. She'll make you very welcome, and in any case, it'll just be me and you during the day.'

My mind flashes back to a time I had a rotten stomach bug when I was about nine. Dad barely left my side for two days. I don't know where Mum or Harry were, I only remember me and him. He mopped me up continually, and I remember us watching The Lion, The Witch and The Wardrobe. We both cried when Aslan died, and I've never felt as close to another human as I felt to my dad.

I know he'll look after me – he won't let anyone hurt me.

30

'Do you remember any of *this*?'

I rub my eyes as we pass through Otley Town Centre, first by the church, then past the Jubilee clock, then my dentist, around the corner, towards the bridge. After being in hospital for what seems like an eternity, I feel really spaced out to have escaped my side room, now to be back in comparative normality. I'll never take anything for granted again.

'Yes – I think I do.' I look out of the window at the other side of the car.

'Well, you've only lived in Otley for seven years, so this is positive. As far as I know, it isn't a town you had much to do with before you moved here.' Dad points from the bridge as we pass over the river. 'This is where you bring the boys to play at weekends. They love to bring their scooters to the skate park.'

'Can we stop for a few moments, Dad? I want to see.'

'It's pitch black at the park,' he laughs. 'There's not much *to* see.' But he pulls up at the side of the road, and I wind down my window, gulping in the blast of cold air as a car goes around us.

'It's so good to have fresh air on my face.' Tears fill my eyes. 'I'm so lucky to be alive. Poor Brad—'

'I still can't believe it.' Dad leans back in his seat. 'He was a lovely lad – it's absolutely tragic. But as for his fiancée—'

'I've been telling myself her attacking me like that was a moment of madness.' I turn to him. 'It's the only way I can come to terms with it.'

'Well, that's pretty noble of you, considering.'

'She was completely maddened with grief, wasn't she?' I gaze out into the darkness. 'And filled with hatred for the fact that *I'm* still living while Brad's dead. All she wanted in that moment was to make someone pay — namely me.'

'She still needs punishing. She could have stabbed you in the eye or anything.'

Instinctively, I rub at my eye, the prospect making me cringe. Then my hand moves back over my now prickly forehead. 'At least my hair's starting to grow back. I look a right sight, don't I?'

'You're my *right sight*. Come on, let's get around there and get this over with.'

'We should have let him know we were coming.' I press the button to close my window.

'It's *your* house. Besides, it'll be a super surprise for the boys. That's if they're not in bed.'

I sit up straighter in the seat. 'I honestly know where we are, Dad. My house is just around the next corner.'

'Can you remember anything else – like where I live?' He points at himself.

'In Ilkley.' I smile. It feels better than I thought to be gaining a sense of reality again, even if I have a long way to go. 'You've got a path running up the middle of your garden and a water feature to the right of it.'

'Yes.' His hands leave the steering wheel as he claps.

'Who's the current prime minister?'

I tell him.

'When did you start work at Bookish?'

'About five years ago. Though my brain would be too muddled to do the job at the moment. I'm still not sure what I did there.'

'Well, this is a relief – clearly it's taken you getting out of that hospital bed for things to start coming back faster.'

'It was coming back in bits and pieces when I was there,' I tell him. 'Doctor Finch said there'd be no rhyme or reason to how quickly I'd remember things.' I stare into the night sky as we approach the final couple of corners. 'But whoever the *old* me was, I'm a *new* me now.'

'There wasn't as much wrong with the old you as you've been led to believe.' Dad glances at me as we reach the final corner. 'Sure, you made mistakes – but haven't we all? Deep down, you're a thoroughly decent person and don't let anyone tell you otherwise.'

'Are you just saying that because I'm your daughter?' Once again, I'm reminded that I'm not the only one anymore. When people ask him about his kids, he'll refer to *two* daughters in the future.

'Admittedly, I'm biased, but no. I'm saying it because I'm proud of you, and I love you.'

I stare at his side profile as he brings the car to a stop. The dad I remember *never* said things like this. But sometimes, until you nearly lose someone, you have no idea what they mean to you.

'So can you remember *this* place?' He pulls the handbrake on.

I glance up at the red brick townhouse, *my* house, and nod. 'We sleep in the dormer room, which looks over the field behind the house, and we've got an ensuite up there. There's a conservatory and a hot tub around the back.'

He tugs the keys from the ignition. 'And what about the boys' rooms?'

'They're up there.' I gesture to the two middle-floor rooms with the blinds down. 'It looks like they're in bed.'

Dad glances at the clock on the dashboard. 'It is going on for nine.'

'What day is it? I've had to ask that question so many times over the last few days.'

'It's Tuesday.' He reaches for my seatbelt, keeping hold of it as it releases over my bandaged arm.

'It's probably just as well that they're not around.' Nerves jangle in my belly. 'We don't know what sort of reception we're going to get.'

'Well, woe betide Daniel if he starts on you in front of me. After all you've been through.'

'It's like he turned, Dad. He was alright with me – and then suddenly he wasn't.'

'Right, I'm going to get that cane thing from the boot. I'll be there to help you out in just a moment.'

Light seeps around the edges of the lounge blind, a blind I remember choosing. I'm amazed at the speed at which things are coming back to me since I've left the hospital, but so far, they're superficial. No matter what I remember, I can't imagine ever being the person I'm told I used to be. I want to be better – I'm going to be better.

Dad presses the doorbell.

'I'm nervous.'

'Don't be.' He winks. 'I'm here.'

'I hope Daniel will be willing to get some clothes together without needing too much persuasion. I'm not sure where anything is.'

'Why wouldn't he?'

'You didn't see what a foul mood he was in yesterday. Plus, I haven't tried getting up and down any stairs since all this.'

'Hasn't your physio done that with you?'

'That was one of our next tasks.'

'But obviously, you've discharged yourself early.'

'Somehow, I'll have to get in touch with Zoe to thank her for all her help,' I say. 'I know her full name from her badge, so hopefully I can find her on Facebook.'

'That reminds me, we've got your new iPhone waiting when we get home. Oh, look, he's coming. About time too.'

My breath catches as the shadow approaches the door.

31

'What are *you* doing here?' Daniel tightens the cord on his dressing gown.

'I need to collect some of my clothes.'

'Now's not a good time.' He looks from me to Dad. 'You can't just turn up like this – you should have let me know you were coming.'

'I've no phone, remember?' I suspected he'd be like this with me, but I'm still shocked by the extent of his hostility.

'She *lives* here.' Dad steps forward. 'She doesn't need an invitation. So are you going to let us in, or what?'

'You're not thinking of *staying,* are you?' Worry lines etch themselves across Daniel's forehead.

I lean on my cane. 'Everything's hurting, Dad. I need to rest for a minute.'

'Get out of the way, Daniel. No, Cathy's *not* staying, but she needs more clothes than the paltry amount you brought to the hospital.'

Finally, he steps aside. 'You can both wait in the lounge.' He points along the hallway.

I should challenge him on who the hell he thinks he is,

telling me where I can and can't go in my own house, but I haven't got the energy for a confrontation. I just need to sit. The smell of steak is hanging in the air as I step onto the doormat. Maybe he's just irritated because we've disturbed his dinner.

Dad guides me into the lamplit lounge, and a blast of warm air from the fire hits me as soon as he opens the door. 'Here, let me help you sit down,' he says. The cane, along with my slippers, sink into the carpet as we make our way towards the closest armchair.

My gaze rests on the large photo of my sons above the fireplace and then another one on the far wall, where they're babies. I don't remember the instances of either of them being taken. Not yet anyway, but I'm more hopeful than ever that everything's going to fully come back. There aren't any photos of me and Daniel, but there's a gap on the mantlepiece where I'm certain our wedding photo was. He must have been serious the other day when he said he'd had enough.

'It's cosy in here,' I remark as I sink back into the chair. 'I don't think I'll want to get back up again.'

'It's just as cosy at our house.' Dad shoots Daniel a look as he hovers in the doorway. 'And at least you'll be properly looked after there.'

'Are the boys in bed?'

'Where else would they be at this time of night?'

'Do you have to be so hostile, Daniel?' I'm so glad Dad's here to help fight my corner.

'Have you *really* arranged to see a solicitor?' I try to turn in the chair to look at him, but my ribs are too sore.

'I can't stay with you anymore, Cathy.'

'I feel exactly the same.' It's a relief to say this. At least he's setting me free from playing *let's pretend*. 'But we have to do things properly, for the boys' sakes.'

'Nothing's going to change for the boys – they're staying right here with me.'

Anxiety bubbles in my belly. This is what I was worried about. It looks like I'm going to have a fight on my hands.

'So effectively, you're trying to turf Cathy out of her own house and separate her from her sons, is that what you're saying?' Dad's expression hardens as he lowers himself to the sofa. 'You'll find that you can't do that.'

'I've got residency of them.'

'Not officially, you haven't. Why the hell are you being like this anyway? She's only just got out of hospital.'

'That doesn't make any difference.'

'I could refuse to leave, Dad. I'm here now. *Then* who'll have residency.' Even as I say it, I know it's out of the question. I need help for at least a few days, and Daniel's hardly likely to offer me any support. I'm certainly in no fit state yet to look after Austyn and Matthew.

'What things do you need? I'll get them, then I'd like you to leave.'

Dad's shaking his head and looks to be trembling. I don't think I've ever seen him lose his temper, so this could be a first if Daniel carries on. We need to collect my stuff and get out of here.

'Clothes, toiletries, shoes,' I point down at my slippers. 'And a coat.'

'You can take *all* your stuff as far as I'm concerned.'

'Just because I'm staying at my dad's, Daniel, doesn't mean I'm just going to roll over and die.'

'She's got rights,' Dad adds. 'Don't forget that.'

Daniel closes the door without replying. Dad and I look at each other. He looks as shell-shocked as I feel.

'Well, you weren't wrong, were you?' He shakes his head. 'The jumped up, selfish, arrogant—'

'He's even more hostile tonight than he was the other day. I don't know what's got into him.' I'm shaking too. I don't need this right now.

'Don't worry, love, we'll get some legal advice. The sooner the better.'

As the floor creaks above us, a woman's cough echoes from the kitchen. At first, I wonder if it's a TV or something. But then she coughs again. I reach for my quad cane.

'Stay where you are, Cathy.'

'No chance.' With every bit of strength I can muster, I hoist myself from the chair. Dad's already out of the lounge door by the time I'm on my feet. Daniel's got a woman here – no wonder he didn't want to let us in. And no wonder he's talking about divorce.

'And you are?' Dad's voice drifts through the hallway as he opens the kitchen door.

'Daniel?' The female voice which calls to my husband sounds familiar. However, I'm struggling to place it. I'm also struggling to get to the kitchen. I hate being so slow and weak.

'I told you to wait in the lounge.' Dad twists around to look at me before turning his attention back to the woman sitting at the kitchen table with the lights turned down. She's clutching the stem of a wine glass like her life depends on it. My kitchen. My table. My wine glass.

Everything is achingly familiar about this house, yet it still feels like I'm having an out-of-body experience. And I know who the woman is – I just know, yet I can't bring the exact memory of her to mind. The effort of trying is making my head crackle with pain.

'Answer my dad's question. He asked you who you are.'

'Oh, don't give me *that* crap, Cathy.' She laughs as she tosses her hair back behind her shoulder. 'Daniel's told me about this false memory thing you've got going on. You know exactly who I am.'

Daniel thunders down the stairs, dropping something at the bottom of them before rushing up behind where I'm standing at the door.

'Mind yourself, love.' Dad rests a protective arm around my good side as he manoeuvres me out of Daniel's way. 'You go steady around her, do you hear me, lad?'

'So what's going on here?' I shuffle further into the kitchen, letting go of my cane and grabbing at the kitchen chair facing the woman. 'Or is that a stupid question?' I look from her to Daniel, who's swapped his dressing gown for joggers and a hoodie.

'Here, let me help.' Dad offers his arm, which I grab as I lower myself to the chair, trying to catch my breath as I clutch my ribs with my good hand. Perhaps Doctor Finch was right. Maybe I should have stayed in hospital for another night or two. My head and ribs are killing me. But if I'd stayed there, maybe I wouldn't have stumbled across what Daniel's been getting up to in my absence. And I'm glad I did – it's definitely a bullet in my gun.

'We were going over my publishing contract.' Daniel hovers near the door as if poised to make a swift exit, should he need to.

'That's what you're calling it? So where is it then?' I glance around. There's no sign of a computer or any paperwork. Just plates from whatever meal they've enjoyed together piled up in the sink.

'We've finished working. So Samantha and I were just having a drink to celebrate.'

'Samantha, eh?' I study her across the table. 'Yes, I *can* place you now.'

She shifts in her seat, hopefully feeling uncomfortable under my scrutiny. What an absolute bitch.

'Congratulations on your new job, by the way. I hope all your underhand methods of securing it were worth it.'

'I don't know what you're talking about.' She looks down, revealing the perfect makeup shadowing her eyes. She's got herself *very* dolled up for a discussion about a so-called publishing contract. And I'm even more aware of the way I look right now. But I won't look like this forever.

'Oh yes you do. What was it you so eagerly told our line manager about? Oh yes, my marital problems.'

'I don't know where you've got that idea from.'

'Marital problems,' I continue, 'for which *you* can claim some responsibility.' I point at her. 'Then there's my so-called drinking problem.' I tilt my head to one side, watching for her response. 'The one you *also* told our line manager about.'

'Who've you been talking to?'

'Bonnie, herself, actually.' Samantha doesn't need to know about my obscure dream when I couldn't make the distinction between imagination and memory. But now we're facing each other like this, further memories are rearing their ugly heads and popping into my mind as fast as a video game.

'Then there's the time you took the credit for my acquisition of the four-book deal that Netflix was interested in.' I lean forward in my chair, wincing again at the pain in my ribs. 'Oh, and the time you went over my head when I'd made an error in one of the contracts to make sure I got into trouble for it.' Still, she doesn't reply. *Samantha the snake*. 'So tell me, what are you *really* doing in my house tonight? I want the truth for a change.'

She glances over at Daniel, her expression imploring him to step in as a flush creeps up her neck.

'We don't owe you any explanation,' he finally says. 'It's alright for you to pursue your ex-husband like you did, but when I look elsewhere—'

'Thank you.' I cut him off as I slap my hand onto the table. 'You're finally being honest.'

'Do you think it's acceptable...' Dad rests his hands on the back of my chair. 'To be conducting this *relationship* when my grandsons are asleep upstairs?'

'They think Samantha's just a work colleague.' Daniel shuffles from foot to foot, his discomfort palpable. Catching him out like this is beginning to feel better than I could have imagined.

'I've certainly got more to discuss with that solicitor now, Dad.' I try to turn my head to him before returning my attention to Samantha. 'I want you out of my house right now,' I say. 'You can conduct your sordid whatever-it-is somewhere else. Not in *my* house where my children are sleeping.'

'So you suddenly give a shit about them now, do you?' Daniel steps closer to the table.

'I've been suffering from amnesia, you bast—' There's a knock at the door. Daniel looks relieved at the interruption – his chance to escape for a few moments.

As I glare at my adversary across the table, not knowing what else I can say to her, the voice at the door pulls me up short.

'Can we come in?'

I glance around to see none other than DI Turner and Sergeant Richards.

The question is, what are they doing *here* at this time of night?

32

'Oh.' DI Turner also stops short when she sees me and Dad. 'I thought you were still in hospital.'

They're a strange sight in here, DI Turner in her stoic trouser-suit and Sergeant Richards in his all-black uniform and huge polished boots. He towers over Daniel.

'I discharged myself,' I explain. 'I'm just here to pick up some clothes.'

'Oh right.'

Sergeant Richards looks decidedly uncomfortable at my presence. What the hell is going on?

'I'm not staying here – in any case, my husband's too busy with his *girlfriend*.' I can no longer look at Samantha. It's not that she's carrying on with my husband, it's more about the fact that she's here, in my home, where my children are sleeping.

It's also that she's here in my house, while as far as *she* knew, I was stuck in a hospital bed. Then there's her underhand behaviour at work. I must have been a real cow before my accident for her to hate me so much. I can't understand why one woman would do to another what she's done to me.

'I'll be staying at my dad's if you need to get in contact,' I continue. 'But, before we go, can I ask why you're *here*?' I look from DI Turner to Sergeant Richards. 'I take it this is something to do with *me*?'

'We can't say at present.' There's a hint of apology in his voice. 'I'm sorry.'

'But we'll call round to see you at your dad's,' says DI Turner, 'we have his address. It will be either before we go off duty at ten, or when we come back on at two o'clock tomorrow. We'll explain everything to you then.'

'Two o'clock *tomorrow*? I can't wait *that* long.'

'I'm sorry, Cathy. Rest assured, we'll be in touch as soon as we possibly can be.'

'But I agree with my daughter,' Dad says. 'If you leave it until tomorrow, it's extra stress for her while she's waiting. She's supposed to be recuperating.'

'I know and I'm sorry, but—'

'If you haven't got the time to make it to the house this evening, could you at least call or send us a message?' Dad says. 'Just so we know what this is about? You've got my number.'

'I'll do my best,' she replies, but there's hesitation in her voice which tells me we'll be waiting until tomorrow unless I push harder.

'Can't you just tell me which one of them you're here to talk to?' I look from Samantha to Daniel, searching their faces for anything that might give me a clue. 'It *has* to be something to do with *me*.'

'Cos everything's *always* about you, isn't it Cathy? You, you, you, you, you.'

'Mr Mason, please.' DI Turner frowns. 'Cathy, Bob, can I ask you to leave us to it please, I know it's frustrating, having to wait, but I promise we'll be in touch.'

'Your bag's at the bottom of the stairs.'

My eyes meet my husband's. That Daniel and I *ever* loved each other seems impossible. That we ever stood face to face, exchanging forever vows is almost laughable and if I hadn't seen photographic proof, I'd have never believed it. One positive thing my fall seems to have done for me is to provide me with a lucky escape. But it's also shaping up to be a messy one. If Daniel thinks I'm going to just limp away and crawl under a stone without putting up a fight for my home and my sons, he's very much mistaken.

'Come on, love.' Dad taps me on the shoulder. 'Let's get going. I think you've had quite enough for one day.' He helps me to my feet and I sense four sets of eyes boring into me as I shuffle to the door. I'm fast running out of energy and Dad's right, I need to rest. Part of me can't bear not knowing what's going on here, but the other part of me just wants to shut it all out for the day and escape into the nothingness of sleep.

∞

'Home sweet home.' Dad turns the keys in the ignition and looks towards his house. The lounge curtains are still open, bathing Teresa's face in the light of the TV, and the porch lamp casts a soft glow over Dad's front garden. It all looks far more inviting than my house did from the outside. Or the inside for that matter.

'Come on, let's get the kettle on while we wait to hear from the police. Or maybe we should have a glass of something stronger.'

'I can't – my painkillers. Besides, my head doesn't feel too good.'

'I bet it doesn't, not after walking into all that. But hopefully, Teresa's got your bed ready, and we can get you settled for the night. You look done in, love.'

I smile. 'I have been, haven't I? Done in, I mean, well, nearly. But I should probably stay awake until the police get in touch.'

'You heard what DI Turner said, it might not be until tomorrow. I think sleep would do you more good.'

'How can I sleep? I need to know what they were doing there. What do *you* think it was about, Dad?' I rest my aching head back against the leather of the seat.

A cat runs out of the garden next door and curls up under the car a few meters ahead of ours. I remember what Teresa said about me having nine lives the other day and just hope I still have a few of them intact.

'I really wouldn't like to say.'

'You don't think *Daniel* could have done this to me, do you?' I point at my head. 'He's admitted we'd been arguing that morning, *and* he knew I'd been chasing after Brad.' Daniel's angry face fills my mind. 'He could have easily left the boys sleeping and followed me to the station.'

'It's more likely to have been that *Samantha*,' Dad replies. 'Daniel's lower than low in my estimation right now, but he wouldn't do something like that – not to the mother of his children. I can't imagine him leaving them on their own either.'

'I've no idea what he's capable of,' I reply. 'In all honesty, I can't say I even know him. What I do know, is *she* was definitely at the station at the same time as me that morning. She catches the same train as me to the office.'

'But can you actually recall her being there? Did you see her?'

'I still can't remember that day, only tiny flashes, but Samantha showed up on one of the CCTV stills the police showed me, now I come to think of it.' I nod affirmatively as I speak. 'Yeah, I bet it *was* her.'

I jump at the tapping on the window and turn to see Teresa's face on the other side of the glass. Dad opens his door a fraction. 'Sorry love, we're just coming in.'

'I thought you were staying out here all night.' She forces a laugh. 'What's going on?'

'I'll fill you in on it all shortly,' Dad climbs out of the car and the blast of fresh air to release the scent of his awful air freshener is welcome. 'Let's just get Cathy settled with a brew and a sandwich.'

'I couldn't eat a thing, Dad,' I call after him as he walks around to the boot for my cane and bag. 'I'll just have a brew. I'm too wired for anything else.'

33

As I stare at the pattern on the chintzy wallpaper, it takes me several moments to work out where I am. What I do know is that every part of me hurts like hell. The double bed in Dad and Teresa's spare room is comfortable enough but I don't think I could get comfortable anywhere – not with my injuries.

I was so exhausted last night, I don't think I've moved since Dad helped me into bed. I hoist myself to sitting, my gaze falling on a cold cup of tea that's been left on the bedside table. I must have been wiped out to fall asleep without drinking it. The inside of my mouth tastes like something's died in it so I've also fallen asleep without brushing my teeth.

I slide one pyjama-clad leg from beneath the duvet, then the other, relieved when my feet connect with the chill of the wooden floor. The sun's filtering around the edge of the blinds and the heating's on. It's warm in here, too warm - more so than in my room at the hospital.

I stand slowly from the bed. My quad cane's downstairs but I'm determined to manage without it today. I'll get to the loo, have a go at making a cuppa with one hand, and then I might be ready to face the day, whatever it's likely to bring. Every day seems to be bringing some fresh hell. Dad's voice carries from his office at the front of the house as I carefully make my way down the sunlit stairs. It sounds like he's on the phone.

Finally, I arrive at the downstairs loo, flinching from my pain as I lower myself to the seat. I need more painkillers and I need them soon. I can't even remember whether I took some before falling asleep.

As I try to recall whether I did or not, memories of yesterday flood my mind. I close my eyes. What a day. Firstly, I found out about Emma being my half-sister. Then I was told Mel Connors had been released on bail. There was Daniel's awful hostility when I arrived at my house, before finding Samantha in the kitchen. I can't believe the extent to which she's double-crossed me. But mostly, there was the police arrival at the house. Were they there to speak to Daniel or Samantha? Even more importantly, *why*?

I shuffle across the tiles to the sink to wash, then fumble with the lock to get back out into the hallway. Hopefully, by now, the police will have been in touch with Dad. Maybe that's why he was on the phone as I came down the stairs.

'Morning, love.' He strides from his office into the hallway, his tense shoulders at odds with his relaxed jeans, woolly jumper and thick socks. 'How are you feeling?'

'Better for having some decent sleep but I could do with some painkillers.' I lean onto the sideboard.

'I'll fetch them from the kitchen while you make yourself comfy.' He points at the door to the lounge. 'With a brew of course. What do you want to eat?'

'Just some toast, please. Where's Teresa?'

'She's at work. Like I said, I'm taking some time off. Nurse Dad at your service.' He takes a mock bow.

I laugh which hurts my ribs. 'For how long?'

'I'm just waiting for the governors to authorise a fortnight for now. Then we'll see.' He laughs at the expression on my face. 'Don't worry – there won't be any problem if I need more time.'

'It's more that I'm in shock. You, being off work, I mean.'

'You're far more important to me than *work*.'

My vision blurs. Tears are never far away at the moment. 'Thanks. I don't know what I'd do without you.'

'It's all part of a dad's job description.'

'I could do with a shower. That's why I was asking about Teresa – I'll probably need a hand with washing my hair.'

'If you can wait until she comes home – or we could get in touch with Emma.' Dad looks uncomfortable as he says her name. I feel more uncomfortable at hearing it. 'She works from home, doesn't she? I think she's back at work, part-time, anyway. She had a bit of time off with her morning sickness.'

'No, let's not disturb her,' I say, quickly. 'I'll maybe wait for Teresa. Have the police been back in touch yet?'

'Yes – we'll talk about that in a minute. But first, you look like you need to sit down before you fall over.'

He helps me into the lounge and into the armchair Teresa was sitting in last night.

'Thanks, Dad.'

'Shall I put another log on that fire, or are you warm enough?'

'I'm fine.' I glance out at the conifers, their needles shimmering in the March breeze beyond the huge bay window. I'm so relieved to be out of that hospital. 'So, how does it feel being home from work on a Wednesday?'

'Strange actually – but it's a good sort of strange. Your new phone's there.' His eyes dart to an iPhone box on the coffee table.

'You're a star. Can you pass it over, though I've no idea how I'll get it all up and running without my old phone.'

'It's all done.' He beams. 'Luckily, you had me listed as a

recovery contact. You just need to reset your passwords for social media and your emails.'

'I really appreciate all you're doing for me.' A tear spills down my face. 'I probably don't deserve it.'

'Oh yes you do.' He reaches for my good shoulder and gives it a squeeze. 'Now let me get you that tea and toast. Then we'll talk.'

As he leaves the room, I brush the tears away with my pyjama sleeve and scan the room. It's a busy room, full of patterns and colour. Teresa's displayed far more pictures of Emma at varying life stages than Dad has of me and Harry. My gaze falls on the last school photo we had taken together. I was nearly sixteen, just about to start my exams and he was eleven, in his first year of high school. We were close then, united in the angst Mum's drinking and depression was inflicting on our home life. Dad was still with us at that point, well, he was supposed to be. He was always at work, or on a course, or as we didn't know until later, with *Teresa*.

There's a photo of Emma at about sixteen – two years before we met for the first time. I look from me to her. Do we look anything like each other? If we do, I really can't see it, or maybe I just don't want to. No doubt she'll be around here over the next couple of days but I can't say I'm looking forward to it, not now that the basis of our relationship has altered so drastically. Watching her and Dad around each other will also be awkward.

It's a struggle to open the iPhone box with just my left hand but I manage it and tip the phone onto my lap. Dad was right, he really has got it up and running. I press into the photos app and begin swiping through them.

There are the photos I've already seen when I looked on Facebook in the hospital. There are lots of the boys – in the park, at the pool, in a soft play area, painting at the table I faced Samantha over last night. Maybe I wasn't as bad a mother as

Daniel has been leading me to believe. Whatever I was or wasn't, I have to try and forgive myself. I was working in London to provide for my family. Perhaps my only crime was hankering after my ex-husband and misreading his friendliness as something else.

'Here we are.' Dad sweeps back into the room balancing a tray. He hooks the coffee table with his foot to bring it closer, placing a steaming mug in front of me and a plate filled with buttery toast. Its aroma makes my stomach growl.

'Thank you.'

He takes his tea and plate over to the sofa, placing it on a nest of tables.

I wipe at the butter which dribbles down my chin. 'Why does toast always taste better when someone else has made it?'

Dad finishes chewing and fixes me with his gaze. I can see Harry in him now. I'll get in touch with him soon, now I've got a phone again. Whatever's gone on between us, I want to sort things out with my brother. Life's too short not to. The last couple of weeks have certainly shown me that.

'Right, let's talk about my phone call with the police.'

34

'DI Turner rang just as you were getting out of bed,' Dad begins. 'It was good of her really, since she's not back on duty until two o'clock.'

'And?'

'They took Samantha to the station last night to answer some questions.' He sips from his cup.

So it was *Samantha* they wanted to speak to. 'Why?'

'She was already on their radar since you recognised her on one of the stills. More so because you mentioned her rivalry with you.'

'On their radar as a *suspect*?' I drop my toast back to the plate. My appetite has vanished as quickly as it arrived. 'For pushing me in front of the train?'

'You need to keep eating.' Dad points at my plate. 'Not only to build yourself back up but you shouldn't take those tablets on an empty stomach.'

'I will eat it,' I insist. 'In a minute.'

'The police also received a message,' Dad goes on, 'someone had filled in a 'report online' form, telling them about

Samantha and Daniel's relationship, and it backed up what you'd already told the police about her work vendetta.'

'So who sent it?'

'It was anonymous, but whoever it was knew about the two of them carrying on, *and* about what was going on down in London.'

'It *must* be someone else from work. Maybe I should give my manager another call – maybe it's even *her* if it's anonymous.'

'I don't think it was – I mentioned your manager to DI Turner and I got the impression they'd already spoken.'

'So has Samantha been kept at the station all night?'

Dad rests his plate on the table. 'Unfortunately not. She was released, pending further investigation, as they call it, just after midnight, which is why they've waited to let us know until this morning.'

I study his face, waiting for more.

'Eat your toast, Cathy. I'm not going to tell you another thing unless you start eating.'

I roll my eyes but pick my toast back up as instructed.

'Samantha's still a suspect, but they just haven't got enough evidence to bring any charges. She admits she was there that morning, she admits to having had a motive, but has emphatically denied that she had *anything* to do with your fall.'

'Bloody hell. What more do they need?'

'Forensic evidence, conclusive CCTV footage, eyewitnesses – and they've got none of that.' He sighs. 'There were around six hundred people on that platform, about to board the train and the view of what happened is completely obscured from every angle.'

'So now what?'

'Hang on.' He takes another gulp of his tea and a bite of his toast. I wait for him to finish chewing. The whole thing feels like one step forward and two steps back. But at least I feel safer here with Dad than I did in the hospital.

I take a sip of my tea. Dad makes one of the best brews – another positive thing about being out of hospital.

'OK, I don't quite know how to tell you this.'

'Now what?' *Can I really cope with any more?*

'DI Turner was preparing to question Daniel after she'd got off the phone with me.' Dad brushes crumbs from his chin.

'This morning?'

'They agreed last night that Daniel would call into the station after dropping the children off at school –to answer more of their questions. Toast!'

'Oh come on, Dad – how do you expect me to eat? They're questioning my bloody *husband* on suspicion of pushing me in front of a train. You said it couldn't possibly be him last night.'

'I know. But listen, they haven't actually arrested either of them, they've both gone in voluntarily.'

'Are they proper *interviews*?'

'According to DI Turner, they're recorded interviews under caution, which means they can be used in evidence. However, to use her words, they're both free to leave at any time as they haven't been arrested. But apparently, they've both been cooperative.' Dad rolls his eyes.

'Oh, I bet they have. It's *got* to be one of them, hasn't it? I can't think of any other people who'd hate me enough to do what they've done.'

Dad doesn't reply.

'Daniel sure put up a good pretence when I first woke up in intensive care. There I was, feeling hopelessly guilty for not being able to remember him when all the time...'

'Don't jump to any conclusions yet, love. Not until someone's actually charged.'

'So what am I supposed to do *now*?'

'While we know exactly where Daniel is, we should get the

ball rolling with some practicalities.' Dad pops the last of his toast in his mouth and washes it down with more tea. Meanwhile, I'm still nibbling on my first slice.

'What do you mean?'

'For starters, we'll get an appointment made for some legal advice,' Dad replies. 'I mean, about the kids and the house. We should also take a look at your bank accounts. Daniel could be moving funds around for all you know. You probably need to get things shored up to keep your money safe.'

'But I don't know any of my logins.'

'Don't worry. We can reset all that. Can you remember who you bank with?'

I stare back at him, my expression probably as blank as I feel.

'Will you have any paperwork back at your house? We know for certain he's not there at the moment so we could have a drive over.'

'My keys will be in my handbag which is still with the police.'

'I've got a key to your house.'

'*She* could be there though. Samantha.'

'Shouldn't she be in London?'

'Well she wasn't in London last night, was she?'

'So what do you want to do?'

'To be honest, Dad, I can't think straight. Can we just make an appointment with a solicitor? Then I'll spend some time today trying to remember what I can about bank accounts and all that. Once I get into my emails and texts, that should give me a few clues.'

'You look shattered, love. You've only just got up and you look like you should go back to bed.'

'My head's banging.' I rub my hand across my stitches. 'I've had my painkillers but they'll take a while to work.'

He rises from the sofa and drags a blanket from one of the

beanbags in the bay window. 'Have a lie-down,' he tells me. 'I'll get that appointment made, then I've got a few other bits I need to do in the office. You rest for an hour, then hopefully you'll be fit to start tackling things.'

I don't need much persuasion. Abandoning my tea and toast. I haul myself up and make my way across the carpet as Dad pulls the curtains together.

'It's a shame to shut the sunshine out, but I'm sure you don't want it glaring into your face.'

'Thanks.' I lower myself to the sofa.

'Do you want the telly on?'

'No, I think I'd rather be quiet.'

'Here, get this under your head. That's it, swing your legs round, let's get you covered up.'

I feel about five years old as Dad drapes the blanket over me before adding another log to the fire. Then, as he clicks the lounge door behind him, a wave of sadness crashes over me and the tears I've been suppressing since I awoke this morning are finally released. I don't care what Dad says – I must have been really, really awful to deserve all this.

Why else would my own husband currently be getting questioned for pushing me in front of a train?

35

'You need to come home, Cathy.' Harry's voice is strangled. 'I don't know what the hell to do.'

'You mean to Mum's house?' Harry might still class it as home – for now, while he's staying there, but he'll be gone in a few weeks when the house he's bought has completed. For me, however, that house ceased to be my home seventeen years ago when I finished university. I hated going back there during my holidays but Mum made me feel guilty if I tried to invent an excuse.

As the years have passed, it's become easier to get out of going back to the place that was filled with so much misery – Mum's misery. 'Why, what's going on?'

'Just get here. Please, sis – there's literally no one else I can turn to – no one else who'd understand.'

'Just tell me what's happened, Harry.' I can only assume Mum's fallen off the wagon after finding out about Dad and Teresa's anniversary party. Or that she and Harry have had some sort of row. 'Tell me what I'm walking into, so I know.'

'Not over the phone.' His voice is heavy with desperation. 'How long will you be?'

'Not long – I'm on my way.'

During the drive, a myriad of possibilities loop through my head. If it's not drink, maybe Mum's taken tablets, or perhaps it's something else entirely. I keep coming back to the notion of her and Harry having fallen out – perhaps it will be as simple as that. He's always trying to persuade her to remortgage the house, saying he needs his share of his inheritance for his property-buying endeavours – now rather than when she dies. Rightly, she usually tells him where to go, which leads to even more of Harry's resentment towards her and guilt-tripping behaviour.

Really, I don't know why he's moved back in with Mum. He tells me how ashamed he is of her bloated face, her waddle when she ventures from the lounge to the kitchen, and her voice which he claims goes straight through his skull. He's right about her weight but there's no need for him to speak about her so cruelly.

Nor do I understand why Mum keeps clinging to him.

I pull up outside my childhood home and for a moment, I can visualise my younger face at the window. A face etched with expectation, waiting for my father to come home. A face riddled with envy at seeing girls skip along the street arm-in-arm with their mothers, while mine lay comatose on the sofa. I have so many visions of my life when I arrive at this house and none of them are happy.

I venture up the path, praying that whatever Harry needs my help with is worth leaving work early for. The silence stops me in my tracks as I reach the door. What the hell am I walking into? I listen for a moment.

Nothing.

I push my way in to find Harry leaning against the kitchen counter, staring at our mother who's slumped on the floor. I rush over to help.

'Mum.' I pummel at her shoulder. 'Mum, for goodness sake, wake up – how much have you had to drink? I can't believe she's fallen off the wagon again – spectacularly by the look of it.'

'You're wasting your time.'

'Help me, will you, Harry? She's just drunk. Let's get her onto the sofa. We can't leave her on the cold tiles.'

But as I look more closely, I know there's zero possibility of raising her from the ground. She'd need to be more than half the size she is for the two of us to stand a chance.

'She's dead.' My brother's voice is flat.

'An ambulance might be our only option – at least they'll have the equipment to hoist her.' I crouch down, reaching for her hand which feels like a cold quiver of jelly as I lift it from the floor.

'Didn't you hear me, Cathy?' Harry's voice rises. 'I said she's dead. Maybe we should just burn the house down like they did in that 'What's Eating Gilbert Grape' film. It's better than the embarrassment of them needing to hire a crane to move her.'

'Just shut up, will you?' I probe Mum's wrist for a pulse. It's not easy to find under this extra weight. 'She's just drowsy – like she often is on an afternoon. Come on, once we get her to the sofa, we'll somehow get some water down her and then let her sleep it off for a couple of hours.'

'She's not bloody drunk.' He slides down the cupboard so we're at the same height. 'She's had a heart attack.'

'What?' I spin around on the floor to check he's being serious. 'Why the hell didn't you say so?' I jump up and sit astride her, positioning my hands ready to perform chest compressions. Harry's right, she's not moving – I don't even think she's breathing. Shit. Shit. Shit.

'Come on, Mum. You're scaring me now. Just breathe, Mum, please.'

'Like I said, you're wasting your time.'

'How can you say that? She's our mother, for God's sake.'

'And you're wasting your energy. She's gone – she's dead. She's been dead for an hour.'

'How can you know that if you weren't even he—' It takes a moment or so for his words to compute. 'Hang on – you were here?'

His face says it all.

'So you've already called for help?' I glance towards the window.

'I called you, didn't I?'

'I meant an ambulance? So where the hell are they?' I snatch my bag up from the floor and pull my phone out. 'Did you call them straightaway?'

'It's no good calling for an ambulance now.' Harry's voice is far steadier than it was when he first rang. 'You'd be better phoning an undertaker.'

I shuffle across the floor, kneeling in front of him as I grip his bony shoulders in each of my hands. 'Did you see this happen, Harry? Did Mum have her heart attack right in front of you – tell me?'

He gazes down at the floor, saying nothing.

'Tell me, I said.' I shake his shoulders.

'She was holding her chest, alright? Then she said she didn't feel too good.'

'What happened next?' My voice is a screech.

'She just crashed to the ground.'

'You called an ambulance though, right?'

'She didn't die straight away.' He closes his eyes and then opens them, fixing me with an unblinking stare. 'She was staring at me, just like we are, making this noise with her breathing.' He rasps in and out, in and out. I stare back at him. Is he trying to tell me what I think he is?

'Did you just leave our mother to die?' I shake him again. 'Did you?'

'She's better off dead.'

'How can you say that?' I yell into his face. 'Oh my God, oh my God. You've knowingly allowed her to die.'

'And I'm better off without her. She wouldn't do a thing to help me – not ever.' He's gabbling now. 'Besides, she's nothing but an embarrassment. Look at the state of her.'

I let go of him and stare down at the twenty-three stone remains of the woman who gave us both life. The one who tried her best to look after us until drink and the grief of Dad not loving her stole her away.

Eventually, when we were both too old to need her in the same way, she was put on Antabuse tablets to prevent her from killing herself. Over the next few months, she switched her addiction from drink to food, justifying her ballooning weight on the fact that binge eating was better than binge drinking. But she never moved, she never went out, she never did anything. Apart from getting on Harry's and my cases for not being a good enough son and daughter. For not visiting her often enough. But all she did was sit on the sofa in front of the TV and eat. Food was her only friend and her complete solace.

'You let her die.' My voice is softer. Part of me seems to have seeped away with her. My mother is dead. She wasn't much of a mother but I'm certain she did the best she could.

'I didn't want to help her.' There isn't a trace of regret on my brother's face. 'I'm glad she's gone and I'd do it all over again if I had the chance.'

'So why call me?' My voice rises. 'Why drag me into all this?'

'Cos you'll sort it out,' he replies. 'You'll know how to handle it. You always do.'

36

'No! No!'

'Hey, Cathy, wake up.' A comforting hand rests on my shoulder. Then another one on my arm. 'It's OK – you're just having a bad dream.'

I'm soaked in sweat as I open my eyes to stare into Emma's. I force myself into a sitting position and glance around the room, hoping to see Dad in the armchair next to the fire.

'How come *you're* here? Where's my dad?'

'*My* dad too, remember?' Her voice is clipped as she perches herself in front of me on the footstool.

I close my eyes again. How could I possibly forget?

'He called to ask me to help you shower.'

'Is he in his office?' Despite being three months pregnant, Emma looks slim and energetic in her yoga clothes. What I wouldn't give to be wearing normal clothes and to be able to exercise, instead of being laid up like this.

'He's been called into work. Something urgent has come up that the school can't deal with without him. But it's fine. I was planning to visit you today, anyway.' She sweeps her gaze around the lounge. 'It feels weird, *you* staying here.'

'Why?'

'This used to be *my* home.'

'It won't be for long – just until I'm back on my feet.'

'Hmm.' She doesn't look at all happy.

I need to change the subject. 'Have you heard about Daniel and Samantha?' It should hurt putting their names together, after all, I'm married to the man. But I feel nothing.

'Yes.' She slides a band from her wrist.

'About *all* of it?' I manoeuvre myself to sit up as best I can against the cushions.

'Yup.' She twists her hair into a loose bun on top of her head which I stare at in envy. My hair will take months, if not years to grow to a length where I can twist it into a bun.

'Did my dad tell you?' I don't care what Emma says – I can't help but put the *my* in front of Dad. If I was talking to Harry, it would be different, but I really can't bring myself to accept this new reality within our family.

She narrows her eyes which suggests she's noticed my faux pas, but she doesn't challenge me. 'Yeah, but just before he set off, someone called him from the police station.'

'And?'

'Apparently, Daniel's also been released – pending further enquiries.'

'Not enough evidence to charge him, I suppose – just like with Samantha?'

'That's what they said.'

'Bloody hell.' I close my eyes. 'So I've still got to live my life looking over my shoulder?'

She nods. 'I'm sorry to be the bearer of bad news but in any case, if they're still suspects, they've probably been told to stay clear of you.'

'Like that's going to stop either of them if they want to kill me.'

'What was going on when I first walked in? What the hell

were you dreaming about? You were shouting, well almost screaming.'

'My mum.' I try to swallow the lump in my throat. 'It's all this memory stuff.' I pause then it all hits me again. 'I don't think it was just a dream though – I'm pretty sure I was remembering something real.'

She doesn't say anything. She just sits on the footstool with her hands together in her lap, waiting for me to continue.

'I was dreaming that *he* killed her. It was all *his* fault.'

'What are you talking about? *Who* killed *who*?'

'Harry.'

'What about him? What do you mean?'

'Harry killed my Mum. I remember it all – it wasn't a dream – it really happened.'

Emma's face doesn't register the sort of shock I'd expect. 'So, this is one of the things that's coming back to you, is that what you're saying?' Emma pulls the footstool closer to the sofa and drops back onto it. 'What your brother did, I mean?'

'You sound like you believe me.'

'I already knew.' Her voice is soft as she tucks a stray hair behind her ear.

'You *knew*? But how?'

'*Harry* told me.' Her face betrays nothing.

'I don't understand why he'd confide in *you*. You barely get along most of the time.'

'He wasn't exactly *confiding* in me.' Emma exhales slowly, as if releasing tension. 'He was *threatening* me.'

'You're joking.'

'He's been off with me for a while – even you noticed, but as you keep saying, you can't remember.'

'I'll take your word.'

'It all started when I was living back here for a bit – when he saw me as being financially subsidised by *his* dad. In his eyes, Bob was spending money on *me* which was rightfully his.'

'But that was years ago. And I remember it as if it was yesterday so it's definitely more than ten years ago.'

'Then, a couple of weeks ago,' Emma goes on, 'just before what happened to you, I caught Harry in my mum's purse, helping himself to one of her credit cards.'

'Oh no. I can't believe he's gone back to that sort of behaviour.'

'Yes, and he got pretty nasty when he realised he'd been rumbled.' She rolls her eyes.

'This is a common theme with Harry at the moment from what I'm gathering.'

'I mean, really nasty.' She gives me a pointed look.

'Go on.'

'He threatened he'd kill me if I told a soul, and you could see in his eyes that he wasn't messing.'

'Oh my God.' I clap a hand over my mouth.

'I should have just walked away but instead, I laughed in his face.'

My brother's angry face fills my mind. 'That will have been like a red rag to a bull.'

'It really was. He grabbed me by my scarf and snarled into my face that he was being deadly serious. He said he'd killed someone before and wouldn't think twice about doing it again.'

I sit up straighter. 'Did he know about you being pregnant?'

'I doubt it. I fought back though.' She displays her perfectly manicured pink nails. 'I sank these into his arm. 'That's when it came out that he'd killed your mum – when he said he'd do the same to me. So yes, I already knew.'

37

I'm engulfed by panic. No matter what, I can't allow Emma, or *anyone* to believe that Harry's some kind of cold-blooded murderer.

'He didn't actually *kill* our mum – he just stood by and never helped her when she was having her heart attack.'

I can't believe how this makes me sound – almost like I'm making excuses for my brother. Perhaps this makes me more complicit in Mum's death. The look Emma shoots me suggests she's thinking the same.

'And I know he regretted it afterwards, but by then, well, obviously, it was too late.'

'That's what he told me but it was hard to believe while he had me by the throat.' She rubs at it as if she's back in the moment. 'Anyway, I managed to fight Harry off and told him I was going to report him to the police.'

'So you believe me then?' No matter how rotten my brother seems to have been, he's still my brother and I can't imagine what could ever kill my big sister instinct.

'Whether I do or I don't, allowing your mum to die like that is almost as bad as actually killing her. So I told him that I was still going to make a report.'

'Really?'

'That's when he told me *you'd* been involved with your mother's death.' It might be my imagination but her voice sounds almost smug. As if she's enjoying having something over me.

'I wasn't *involved*.'

'But you knew what he'd done and you didn't tell a soul.'

I bow my head, shame rushing through my veins. 'The details of exactly what happened are sketchy.'

'Oh, come on, Cathy.' She slaps her palm against one of her lycra-clad legs. 'This memory stuff is starting to get tedious.'

'Let's say I *had* told everyone what he'd done, it wasn't as if it could have brought our mother back. He's my little brother, Emma – I've always looked after him.'

A shadow crosses her face as I'm once again reminded that he's now *her* little brother as well. And she's possibly wondering whether I'd go to similar lengths to protect *her*, now that we know we're half-sisters.

'The truth is, Cathy, that if *you* hadn't been part of his cover-up, *nothing* would have stopped me from reporting him.'

I continue to stare at the floor, unable to meet her eyes.

'Your brother is one nasty and messed up individual.' She folds her arms across her chest. 'The day before I caught him in my mum's purse, he'd been hassling *her* for this loan. Everyone else had said no so he thought he could bully her.'

I can't imagine *anyone* bullying Teresa but it's best if I stay quiet and let Emma vent.

'For as long as I've known Harry,' Emma goes on, 'he's just been out for himself. And to be honest, Cathy, at times, you haven't been much better.'

'What's that supposed to mean?' Great, it's my turn to be criticised.

'Everything's always about *you.*' The gentleness of Emma's voice is completely at odds with her words. 'Even your dad, *our* dad had started to keep you at arm's length.'

'No, that's not true.' My stitches pull against my scalp as I frown. 'Just because it's turned out that I'm having to share my father with you, don't think you can drive a wedge between us.'

'If you don't believe me, go ahead and ask him.'

'I saw the messages that were sent between the two of us. He wished me luck with my interview. He was involved in my life. He cares about me.'

'He's that type of man,' she continues. 'He cares about everyone and always wants to do the right thing.'

'Are you saying you know my father better than I do?' My tone is filled with caution.

'You forget – I've lived with him as an adult.' She tilts her head to one side as if trying to get a better view of my reaction. 'Not only when I was home at the weekends from uni, but also before I married Joel.'

'It's not some kind of contest.' I glance at the clock. 'Look, forget the shower – I'll manage. I just want to be on my own if you don't mind.'

'So you're telling me to leave?' She smiles. 'It doesn't work like that in this house.'

'In that case, I'll go to my room.' I just want to get away from her – I've had enough.

'Just remember that I've got just as much right to be in this house as you have. If not more. *Both* of my parents are here, after all.'

She doesn't move out of my way as I lean on the arm of the sofa to get to my feet. Nor does she help me. As I blink back tears, it dawns on me what's happening. I lean back against the cushions. 'Come on, Emma, I can't believe we're falling out like this. Let's sort it out – we're supposed to be friends.'

She folds her arms across her chest. 'You just don't want me repeating your sordid secret to anyone, do you? Which is ironic really, since you've already threatened to blow the whistle on Harry yourself.'

'What are you talking about?'

'The day before you ended up in hospital. You told Harry that telling the truth about what he'd done to your mum would be worth it to get him out of your life.'

'I wouldn't have said that.' I lock eyes with Emma.

'You said it when he was hounding you for money.'

I'm facing Harry in my hallway. We're standing at the front door but I'm not inviting him further into the house. My body language is defensive and the back of my neck prickles. I want to be well away from him. His hands are balled into fists but he'd never hit me. He never has. He never would.

'You also repeated what our dad had said about him, didn't you? A *waste of space*, wasn't it?'

'I don't remember. I need to think.'

'Look, I'm sorry if I've sounded harsh but all this needs to be brought into the open.' She folds her arms across her chest.

'How do you know all this?'

'Harry told me, that's how. While you were out of it.'

I'm beginning to wish I still was. 'Like I said before, Emma, I could do with some quiet. My head's killing me. I'm going upstairs.' I sit forward on the sofa.

Emma shuffles on the footstool, clearly unsure about her next move. 'I might as well go.' Slowly, she gets to her feet but the expression on her face suggests that she's still got something left to say.

'I'm sorry it's come to this today.' I grip the arm of the sofa. I can't recall a time when Emma and I have ever fallen out.

She threads her arms into her coat. 'Before I go, shall I tell you what I think?'

'If you must.' I get the sense that she's going to whether I like it or not.

She wraps a scarf around her neck. 'Do you *really* want to know?'

'Probably not, but you're going to tell me anyway?'

She zips her coat. 'OK.' She allows a maddening pause to elapse. 'If you want to know who might have had the greatest motive to push you in front of a train that morning,' She leans in so close, I can feel her breath on my face.

'Who?'

'Look no further than your brother.'

38

'Do you know what your problem is?' My brother squares up to me, the veins popping in his temple – if he were to lose his temper, I'd be no match for him these days.

'No, but I'm sure you're going to tell me.' My head feels like it's being squashed against the wall behind me as Harry closes the gap between us. I can't get away from him.

'You think you're a cut above everyone else, don't you, Cathy?'

'I don't know what you're talking about.' I try to push him back but he's holding firm. He follows me as I step to the side.

'You might want to look like a respectable person with their shit together, but I grew up with you, remember? You're as messed up as I am, if not more so.'

'People improve themselves, Harry. You should try it sometime, instead of being the big, I'm gonna...'

'What's that supposed to mean?'

'I'm gonna buy this flat, I'm gonna flip that house, I'm gonna do this, I'm gonna do that. And what have you done? Apart from coming to me and Dad for handouts? You haven't even paid me back from the last time.'

'I'm sick of you looking down your nose.' His spittle lands on my face.

I raise my hand to wipe it and he flinches as if I'm about to hit him. 'And I'm sick of you blaming me for everything that's wrong with your life,' I reply. 'I had the same start that you had, the mother who couldn't get her act together...' Mum's miserable face invades my thoughts and I blink it away, 'the father that moved on from us, the guilt after what you did.' I point at him.

'If you just do this one thing for me, that'll be it, sis. I'll never ask you for anything else.'

He always calls me sis when he's trying to worm around me. Either that, or he refers to me as his second mum. He knows it pulls at my heartstrings. That's the trouble with my brother, he's too familiar with my weak spots.

'What part of the word 'no' are you having difficulty with?' I stand up tall. 'There's no way you're getting another penny. So leave me and Dad alone.'

'I'd strongly advise you to reconsider.' His jaw throbs with the tension that seems to be coursing through his body. 'Because, if you don't—'

'Cathy, love – DI Turner and Sergeant Richards are downstairs.'

I force my eyes to open. If the two of them are back on duty, it must be after two o'clock. I'm sick of spending so much of my time sleeping – what a waste of life. I'd give anything to be living a normal life instead of *this*. Whatever my 'normal' is.

I haul myself up to seated.

'Is Emma still downstairs?' I grip the bannister with my good hand.

'No,' he replies. 'Did she help you to shower?'

'She was in a rush.' I reach the bottom, relieved she hasn't stuck around.

'We're sorry to disturb you, Cathy.' DI Turner is standing by the window as I enter the lounge. 'But we just wanted to talk through where we're up to with the case.'

'How are you doing?' Sergeant Richards's at her side, his hands thrust deep into his pockets.

I make my way back over to the sofa. 'I've been better, to be honest.'

'Do you mind if we sit down?'

'No, of course, take a seat.' Dad gestures to the two armchairs as he helps me to sit and then takes a seat beside me.

DI Turner's expression appears to be loaded with even more sympathy than normal. I suppose it would be after what came to light last night. My husband and my former work colleague. And here I am, reduced to sleeping at my father's house. I must look a fright as well. I'm wearing my pyjamas, I still haven't showered and the scar on my head makes me look like something from The Living Dead. I wish I could regain the positivity I had when working with Zoe. But that's all evaporated.

'Before we go any further, can I ask a question?' All eyes turn to me.

'Sure. Ask away.'

'Did you take a statement from my brother, Harry?'

I glance at Dad whose face creases into an expression of puzzlement. 'What's that got to do with anything?'

I'm going to have to tell him, and *them* what's come back to me, no matter how awful it is to face the facts and to be honest about my part in Mum's death. If Emma's hunches are right, if it *was* Harry who pushed me that day, he needs to be stopped, locked up, or whatever, before he can cause me any more damage. I have those boys of mine to get better for. To *fight* for.

'We've spoken to your brother, of course we have – we asked him the same questions as we have the rest of your family.'

'Why?' The expression on Sergeant Richards's face suggests

he's picked up that I'm getting at something important. 'What is it?'

'OK – look – I'm going to tell you *everything*.' I inhale slowly in an attempt to steady my breath.

∾

'OK, thanks. Keep us posted.' Dad's words reverberate through the hallway walls as I stare at the photo of my brother's cherubic face, taken in the short time we were together at primary school. His blonde hair and blue eyes display none of the anger and resentment he's come to harbour in later life. He'd have been about five in the photo, me ten, and I can recall how much I enjoyed being one of the few in my class who were having a sibling photo done when the school photographer visited.

Harry and I used to seek each other out at playtimes when he first started school. We were supposed to remain in our separate key-stage playgrounds, but I adored my little brother and being one of the smallest and youngest in his class, I wanted to make sure he was alright.

As Dad returns to the lounge, it's impossible to tell what he's thinking. He lets out a long breath, his eyes flickering shut for a moment as he lowers himself into the chair Sergeant Richards just vacated.

'Talk to me, Dad.'

'I'm just trying to get my head around it all.' He checks his watch. 'Teresa will be home in half an hour.'

'All the more reason for us to talk before she gets back.' I don't take my eyes off his face as I search for a glimmer that he isn't blaming me for everything. 'Look, I'm really sorry.'

'For what?' He leans back in the chair and clasps his hands behind his head.

'All of it – protecting Har—'

'I'm not blaming you in the slightest, love. You've always had your brother's back. But I can't deny that it's come as a shock.'

'Mum was already long gone when I got to the house.' A memory of her huge body sprawled across the kitchen tiles fills my mind. 'Nothing I could have done would have made any difference.'

'It's OK, love. I know it wasn't you.'

'Are you going to tell Harry that you've found out?'

He lowers his eyes to meet mine. 'To be honest, I still need to work out how I feel. I can't even think straight.'

'I'm really sorry, Dad.'

'Will you stop saying sorry?'

'Sorry.'

He smiles, despite the increasing awfulness of it all. Mum, in her more lucid moments used to tell me that she should have given me *sorry* as my middle name. *Stop being such a people pleaser,* she would often say. *People won't like you any more for it – they'll just have a better excuse to walk all over you.*

'After what you told the police about your argument with Harry.' Dad lets out a huge sigh. 'And how angry he's been over our refusal to lend him the money...' His words hang in the air. 'What I mean is, if he can do what he did to his own mother, then—' He stops, but I know what he was going to say.

'It's OK. You're only voicing out loud what we're both thinking.'

'It isn't good from where I'm sitting.'

Still, neither of us can say the words. That my own brother might have pushed me in front of a train.

That for whatever reason, Harry hates me enough to want me dead.

39

Teresa replaces the shower head before passing a fluffy white towel from the rail. 'There you are.' She's barely spoken to me as I've showered and the expression on her face says she'd rather not have been forced into helping me. She holds the edge of the towel as I manage to wrap it around my back.

'Thanks for giving me a hand. I know you must be tired after work.' Here I go again – people pleasing.

'Well, somebody had to help. You're a bit long in the tooth to be bathed by your dad.' There's more of an edge to her voice now we're on our own together and she can't be overheard.

'You don't mind me staying here, do you, Teresa?' I cast my gaze around her pristine white tiles. I'm sure I've got similar tiles in my bathroom but I'm struggling to remember.

'Well, obviously it's not ideal – I mean, with Bob having to take time off work, especially when you've got a home of your own to go to.' She holds the shower head over the bath to rinse it.

'Dad said you were happy to have me here.' Great – she *isn't*. Really, I should have known.

'When are you seeing the solicitor?' She turns to face me.

'We've got an appointment tomorrow. Don't worry, I'll be out of your hair as soon as possible.'

'It's just that we've had a lot going on lately. There's this thing with Emma and your Dad, and—'

I grip the towel where its edges meet under my arm. I'll wait until she's gone and then I'll manage dressing on my own. I thought Teresa was willing to help me but Dad must have been making it up to make me feel better about coming here.

'It was a shock to find out about Emma.' I'm glad to change the subject. 'That she's my half-sister, I mean.'

Some people would tear a strip off this woman for her secrecy and lies over the years, not to mention what her very existence did to my poor mother. But there seems little point in causing any more friction within the fragments of my family.

'Yes, well, at least everything's finally out in the open.'

'Why didn't you tell Emma when she was younger?'

The look on her face suggests I've overstepped the mark but then as quickly as it arrives, her mouth relaxes and I get a sense she might be straight with me. 'There comes a point where too much time has elapsed.' She sits on the edge of the bath, gripping it with her bony fingers. 'When the longer something has gone on, the harder it is to upend things.'

There's probably also the hefty divorce settlement I heard she wheedled out of her ex-husband, not to mention the even heftier maintenance payments he made for Emma for so many years. He might have lingered on the outskirts of his daughter's life in a physical and emotional sense, but financially, he appears to have been forced to cough up handsomely. Perhaps, he'd have grounds to take Teresa to court if he were to find out she'd spent years hiding the truth about Emma's suspected parentage. Of course, I don't say any of this out loud.

'Whatever's happening between Bob and Emma should be the least of your concerns.' Teresa rises from the edge of the bath. 'You should be more worried about whether the police have caught up with your brother. Because if they haven't, he could still turn up here.'

'Is the front door locked?'

'It should be but I'll double-check.'

'I don't know whether it's a positive thing or not that we haven't heard from them,' I say as she opens the bathroom door.

She pauses to look back at me. 'It probably means he's still being questioned.'

~

'Are you decent, love?' Dad taps at the door to the room where I'm staying. I don't feel like I can call it *my* room – not now I know that I'm not as welcome as Dad led me to believe. Part of me wants to mention this to him, but the greater part doesn't want to cause any trouble.

'Yeah, I'm just watching telly.' I signal towards it with a flick of my wrist. 'I thought I'd give you and Teresa some space.'

'That's very thoughtful,' – he comes further into the room, – 'but you don't have to do that. I've only been in my office.'

That's even more of a reason for me to hide away. I don't exactly want to be stuck in a room alone with my stepmum. But I can't, and I won't repeat this to Dad.

'Teresa's gone to see Emma,' he adds.

'Oh.'

I'm sure they've got plenty to talk about. Again, I don't say this to Dad. If anyone's going to look like a trouble-causer in this cesspit that's become our family, it's not going to be me.

'The police have just rung,' he says. 'They've suspended the interview with Harry and DI Turner is driving over.'

'Here? Again? Why?'

'Some new evidence has just come to light that she's wanting to discuss with you before they go any further.'

'This is going to be either really good or really dreadful.' I drag a pillow over my stomach. 'Either they've got something major on *him*, or...' My words taper off into nothing.

In spite of it all, I'm tormented by the knowledge that my brother's in a police interview room. I still can't let myself believe he'd be capable of hurting me. Until he admits it or is charged and found guilty, I can't accept he could want to kill me.

'Come on, I'll put the kettle on while we wait.'

Tea. Dad's answer to every problem.

∼

'I'm sorry to bother you again, Cathy but I have a couple of things I need you to look at.'

DI Turner clutches a brown folder which she lays on the kitchen table as she stands facing us. 'As we mentioned, we've been analysing CCTV footage,' she says. 'We've shifted the focus to passengers arriving from internal trains rather than through the main barriers.'

I wrap my fingers around the hot mug of tea as if it might bring me comfort.

'And we've got a clear shot of someone we'd like you to identify.'

Every part of me tenses and a prickling sensation crawls up my spine. *Do I want to look at this?* Dad cranes his neck as DI Turner tugs the photograph from her folder and turns it around.

40

'As you can see, the person in the photo has briefly lifted his hat to scratch his head. Which was long enough for us to obtain this image.'

Dad glances at the photo and then averts his eyes. 'It's Harry – one hundred per cent.'

'Can you confirm this as well, Cathy?' DI Turner looks at me, her bobbed hair swaying with the motion.

'Yes.' I close my eyes. 'It *is* my brother. But what does this mean?' Unless I see actual footage of him pushing me from the train platform, I can't accept what's going on here. *Not* my little brother.

'I got this rushed through after what you told us about him this morning.'

I can't believe I'm feeling guilty for what I've said. It's ridiculous but guilt seems to be my default setting.

'Can either of you think of a reason why Harry might have been at Leeds train station at seven in the morning of Monday the third of March?'

'He's self-employed.' Dad scratches his head. 'Well, kind of. He's been in a mess with things – money, I mean. But no, he's got no reason to be catching a train, not that I know of. He drives, in any case.'

'We've now also got copies of the transcripts from your phone, Cathy.' DI Turner reaches back into her folder. I like her jacket. It's the sort of thing I wore as a journalist – in my happier days when I was married to Brad. It's funny what you remember at a time like this. It's looking like my own brother's tried to kill me and I'm here, admiring a detective inspector's jacket.

'They've taken their time,' says Dad.

'Two weeks is quite normal,' she replies. 'You should see how long it takes for items which aren't expedited.'

'What are you showing me?' I squint at the page of print as she slides it in front of me. 'I don't even know whether I'm supposed to wear glasses.' I try to force a smile but it's not happening. There's not a great deal to smile about. It's like the *only* person I can count on is Dad, yet *both* Teresa and now Emma are trying to get between us.

'Normally you do wear them,' Dad tells me. 'For reading anyway.'

Emma must have been talking crap when she was leading me to believe that Dad keeps me at arm's length. He knows so many details about me that he couldn't if we didn't see each other regularly. At least I'm aware of her reasons now – that she probably doesn't want to share him with me, any more than I want to share him with her.

'It's alright. I can just about read it.'

'This is a transcript of text messages from the second of March,' DI Turner explains. 'Between you and your brother.'

Not that I need telling. As soon as I read the first line, I know what I'm looking at. Dad hangs over my shoulder.

> I hear you've been bleating to Dad.

About what?

> You'd warned him that I might ask Teresa for the loan.

She told you that, I take it?

> You're even more of a weasel than I thought.

For God's sake, Harry – I'm your sister. Please don't be like this. Just because I won't stump up the kind of money you want doesn't mean I don't care.

> You only care about yourself. You could easily afford to help me get this property. With your posh house, your fancy job and all the investments you keep bragging about.

No I don't.

> I hope you remember what I said to you the other day.

About what?

> About how, if you won't reconsider helping me, you can count me out of your life for good. I mean it, Cathy. You mentioned families – and families are supposed to help each other.

Haven't I already helped you enough over the years? Bloody hell, you don't know how much it's all dragged me down at times.

> You're talking about what happened with Mum?

What happened??? That's bloody putting it mildly! You stood back and watched her die.

> And I'd do it again. But I'll do it with you next time.

> What????? What the hell are you saying?

> You say you've had enough of my shit, well I've had enough of yours. You'd better watch your back, 'sis.'

'Surely not. Not my own *brother*.' I push the sheet of paper back across the table. 'He can be a nasty piece of work but what he's typed there, he won't have meant it literally – no way.'

'It must be a shock, but nevertheless, we've probably got enough to dig deeper and ultimately bring charges.' She glances at the clock. 'But I came here because I wanted you to see what we've got so far, first hand, to help you to understand why we're putting this evidence in front of the Crown Prosecution Service.'

'No.' Dad pushes his glasses to his forehead and rubs at the bridge of his nose. 'My son's *many* things but I can't accept he'd push his sister in the path of a train.'

'Unfortunately, Mr Wheeler, these messages show his feelings towards Cathy only the evening before it happened.' She draws the page back towards herself and slides it back into the folder.

'Presumably, Harry will have known when and where Cathy caught her train every week?' She looks at Dad with questioning eyes as he nods and averts his gaze to the floor. A cloud of silence hangs between us all for a few moments as the enormity of what's happening envelops me. I'm still hoping there'll be another story here – one that doesn't involve my brother.

Dad clears his throat. 'OK, there's maybe more to all this.'

'What?' I try to relax my jaw and my shoulders. I'm no doubt causing myself far more physical pain with the tension

I'm holding. But this is the stuff of nightmares and a hundred times worse than what Harry did to our mum.

'He has even more of a motive than you've probably been told about.' Dad's voice is uncertain as if he can scarcely believe what he's saying. Effectively, he's turning his son in to save his daughter.

'What?' We both look at him.

'Money,' Dad replies. 'He knows he stands to gain from your will.'

'Are you sure? I don't even recall making one.'

'It's probably filed in your head along with your bank accounts,' he says. 'But yes, I'm positive.'

'What am I leaving *Harry* money for?' I lift my arm in its sling onto the table. 'I've got a husband and two kids who would come well before him, surely?' I stare at the side of Dad's unshaven face. He never goes a day without shaving which shows how the stress of everything must be getting to him.

'You've always been like a second mum to Harry, especially during everything your mother put you both through.' Dad sinks to the chair beside me. 'God knows, he's never deserved it. All he's ever done is take, take, take from you. Well – from everyone.'

I can't get my head around this.

'You've split what doesn't automatically go to Daniel, for instance, in places like your joint account, four ways,' Dad explains. 'Money in places like your current account, and in your personal investments and savings, are to be divided between Daniel, Harry, Austyn and Matthew – according to your will.' He touches the table in front of him in four places to illustrate how things will be divided into quarters.

'And Harry *knows* about this?' DI Turner arches an eyebrow.

'He was there when Cathy asked my wife to be one of the witnesses to her will.'

The pain in my head seems to have tripled in intensity since

I sat at this table. 'I just don't remember any of this – bloody hell.' I slap my palm against the table and glance at the clock. As soon as she's gone, I need more painkillers.

'So we know he's already been inclined to let someone, his mother, die for his financial gain. We now know he could also be driven by financial motivation with *you*, and lastly,' DI Turner holds up the still showing Harry. 'As you've confirmed, we've now got concrete confirmation of Harry's whereabouts at the time of your fall, *and* the fact that he had no other business being at Leeds train station that morning.'

Dad and I exchange glances. His eyes are flooded with tears.

'So I'm really sorry to put it like this, but your brother will no doubt be charged and will be unlikely to have his bail application accepted, so he will be remanded into custody,' – she moves her attention from Dad to me, – 'for your safety.'

∼

'I wonder what's going on with Harry.' Teresa glances up from scrolling on her phone. 'And whether they're definitely going to charge him.'

I wish I could tell her to butt out, but she's part of all this whether I like it or not.

Dad tugs his phone from his pocket and his expression changes. 'That detective's just messaged — well five minutes ago.'

'Read it out then.' Teresa shuffles along the sofa towards him as he reaches for his glasses.

He clears his throat. '*Mr Wheeler, it's DI Turner. We're still holding your son at Weetwood Police Station and are awaiting the CPS decision on whether we can charge him with attempted murder.*' Dad's voice is wobbling. '*He's currently in a cell with his solicitor and I will keep you informed.*' Dad lifts his glasses and wipes his eyes. 'He can rot for all I care.'

I've rarely seen my dad cry before today. But then it's not every day you discover your son allowed his mother to die and a couple of years later tried to kill your daughter.

'Come here, you.' Teresa reaches for Dad's shoulder. 'We'll get through this.' However, the chill in her eyes, as she glances towards me, suggests my exclusion from this supportive cocoon. In a couple of days, when I'm more on top of my pain and managing things better with just one hand, I'll get home to my boys. By then, my memory might be returning even more. The sooner I get out from under Teresa's roof, the better.

So tomorrow, I will find the strength and energy to get into my bank accounts and speak to the solicitor to work out how best to handle things with Daniel.

Today I've turned to jelly. Tomorrow, I will be steel.

41

'Did you manage much sleep last night, love.' Dad's filling the kettle as I walk into the kitchen. 'I didn't.' He looks exhausted and has now got two days of beard growth, sending me to my modus operandi of being riddled with guilt for something I haven't even done.

'Yeah, I've gone from struggling to sleep to struggling to stay awake.' I yank a chair from beneath the table and sink onto it. 'Whatever they did to me during that operation has knocked me sideways.'

'A craniotomy,' – Dad drops tea bags into the pot, – 'isn't exactly a minor operation.'

'At least sleep helps me to escape from it all – what's going on with Harry has hit me like a—' I stop short, horrified at what was about to come out of my mouth.

'You were going to say *train*, weren't you?' The corners of Dad's mouth are slightly upturned as he looks up from filling the teapot.

I nod and stifle my own smile.

'At least we haven't lost our warped sense of humour.' He

pulls a teaspoon from the drawer. 'Despite how horrendous it all is.'

'Have you heard anything else?'

'My phone seems to be on the blink,' he replies. 'I can't get it to charge, let alone switch on. I'm going to have this tea, and then nip down to the phone shop to get them to take a look.'

'To be fair, Dad, you should treat yourself to a new phone. That thing you've got ought to be in a museum.'

'It does the job, doesn't it?'

'Well, clearly not.' I smile, relieved that somehow, I've still got it in me to smile. More and more snippets are returning to me about Austyn and Matthew, and all that matters now is getting myself right and being a brilliant mum. They'll be my reason to smile and I'll be their reason. And if Daniel thinks he can come between us, he's in for a shock.

'Will you be alright if I pop out for half an hour?'

'Is Teresa in?' I glance up at the clock. It's after nine but I'm not sure what day it is.

'She left for work an hour ago.'

'I'll be fine,' I tell him. 'Lock the door after yourself, just in case. What time's our appointment with the solicitor?'

'Not until this afternoon.'

This afternoon. My brother could be in a G4 van on his way to prison by then if he's remanded. Even though it shouldn't after what he's done, the thought kills me.

'When you get back from sorting your phone, will you help me with all this money stuff? I've remembered who I bank with – at least, I hope I have.'

'I'm so proud of you, you know, love.' He stirs the teapot. 'Now that you've reminded me about that appointment, I'll go and get this phone sorted straight away. I'll have my brew when I get back.' He hands me my mug. 'The quicker I can get back, the sooner we can get the bank business sorted. I just hope it isn't already too late to prevent Daniel from doing his worst with your money.'

'Me too, but the bottom line is that it's only money. All that matters is that I'm alive and I'm going to get better.'

'I don't think you and your brother could be any more different.' Dad pauses as if only seeing me for the first time. 'Right, I won't be long. Oh, hello, I'm actually just on my way out.' He jumps as he reaches the kitchen door and nearly collides with Emma. 'I keep forgetting you have a key. Have you locked the door?'

Great, not only is Emma the *last* person I want here – for a variety of reasons, but one of them is that once again, her plaited hair and lovely clothes only serve to remind me of the state I'm in. I glance down at myself. I need to get showered and out of these pyjamas.

'No – why? Should I have done?' Her face is pouty. Perhaps she's thinking that Dad hasn't offered her a warm enough welcome.

'I'll let Cathy fill you in with the latest.' He waves towards the kitchen counter as he leaves the room. 'There's tea in the pot.'

'Great.' She stomps into the kitchen. 'I'm just a nobody to him, aren't I? I could have been *anyone* just then. He can't even bring himself to look at me.'

I stare down at the table, unsure how to answer.

'So what's going on? How come the door needs to be locked?' She ignores Dad's invitation to make herself a brew and sits heavily in the seat opposite me. The warmth I once knew in her face has completely disappeared since she's revealed that she's also Dad's daughter. Maybe I haven't given her the reaction she wanted to the news either, but I can't help that. I feel how I feel but she's making it even harder with her jealousy and bitterness.

'You were right about Harry.' I gaze out of the window,

hoping the blue sky beyond it might somehow help me to feel more positive. 'We're waiting to find out if he'll be charged.'

'Yet I'll probably still be treated like the black sheep, won't I? It's all I've ever been with everyone.'

This is definitely what Zoe would call Debbie Downer talk. I, for one, can do without it today.

'I won't be long,' Dad calls and the front door bangs after him.

'I heard what he just said.' Her tone's accusatory.

'About what?'

'*I'm so proud of you, love.*' She mimics his words. 'He's not proud of *me* though, is he? No one is.'

'Oh give over, Emma.'

'What have you got that I haven't? That's what I want to know. What have I got to do to get him to notice *me*?'

'He's just trying to help me to feel better.' Here I go again with my appeasing ways. As Dad and I discussed in hospital, I definitely need to get myself in for some therapy. Sooner rather than later.

'He's never said anything like that to me.' Her face darkens even more. 'It's not fair. Why do you get all his time and attention while I get *nothing*?'

'It's because of what's happened to me, that's all.'

'He didn't want to know me even before that. I'd have thought he'd have wanted to make up for lost time with me but he doesn't give a shit.' She drops her head into her hands.

'You need to talk to him directly, Emma. I really don't want to get involved.'

'What's so bad about me?' She raises her eyes to meet mine. 'My own dad, well the man I *thought* was my dad has done his best to ignore me my whole life. And Bob knows this.'

'He's had a lot on his plate.'

'With you, you mean. It's always about *you*, isn't it?'

She's not the only person to have said this lately.

'Look, he'll still be getting his head around you turning out to be his daughter.'

'It shouldn't need any *getting his head around*. He should be pleased. Instead, all he cares about is you.' She points at me. 'And your murdering brother. What do I have to do to make him *proud* of me?'

The silence hangs between us for a few moments. I don't know how to reply to her – I don't *want* to reply to her.

Emma's expression suddenly changes to look smug. 'I can't imagine him being so *proud* of you if he knew about your cover-up over the last two years.'

I stare at her. It's clear from the look on her face she's considering using this information as a weapon in her arsenal.

'So maybe I'll be the one to enlighten him.'

Thankfully I'm already one step ahead. 'If you mean what I remembered about Harry letting our mum die, you needn't concern yourself. I've already told Dad. *And* the police.' *Take that, you cow.*

'Why the hell would you do that?' Her voice is strained. 'Aren't you bothered about what might happen? After all, you're implicated – you're an accessory to murder.'

'I just wanted everything out in the open.' I tug at my sling where it's rubbing at the back of my neck. 'Anyway, nothing's going to happen to either me *or* Harry – not for my mum's death anyway.'

'Really?' Her widening eyes suggest she doesn't believe me.

I hold her gaze. 'According to the police, neither me or even Harry did anything that breaks the law. It might have been morally or ethically wrong, but that's as far as it goes.'

'Surely he should be done for manslaughter. After all, he stood back and just watched your mother *die*.' She rises from the chair and pushes it back with a scrape. 'If he *had* called for help, she might have lived.' She marches across to the teapot. 'And if *you'd* spoken up at the time,' – she swings around and points at me, – 'Harry might have been held to account for taking away her chance of survival.'

'Don't you think I already know this, Emma?' She's turned her back and is pouring her tea. 'The bottom line is that whatever I did was never going to bring my mother back – so in the end, I was simply protecting my brother, just as I always had.'

'Does Daniel know what you did?'

I can't believe the change in Emma since she told me about Dad. I wish I'd swapped details with Zoe as I could really use a friend. That's if she'd be allowed to keep in touch. There's probably a staff-to-patient boundary line she won't be allowed to cross.

'What difference does *Daniel knowing* make?'

'I'm just wondering if it's part of the reason why your marriage has been going down the pan.'

Gosh, she's not mincing her words.

'I've no idea if I ever told him.' A shake has entered my voice. Being around Emma is really not doing me any good today.

'From what I can gather, he's got a pretty low opinion of you right now.' She swings around to look at me. 'And he's not the only one.'

'I really don't care. I'm not the person I was before, Emma. So just leave me alone.'

'What's *that* supposed to mean?'

'It means that you, your mother, my husband, Samantha, Harry, or *whoever,* can tell me how awful I might have been to your heart's content – but I'm not going to let *anyone* bring me down any more. So do your worst.'

42

'Look, I'm sorry.' Emma places her cup on the table and sits down. 'I don't want things to go sour between us any more than you do.' She rests her hand over mine but I tug mine back.

'I don't know what's happened over the last couple of days, Emma.' A flood of tears wells up behind my eyes. 'You seem to have turned against me.'

'It's probably my hormones. And I've got other stuff going on. Joel's as good as deserted me – he barely comes home anymore.'

'That must be rough,' I say. 'I haven't much memory of being pregnant, but that, I imagine, is when you most need your husband.'

'Then in the last few weeks,' – She fiddles with the end of her plait. 'I've found out I'm not even who I thought I was – that my dad isn't even my dad.'

'It must have been a huge shock.' I don't add, *it was for me.*

'At first, I was quite excited, but then trying to get Bob to notice me has been mission impossible.'

I'm glad she's called him Bob. I guess to start calling

someone Dad for the first time when you're forty doesn't come naturally.

'*You're* all he cares about,' she adds.

'That's because I nearly *died* two weeks ago.' As if I'm even having to remind her. 'And it's looking like Harry's responsible. It's the only thing on my dad's mind – surely you can understand that?'

'He's as much *my* father as he is yours and Harry's.'

I take a sip of my tea at the mention of my brother's name, struggling to swallow it with the lump that's still filling my throat. I wish I could talk to Emma about what's going on at that police station and how wretched I feel, but she's too busy wallowing in self-pity. I can't imagine our relationship coming back from this.

'Do you think you might be directing blame at the wrong person?' I rest my mug back on the table.

'What's that supposed to mean?'

'You seem to be hitting out at me, my dad, Harry…'

'So what? I've got every right to *hit out*.'

'Your *mum's* known for your entire life of the chance that the man you were calling Dad, wasn't your dad.'

'But, as she's explained—'

'I don't buy all this, *the longer it went on, the harder it was to tell her,* crap.' I mimic Teresa's voice then immediately regret it as I sense a fresh hostility emanating across the table.

'Did *she* tell you that?'

'It's about *all* she's said to me on the subject. As you know, she doesn't talk to me a great deal.'

'I wonder why.' There's a slight curl to Emma's lip as we continue to stare at one another. 'You're all going to have to accept that I exist and that things have changed whether you like it or not.'

'We'll talk about this stuff another time – I've got enough

going on with Harry right now.' I rise from my chair. 'I'm going up to have a shower and get dressed.'

'So why are you staying *here* if you can manage to do that on your own?'

'I can't really,' I turn back to her. 'But I'm going to have a damn good go. You can show yourself out.'

'Like I've told you before.' She bangs her mug down. 'This is *my* mother's house. So I'm going nowhere.'

'Suit yourself.' Resisting the urge to slam the door behind me, I shuffle across the hallway tiles and towards the front door. Before I head upstairs, I need to get outside to stop myself from crying and to dig deep within myself to cope. I twist the lock and throw the door open, gulping in the morning air like its life-saving oxygen. Here, in Dad's street, life goes on. The neighbours are oblivious to the misery that's swirling within what's left of our family.

'Good morning, love.' The elderly next-door neighbour waves from her kneeling pad on the lawn and then returns to what she's doing. She's probably too polite to enquire as to why half my head is shaved and why I'm covered in cuts and bruises. If she hasn't heard what happened, she might think my hairstyle is a new fashion craze.

A man across the cul-de-sac is washing his car and the postman is zipping from house to house, whistling as he walks. I'd love to have that kind of bounce in my step, but perhaps I'll still be able to find it if I fight hard enough. I stare into the sky which couldn't be bluer today. There's still a chill in the air but the promise of spring is just around the corner.

I think of my boys who'll be sitting in their lessons, or perhaps running around their playground beneath this same blue sky and my heart pines for them. It's the first time since I've woken from the coma that I've viscerally felt like their mother. And I like it. This, in itself, is well worth fighting for, even if the person I have to fight is Daniel. And now Samantha too, by the sounds of it. Hopefully, she'll want Daniel all to herself and will leave my children well out of things. She's caused me enough damage.

I let out a deep sigh. I think I knew deep down that the police were barking up the wrong tree when they were questioning her and Daniel. But never in a million years would I have suspected that my would-be killer could be Harry.

Some clattering around in the kitchen jolts me back into the present. Emma could be out here, in the hallway at any second. So to avoid any further confrontation, I'll make myself scarce while I've still got the chance. I click the door closed again and head, as fast as my broken body will allow, to the foot of the stairs.

It's not that I can't walk, it's more that everything hurts with *any* exertion, especially my ribs. And whichever way I try to slice it, I'm light-headed and utterly exhausted. It's a kind of mind-numbing, bone-burrowing exhaustion, and I think I could sleep standing up if I had the energy to stand for long enough.

I head to my room, bending to the floor to retrieve yesterday's leggings and hoodie, my head swooning with the movement. I only wore my clothes for a few hours yesterday, so they can go back on.

Next, I head for the bathroom, cursing the fact that there's no lock on the door. I guess with only the two of them living here, they feel they don't need one. Hopefully, Emma, or Dad when he returns, will hear the shower running and will leave me to it.

As I'm working out the logistics of how I'm going to manage this, there's a tapping at the bathroom door. 'Can I come in?'

Bloody hell, she just won't let me be. I step towards the door and peer around it. 'I'm about to have a shower.'

'Let me help you,' Emma's forcing a smile. 'You need my help.'

'I'm fine. I can manage, thank you.'

Her mouth twists into a scowl. 'So my help isn't good enough, is that what you're saying?'

'You want me to go home, don't you?' I lean against the doorframe. 'So the quicker I can do things on my own, the better.'

'I'm just not good enough, am I?' Her voice hardens. 'For *you* or for *Dad*?'

I really can't get used to her calling him *Dad*. I don't think I ever will. 'Please, leave it, eh, Emma? Go home.'

She steps closer to the door and suddenly, she's right in my face. 'I see you so clearly, Cathy. Don't ever forget that. You're nothing but a spoilt, self-centred little bitch.'

'Leave me alone,' I shout and kick the door shut, wishing there was a lock on it. I stare at it for a few moments, half expecting her to burst in and have another go at me but as I hear the floor of the landing creak beneath her weight at the top of the stairs, my breath begins to even out. Finally, she's taken the hint. Hopefully, she'll leave me alone now.

Getting undressed and into the shower is more difficult than I could have ever imagined. If I don't bother washing what's left of my hair, I should be able to keep the cast on my arm dry like I'm supposed to.

The heat of the water feels good on my skin, as if it's washing away some of my angst and misery. Life keeps veering between feeling hopeful and then dreadful, so I have to appreciate the small wins to keep myself going. Things, like the sun shining and a good cup of tea, or like now, managing to get myself into the shower. I'll have no doubt taken everything for granted before my accident. Why do I keep calling it an *acci-*

dent? Before my brother tried to kill me would be a more correct summation.

This reminder washes over me with the water, threatening to drown me in its reality. I close my eyes as it runs over my face and mingles with my tears.

Then, as I open them again, the bathroom door is pushed open.

43

Bloody hell – I'd hoped Emma was leaving.

'Can't I have a shower in peace?' I glance around for a towel but they're all hung over the towel rail at the other side of the bathroom. I've been undressed in front of my stepsister before, when we've been swimming together, or when we've been getting ready to go out, but things are different between us now and my nakedness makes me feel extremely vulnerable. 'What do you want?'

'Just to say sorry.' Clicking the door behind her, she crosses the bathroom tiles and perches on the edge of the bath next to the shower screen. She's sitting in the same spot her mother sat in yesterday. She twists herself around to look at me.

'OK. Apology accepted. Now can I get on with my shower?' I turn myself away, hoping she'll take this as her cue to leave.

She doesn't. 'I don't trust you not to tell Dad about us arguing.'

'Oh, for God's sake. I've got more things to worry about than telling tales on you.' I need her to get out of here – I'm struggling to keep my cast dry and should probably just get myself dried and dressed again.

'You're going to go bleating to him, aren't you? You're going to turn him against me even more.'

'I think you'll do a good enough job of that all by yourself.' I regret my words as soon as I've said them. I wanted her to leave me alone but I can tell from her face that what I've just said has been like a red rag to a bull.

'What did you say?'

'Look I'm sorry. It's just—'

'You're lucky to be alive, you know, Cathy. *Very* lucky.' There's a darkness in her eyes I've never seen before.

'I know I am but please – this has gone far enough. Look, I'm not going to say a word to... Dad and I accept your apology but now, I'd like you to leave me alone.'

'Maybe I can't do that.' Emma stands from her perch. 'Maybe you've completely blown it with me. You and your psycho brother.'

'He's your brother as well!'

Her face twists as she slams one of her denim-clad legs inside the bath, and then the other. 'Maybe I want *both* of you out of my life.'

'What the hell are you doing?'

'Helping you with your shower, of course.' Our gazes are locked onto one another's and the darkness in her eyes seems to be intensifying.

Anxiety pools in my belly. 'I've already told you. I don't need—'

'I don't want you here, Cathy.' She closes the already tiny space between us. 'Haven't you worked that out?'

'I'm leaving over the next couple of days.'

'I don't want you here – full stop.'

'I'll be going home. Just as soon as my dad—'

'He's *my* fucking father.' She swipes at the shower head behind me and wrenches it from its holder. 'You shouldn't even be here anymore. You were supposed to die under that train.'

Despite the steam which has filled the bathroom and the heat of the water, icy dread snakes over me. 'Are you saying what I think you're—' My words fade out, evaporating like the steam that's filling the space between us.

'Yes, I was there that Monday morning.' Her voice is acidic as she points at herself. 'And it was *me* who put Harry in touch with a loan shark in York for a breakfast meeting. I even booked his train ticket for him.' For a split second, she looks almost smug as she spills the plan she hatched and executed.

'What are you talking about?' I shiver. Unless she spells this out, I won't believe it. Emma's my friend when all is said and done. So why is she saying these things?

'It was *me* who pushed you.' She pauses as if allowing time for her words to sink in. 'And you weren't supposed to *survive*.'

'It was *you*?' I stare at the woman I believed to be one of my closest allies. This makes no sense. 'But why?' My voice is a husk. What a stupid question. Could there ever be a reason?

Silence hangs between us for a moment, broken only by the hiss of the still-running shower.

'You've had it all.' Her eyes skim over me, full of revulsion. 'For your whole life – you *and* Harry have. You had *my* dad. And I want him back.'

I raise my hand to shield my face from the spray as Emma holds the shower head directly towards me.

'Maybe I wanted to be the centre of attention for once.' Her other hand flies to her midriff. 'Me and my baby.'

'I don't believe you, Emma. You wouldn't have done that to me. You're just making this up to hurt me.'

'Push you in front of that train?' She laughs. 'You can rest assured I did.' The humour fades from her face as quickly as it arrives. 'And you'll be doing a lot more *resting* where you're going.'

Her words send an icy chill up my spine. But she doesn't mean it. She's just saying this to hurt me – to scare me. She must know she can't get away with trying to hurt me here – in this house.

'Cat got your tongue, Cathy?'

'I don't understand why you've even told me this – you must know I'll be going to the police. It's *you* who should be locked up, not Harry.'

A slow smile spreads across her face – a face I thought I knew so well. 'I just couldn't resist seeing the look in your eyes when you realise you're no longer going to be daddy's girl.'

'What are you talking about?'

'Instead, I am.' She points at herself again. 'It'll be *me* who gets all this,' – her hand hits the shower screen as she waves it around, but she doesn't seem to notice, – 'their house, their money, everything – when *they're* gone. But we're going to have many happy years together before that time comes.'

'Just get out of my way.' I lunge forward but she shoves me back against the wall. I cry out as I slam into the tiles – agony spreading through my ribs. I barrell myself towards her again but she's unmovable – her body and the shower screen forming a barrier against my escape.

Where the hell's my dad? He said he wouldn't be long. *Where is he?*

'Emma, please, don't do this to me.' I try to surge forward again but this time, her push is much more forceful as my spine smacks into the shower's heat dial. The pain in my torso snatches my breath, sending waves of nausea crashing over me. I battle with the urge to sink to my knees. I must somehow get past her and out of this bathroom so I can call for help.

'You're going nowhere, Cathy.' Her face is right in mine. 'And *this* time, you won't be getting back up.'

'You can't do this.' My voice is a wheeze as I struggle for breath. She's going to kill me. She's *really* going to kill me.

'Soon, *you'll* be six feet under and your beloved brother will be inside. Meanwhile, the rest of us are going to live happily ever after. Me, my parents, and my baby.' She pats her stomach.

'Then think about your baby, Emma.' My voice takes on a renewed strength as I bargain with the only bartering power I have left. 'Do you want it to be born in prison, Emma?' Her name feels foreign in my mouth. To think I ever trusted this woman. If she *does* manage to kill me, Harry may well continue to take the blame for something he hasn't done.

'Letting you out of here isn't an option. It'll be born in prison anyway once you go bleating. Like I said, I just wanted to see your face when you knew the truth.'

'You won't get away with this, you know. How can you? There's only me and you in the house.'

'I'll be telling them how frustrated you've been.' She raises the showerhead aloft. 'How you were bashing yourself in the face with the shower head after seeing yourself in the mirror. Everyone knows how vain you are.'

'Please, no!' But I'm powerless to block Emma's next move as she smashes the metal into my face. I scream as it collides with my nose, blood exploding into the stream of water as she lifts it back to have another go. 'No. Stop. Please.'

The shower head rams into my mouth and then again onto my forehead. I'm so dizzy, I can no longer stand. She beats me over and over as I slide down the tiles, slumping onto the floor of the bath.

'Look at this, Cathy.' Her voice sounds far away as I force my eyes to open, for what might be the final time. She's holding a magnifying mirror in front of my face. With my bust nose, swollen lip and egg coming up on my cheekbone, I look like Elephant Man. 'Just look how ugly you are. It's no wonder Dad's going to see me in the years to come and know I'm the daughter he always should have had. He'll forget all about you.'

I close my eyes again. How ugly I may or may not be hardly matters at this moment. There's a crash as the mirror hits the floor of the bath, sending shards of glass spraying over me, then she hits me on the top of the head with the showerhead. I slump forward. This is it. I'm going to die. My brother will be sent to prison and I'm never going to see my little boys again.

My name is being shouted but am I hearing it for real? The voice is probably calling from the void between life and death, beckoning me to the other side. I slump further down. This is it.

44

'Oh my God! What's happened to her?'

I force my head from the floor of the bath at the sound of my brother's voice. 'Help me,' I croak. There's no way I can survive another slam of that showerhead. It's a miracle I'm still conscious.

'I found her like this,' Emma cries. 'She must have fallen – I told her not to try showering on her own.'

'She—' I raise my arm out of the broken glass, – 'did – this – to – me.'

'Get the hell away from her.' Harry's footsteps pound across the tiles. 'What have you done to my sister? Then he cries out in pain. She must have belted him on the back of the head while he was bending over the bath.

Grappling with the edge of the bath, I hoist myself up so I'm resting on one hip, shredding more of my flesh on the broken glass as I move. There's blood everywhere but Emma hasn't finished me off yet. While I've still got breath, I've got fight.

'You evil bitch.' Harry reaches over me and wrenches the metallic hose to the shower from where it attaches to the piping. Emma's fingers whiten around her makeshift weapon as she and Harry face each other, clutching either end of the shower like they're about to play tug-of-war.

'No,' I shriek as she slams the showerhead into my brother's face. There's an explosion of blood as he yells out again.

But he's straight back at her, throwing his body weight onto her, forcing her knees to buckle as he sends her crashing backwards. Her head smashes onto the tiles as she hits the floor. But she's still gripping the showerhead – and she's still trying to hit him with it from where she's lying beneath him, shrieking with the exertion.

'It was *her* Harry,' I try to get up out of the glass but the room's spinning. My voice doesn't sound like my own. 'If I don't survive this, you need to know. It was *her* who pushed me under the train.'

I don't want to die – I really don't want to die – but who knows what damage those blows to the head will have caused. I'm forcing my eyes to stay open. My head's probably bleeding inside. I rest my head on the edge of the bath.

'Get off me – my baby.' Emma writhes around as she attempts to hit him again.

He yanks the showerhead from her hand. 'You think you're going to get back up off this floor, do you? After what you've done to my sister.' As she raises her head and tries to twist from under him in what seems to be an attempt to throw him sideways, he hooks the hose beneath her head and grasping it within his fists, he tightens it around her throat. 'And after what you've done to our family.'

'No – Harry – don't.' Time seems to slow as I attempt to get up from the floor of the bath but slip in the mix of water and blood, before landing badly on my arm, shredding the other side of my body in the pieces of shattered mirror. I cry out, fighting once again with the urge to yield to the darkness which is trying its best to envelop me. No matter what she's done to me, her baby deserves to live.

But Harry's gritting his teeth as his fingers whiten on the hose and he pulls even harder. 'Good riddance to you – bitch,' he snarls.

'Harry – stop – her baby,' I gasp from the bath. 'If you kill her, you'll kill the baby.'

He relaxes his grip and falls back from her, turning to me with wide eyes as she writhes and gags on the floor.

'What baby?'

'She's pregnant.'

He stares at her as she wriggles around, her gasps deepening as she begins to get some breath back into her lungs.

'Her baby doesn't deserve to die. Just call the police. And an ambulance.'

Harry's panting as he slides his hand into his pocket. 'OK, OK, I'm calling them now.'

But as I try once again to move, I'm overtaken by a surge of pain in my head. 'Help me, Harry.' I slump further down into the glass. I can hear it cracking beneath me but can no longer feel it. All I can feel is the agony of what feels like a dozen hammers battering against the inside of my skull. My brain's going to explode here in this bath. I can't open my eyes – no, no, no, I'm going to die. Emma's finally achieved what she set out to do. Bile rises in my throat and it's my turn to gag.

'Cathy, please – don't close your eyes.' Harry's voice is becoming more distant. 'Stay with me, do you hear? Oh my God, oh my God. Yes – police and ambulance. I need them here now – straightaway.'

'Cathy!'

As my world fades, the last thing I hear is my father calling my name.

45

'CATHY. Oh, thank the Lord. Doc – she's waking up.'

Through the slits I've forced my eyes into, the blurry faces of Dad and Harry come into view.

'Where am I?' Every bit of my face aches as my mouth forms the words.

'You're back in hospital, love. It's OK – don't try to move.'

'If you could both just stand back for me please?' Another kindly, but blurry face replaces theirs. 'Hello, Cathy, do you remember me? Doctor Finch?'

I nod – at least *him* being here means I'm not back in Intensive Care. I'm on the normal ward – the same one I was on before I discharged myself.

I scrunch my eyes back together as he shines a torch into them.

'If you could just try and keep them open a little for me.' He shines it again. 'Perfect, well done.'

'Am I going to be OK?'

'We've had to repin your arm and keep that head of yours under surveillance, but I think we can now safely say you're going to be alright.'

'How are you feeling, sis?' Harry's moved around to the other side of my bed. I stare into his eyes – eyes that are filled with a mixture of relief, regret and pain.

'Groggy.'

'We've upped your painkillers again, Cathy.' The doctor gestures to the drip which leads to a cannula in the back of my hand.'

'How long have I been here?'

Dad twists his wrist to look at his watch. 'We brought you in at around half past ten this morning – so, six or seven hours. You were out of it to start with and then, obviously, they anaesthetised you in theatre when they operated on your arm.'

At least they're not saying *a week* this time. 'What about my head?'

'Miraculously, given the blows you've sustained,' begins Doctor Finch. 'The two scans we've carried out show no further brain trauma.'

'They had to hunt for a while to find it though.' Harry lowers onto the seat beside me. 'Your brain, I mean.'

I smile, wincing with the pain it causes, both physically and mentally as the reality of how me and Harry have been slams into my mind. His nasty messages, his ultimatums, the hassling me for money, him letting our mum die. It's no wonder I believed he was capable of pushing me from the platform that morning.

But he saved me from Emma. Our half-sister. My eyes scan the room and beyond the windows, as I try to swallow the sudden panic that's engulfing me. The last time I woke up, when I was in intensive care, Emma was waiting at my bedside.

'Where is she?'

What if she got away and comes back to have another go? It could be third time lucky for her.

'Emma's been locked up, love.' Dad appears back at Doctor Finch's side as he's busy writing something. 'She won't be getting anywhere near you.' I feel the warmth of his hand as he rests it over mine.

'But what about her baby?' The heat of tears prickles at the back of my eyes. 'And what about my two – what do they know about this?'

'Shush, for now, Cathy.' Dad's voice is as soothing as it was when he looked after me in my younger years. 'All that matters right now is you.'

'And you need to rest tonight.' Doctor Finch's voice is authoritative. 'We're keeping you in for observation for a couple of days.'

'And then I can go?'

'All being well. Anyway, I'm going to continue with my ward round, but I'll be back in the morning to check in on you.'

I slide my hand from beneath Dad's and raise it to my face, touching the swell of my lip and the prickle of stitches on my cheekbone and above my eyebrow. 'As if I didn't look bad enough before,' I try to smile. 'Can I have some water, please?'

'You're still here – that's the main thing. When I think of how close she was – again – to killing you.' The anguish in my brother's face is undisguisable and I can tell he's fighting back tears. He's many things but I think I always knew, it could never have been *him* who would have pushed me in front of a train.

'Thank God you got to the house when you did, Harry.' Dad holds a straw from a cup of water to my lips. 'If the police hadn't let you go...' His voice trails off. He doesn't need to say anymore. Without a shadow of a doubt, Emma would have killed me.

'Well thankfully, they didn't have enough to charge me, did they? They *had* to let me go.'

I close my lips around the straw but can't drink much without the pursing action hurting my entire face. 'Where's Teresa?'

'She's at home,' Dad replies. 'We felt, in the circumstances, that she should stay away, for now, at least.'

'What's she said about it all?' I'm suddenly consumed with a need to know Teresa's reaction after what her daughter's done to me.

'Like the doc said.' Dad rests the water back onto my overbed table. 'You need to rest. Nothing's as important as you getting better and getting you back home again.'

'But she doesn't even want me at your house, Dad. She told me that herself.' There – I've said it. At least with the state I'm in, I'll probably get away with saying this. But I'm struggling to even keep my eyes open as I wait for Dad's response.

'We can discuss all that tomorrow. When you've got over this a little more and when we've all had some rest. It's been quite a day.'

'And some.' Harry moves his chair closer to my bed with a scrape. 'I'm so sorry for everything, sis. I've been a right—'

'Leave it, Harry.' Dad frowns at him. 'There'll be plenty of time for us to talk about everything soon enough. But not tonight. Anyway, I don't know about you but I could do with a stiff drink.'

Harry's face relaxes into a grin. 'If you're buying, Dad.'

'I wish I could come with you,' I turn my head from Dad back to Harry. 'But I'm just soooo tired.'

'The doc said it would take a while for the anaesthetic to completely wear off,' Dad says. 'You're doing pretty well, considering.'

'And you're pumped full with painkillers,' Harry adds.

'Right, we'll let you get some sleep. We'll be back in the morning and hopefully, we might be able to take you back home either then or the day after.'

'I hope so.' I don't know if I'm saying or just thinking the words as before Dad and Harry leave the room, I've already drifted away.

46

'You just can't stay away, can you?'

I flutter my eyes open to a very welcome face. 'Zoe.' I try to smile but it hurts. 'It's so good to see you.'

'Under better circumstances would have been preferable,' she says. 'Perhaps bumping into one another in a pub – not on Ward Twenty-One.'

'I was going to find you and message on Facebook,' I say. 'Since I didn't get a chance to say thank you or goodbye when I discharged myself.'

'So what happened?' Zoe frowns. 'You left in such a rush.'

'It's a long story. But I could use a friend if you've got time to listen to it?'

∽

'Hey.' I must have fallen back to sleep for this time it's a different voice. A voice I don't particularly wish to hear – Daniel's. However, it sounds far more amenable than the last time we came face to face. And at least he's made the effort to visit.

I shuffle up onto my pillows, disappointed when I don't see the boys file in behind him. 'Where are Austyn and Matthew?'

'They're in school,' he replies as he reaches my bed. 'I thought I should visit you on my own before bringing the two of them in with me, no matter how much they wanted me to.'

'This sounds ominous.'

His gaze starts at my legs, covered in cuts and bruises after being shredded by the glass in the bath, then it travels up to my battered face.

'I can tell what you're thinking.'

'I'd like to say you're looking well, Cathy, but you're looking decidedly worse than when I last saw you.' Despite what our marriage has become, his eyes are warm and sympathetic. 'How are you bearing up?' He rests a bag of grapes on my table. I can't fathom the difference in him after his hostility the other night. But I guess I'm about to find out.

'Grapes – great, cheers. The fresh injuries look worse than they are, so I'm told. But to say I'm sore is an understatement.'

'I couldn't believe it when I heard – the full story, I mean.'

'Who told you?'

'Your dad – he's told me *everything*.' He lowers himself to the chair Harry was sitting in last night. 'He and Harry came to see me after they left here.'

'What's going to happen to *her* and the baby?' I'm struggling to say Emma's name, now what she's done has begun to sink in. However, I can't stop thinking about the baby. If it wasn't for her being pregnant, perhaps I'd have let Harry strangle her with that shower hose. When I said this to Zoe, she said Emma would be better punished by spending a hefty amount of time behind bars.

'She's waiting for a date for her plea and trial preparation hearing. We were all in court to watch her be remanded first thing this morning. So it looks like she'll be having her baby in prison.'

'At least it's alright.' Relief courses through me. Living with Mum's death on my conscience is punishing enough without adding another death into the equation.

'Who knows what sort of life the baby's going to have.' Daniel's eyes have a faraway look. 'Starting its life in a prison. *She* deserves it – the baby doesn't.'

'I know.'

'And just for the record, I've ended things with Samantha. I can't tell you how sorry I am. For the other night as well.'

'Sudden change of topic.'

'We only slept together once.'

I should be furious. I should be hurt, jealous and vengeful. He's freely admitting to sleeping with my former work colleague, not to mention, my adversary, while I was laid up here in hospital. Yet I can't, and I don't feel a thing.

'So when did it happen?' I'm more *curious* than jealous. After all, knowledge might be a bullet in my gun if Daniel reverts to obstructing me from going home and being with my sons.

But his demeanour is completely different to what it was the last time I saw him at the house. He shifts in his seat, looking uncomfortable – as well he should. 'It was the night before– oh, what does it matter when it was? She just turned up at the house and—'

'I suppose you're going to say, *one thing led to another*.'

His expression of shame is good enough for me. He's struggling to meet my eyes. Samantha is an absolute bitch and she hasn't heard the last of me, that's for sure.

'What were you going to say, *the night before* when?'

'You were working with your physio.' His head tilts in the direction of the side room across the corridor which I discharged myself from only two days ago. I can't believe how much has happened since then.

'Ah – no wonder you were so *off* with me that day, and the

next time you visited too. Your conscience couldn't handle being around me, could it?'

'It's more than just that, Cathy. Things haven't been great between us for a while. But jumping into a new relationship, especially with my publisher, wasn't the answer.'

'I'm more upset by how you've been carrying on with her while our sons are in the house. I take it they were there?'

'They were at my mother's the night she stayed over.'

I think back to what I now know about chasing after my ex-husband. Pot, kettle, black, and all that. I can hardly be mad with Daniel.

'It sounds like I wasn't much better,' I say.

He meets my eyes now.

'I can't remember too much about the weeks before my accident but how I was carrying on over Brad isn't anything to be proud of.'

Daniel's face relaxes as if he's on safer ground discussing *my* indiscretions instead of his own. 'His fiancée messaged me – when you were down in London - during your final week there. She told me how you were following him around – doing whatever you could to get his attention.'

'I get flashes of it all, but then, I'm getting flashes of lots of things.'

'Will your memory fully come back?'

'Hopefully – but whether it does or it doesn't, I'm on a waiting list to speak to someone. I want to be better than I was before.'

He moves the chair closer to my bed. 'Will you speak to them about me, Cathy? And our sons?'

'I love Austyn and Matthew – I know I do. My memories of them might be hazy but feeling like their mother came flooding back last week.' I touch my chest. 'I feel it in here.'

'But what about me?' His voice is soft. 'Look, I know I shouldn't have gone anywhere near Samantha, but we've both, me *and* you, – he points from himself to me, – made mistakes. But the bottom line now are those boys.'

'Boys who could still be just as happy, even if we aren't together, Daniel.'

His eyes cloud over.

'This will be tough for you to hear, but I need to be honest.'

He sniffs. 'I suppose I should be grateful.'

I hesitate. What I'm about to say is pretty brutal but he needs to hear it so he can move on. 'I just don't love you, Daniel, and I can't remember if I ever did – I'm really sorry.'

His shoulders slump. 'But we're married – and I'm the father of your children.'

'So clearly you meant something to me *once*.' My eyes don't leave his. 'Therefore, the kindest thing I can do is to set you free to find someone who wants you as much as you want them. I'm sorry, but that just isn't me.'

I can't be certain but his eyes look to be welling up with tears. 'So where does that leave us?'

'As two adults, wanting the best for ourselves, the best for each other and the best for the boys. Surely we can do an amazing job of this without having to stay *together?*'

He stares down at his hands, twirling his thumbs around and around each other. 'You've changed. You've really changed.'

I take a deep breath. 'And for the better, from what I can gather. When I first woke up, you told me that I've never been satisfied with my life – that I've always been unable to count my blessings. That cut deep and I don't want to be that person.'

'I'm sorry – it's just that it's always been the *what*, rather than the *who* with you.'

'When you said I've changed a moment ago, you were spot on – all I want is to be the mum those boys deserve.'

'And what about your work? What about your publishing career?'

'I'd rather have a job stacking shelves if it means I get to take Austyn and Matthew to school and to pick them up every day. I want to tuck them in each night. Well, the nights you haven't got them, that is?'

'What are you saying?'

'We can share them, can't we? We can make this work. It sounds like we'll be a million times better apart than we ever were together. It's better for them to *come* from a broken home rather than to *grow up* in one.'

EPILOGUE

I'VE PURPOSEFULLY AVOIDED SWITCHING the radio on as I'm scared of what the announcement might be in the news bulletin. Usually, in the afternoon, I like music and voices in the background of my sunny kitchen while I work at the table.

I'm enjoying being back with Bookish on a part-time basis, and working from home – as was offered to me, just doing a little editing. Presently, I'm working on Daniel's book. He decided he didn't want Samantha anywhere near it, and my boss, Bonnie agreed now that we've formally separated with a professional distance between us, I can be his editor.

Because I don't ever remember loving Daniel, we've had one of the most amicable separations probably known to a divorcing couple. Love and hate are two sides of the same coin, so it stands to reason that without love, there can be no hate.

I glance at the clock, then my eyes wander to the boys' latest school photo on the fridge. They've got their arms around each other and a light in their eyes which Daniel said wasn't there until I moved back into the house and began taking care of them full time. Well, apart from each weekend when they sleep at Daniel's new apartment. But we do things together as a family at the weekend now, and Daniel says the two of us get on far better than we ever did when we were together. I could *grow* to love him – but only as a friend – nothing more.

Maybe I *should* switch the radio on. But *no news is good news*, as Dad always says. Teresa paid for the best solicitor money can buy for her only child, so there's still every chance, that with only *my* testimony, and the lack of forensics and CCTV that Emma could be acquitted. Especially with the medical testimony about my memory loss problems. She's bang to rights with her attack on me in the shower but won't necessarily go to prison if that's the only guilty finding.

Then, of course, the jury might feel sorry for her, especially with her seven-month pregnant belly.

As our eyes met when she arrived in the dock during my evidence-giving last week, I was struck by how she couldn't look any less of a hardened criminal. With her blonde hair in plaits, her demure skirt, patterned blouse and kitten heels, she looked more as if she were going to a job interview than standing trial for attempted murder.

'Knock, knock.' Harry and Dad appear at the back door which leads into the garden, darkly dressed in their suits.

'I take it the verdict's been announced.' I look from one to the other, trying to read what it could be from their faces. Harry always grins when he's under scrutiny, no matter how sombre the situation, so his face isn't the best one to assess.

'Did you stick to your guns about the radio?' Dad nods towards the kitchen windowsill.

'I wanted to hear the verdict from you.' I close the lid on my laptop and gesture to the seats on my left and right.

'Have you got a beer, sis?' Harry nods at the fridge.

'Not beer – but I've got some gin in a tin.'

'That'll do.' He strides across the kitchen.

'I'll have one as well.' Dad hitches his trousers before sitting. 'And you might want one yourself.'

'I can't. I've got to collect the children in an hour.' At least everyone at the school gates has stopped staring at me now that my hair's grown back a couple of inches. I had the other half cut off to the same length so I've got a short pixie style that people say suits me. 'Besides, I can't drink on a *Monday* afternoon.'

'Trust me.' Harry plucks the cans from the fridge. 'You're going to need one.'

'We can walk around to the school together,' Dad says. 'But without breathing gin fumes over any teachers.'

'What's happened then?' My heart's beating ten to the dozen. Surely Emma's not walking free. *Twice*, she's nearly killed me. They can't let her get near me again.

'OK, well as you know from when you gave your evidence, the defence barrister was making *mincemeat* of the prosecution,' Dad begins.

'I remember.' Last Monday isn't a day I'd wish to repeat. I stood in that witness box like *I* was the criminal instead of Emma.

'Well it got far worse on Tuesday, then worse still on Wednesday,' Harry says. 'It was looking like she was going to get off with everything. I was keeping a close eye on the expressions of the jurors.'

'Why didn't either of you tell me?' I open my ring pull with a click and a hiss as I look from him to Dad before pouring the drink into a glass.

'We didn't want to upset you, love,' he replies. 'You've already been through so much. You're only just starting to find some semblance of normality.'

'Tell me what's happened.' I'm desperate to know, yet also desperate not to know. Especially if Emma's walked free.

'An unexpected witness stepped forward,' Harry says.

'Someone who wanted to do the right thing in the end. She started as a witness for the defence, but ended the trial as the key to Emma being found guilty.'

'She? Guilty?'

Silence hangs between us for a few moments.

'Teresa.' Dad's avoiding my eye.

The two of them separated not long after Emma was initially remanded. What had happened blew them apart. Dad's rented a house near his school for now and Teresa's taken early retirement. Neither me nor Harry have been sorry to see them split, however we've kept our opinions from Dad. Things have been messy enough. One thing is for certain, I'm relieved I don't ever have to see Teresa again.

'Tell me.'

'She knew what Emma did to you that Monday.' Dad hangs his head.

'You're kidding me.' I look from him to Harry.

'I couldn't believe it either.'

'I'm so sorry, Cathy.' Dad's voice is trembling. 'I had no idea – not until she stood in that witness box first thing this morning.'

'The jury was only out for thirty minutes,' Harry adds. 'After what Teresa told them, there won't have been much deliberating needed.'

I take a huge swig of my G&T. Dad was right – I'm glad I've opened it. The bitterness hits the back of my throat, mirroring my sentiment towards Teresa.

'Emma told her mother what she'd done to you,' Dad begins. 'The same day she did it.'

'And they were *both* willing and happy to watch *me* take the blame,' Harry adds. 'And for you to believe I was capable of trying to kill you – thank God there wasn't enough evidence for the police to charge me, that's all I can say.' He gulps his drink.

'Gosh there's not exactly a lot in these tins, is there? I might need another one.'

'You're supposed to savour it not down it.' I force a laugh. Then we all sit in silence for a moment. No wonder the woman didn't want me to stay at her house when I came out of hospital. But why did she even bother visiting me? Teresa sat at my bedside, yet all the while she *knew* it was her daughter who'd tried to kill me. She's also got *Brad's* blood on her hands. 'How could she have kept quiet all this time.'

'She claims it was because of Emma's pregnancy,' Dad replies. 'She didn't want her grandchild to be born in prison.'

'I hope you're not defending her.' Harry's eyes narrow.

'Of course not – I'm just relieved she spoke up in the end.' Dad's face is grave as he pours the dregs from his can into his glass. 'She said she couldn't live with herself.'

'She also said that Emma shouldn't get away with what she'd done and that she'd pose a risk to Cathy, *and* even to me, – Harry points at himself, – 'if she was to be acquitted.'

'And it was looking like she could be,' Dad continues. 'If Teresa hadn't told the truth, I don't know where we'd be now.'

'Bloody hell.' I wrap my warm fingers around the chill of my glass. 'I suppose I should be almost *grateful* then. Will anything happen to Teresa – for lying, I mean? It's been four months since it happened.'

'The judge said she'd be charged with perverting the course of justice.'

I trace the pattern of the tablecloth with my finger as I struggle to take it all in.

'The defence barrister said Teresa could be looking at a custodial sentence.'

'Wow.' It's hard to imagine Teresa in prison clothes and living in a cell but I don't say this. I expect Dad's miserable enough already.

'Brad's fiancée was there too.' Harry swirls the dregs of gin around his glass. 'Just for the verdict.'

'I'm even more relieved I decided to stay away then. She'll be having *her* day in court next week, won't she?'

'I can't imagine she'll be sent to prison. I asked our barrister who said the worst she'll probably get is a suspended sentence – especially since she pleaded guilty.'

'As long as she continues to stay away from me. Anyway, what about Emma?'

Harry drains his glass. 'Because of Teresa stepping forward at last, Emma was found guilty of one count of attempted murder and another of grievous bodily harm.'

'The second charge was downgraded,' Dad adds. 'It started as two counts of attempted murder against you, but there must have been some kind of plea bargaining going on behind the scenes.'

'What about Brad's death?' Tears pool in my eyes. 'Surely she should be punished for that.'

'I thought the same,' Harry replies. 'But no, unfortunately not.'

'We asked our barrister about that as well,' Dad says. 'But there was no basis in law for additional charges to be brought. Emma didn't *directly* kill Brad.'

'But if it wasn't for what she did to me...' My voice fades.

'I know.'

'How long did she get?' The million-dollar question. How long can I lead a normal life without having to look over my shoulder the whole time?

'We don't know yet. Her case has been adjourned for sentencing in ten weeks.'

Ten weeks. Her baby will have been born by then. Joel visited me a couple of weeks ago, telling me he's started divorce proceedings against Emma, as well as a fight to bring the baby up on his own after it's born. I can't imagine there's a judge in the land who'd rule in favour of a murdering mother raising a small child in prison, over a single dad raising him or her in an affluent household.

I'll never understand Emma as long as I live. We could have got beyond any resentment at sharing our father. We could have stayed friends. But to use Daniel's words, it was *Emma* who wasn't satisfied with her lot, Emma who couldn't count her blessings. Emma who so nearly killed me – twice.

My friend – my half-sister – my nemesis.

But I can't dwell on her any more – she's caused more than enough damage. I stride towards the radio and switch it on. 'It's my song.' There are tears in my eyes as I swing around to face Dad and Harry. 'I Don't Like Mondays.'

I turn the volume up high.

Before you Go

Thank you for reading *I Don't Like Mondays* – I hope you enjoyed it!

If you want more, check out *Ties That Bind on Amazon*, my next psychological thriller, where you'll meet Oliver and Ellen, a couple who are struggling to conceive.

A chance encounter with someone who can help them seems like the end of all their problems until this third party changes the rules. Suddenly, not only is the couple's chance of having a family in the balance – but their entire marriage is at stake, and for one of them, their life.

And for a FREE novella, please Join my 'keep in touch' list where I can also keep you posted of special offers and new releases. You can join by visiting my website www.mariafrankland.co.uk.

BOOK CLUB DISCUSSION QUESTIONS

1. How did the fragmented narrative and unreliable memory of the protagonist shape your understanding of the story?

2. Which character did you find most suspicious, and why? Did your suspicions change as the story unfolded?

3. How does the title *I Don't Like Mondays* connect to the events and emotions in the book?

4. Cathy struggles with her identity as a wife and mother. How does this theme impact the tension in the novel?

5. How did the setting of the train station contribute to the suspense and mystery of *that* Monday morning?

6. Were you satisfied with the resolution of the story? Why or why not?

7. Discuss the role of secrets and grudges in the relationships depicted in the book. How do they drive the plot?

Book Club Discussion Questions

8. If you were in Cathy's position, who would you have trusted – or mistrusted – and why?

9. How does the novel explore the concept of memory and its reliability?

10. Were there moments in the story where you questioned whether Cathy was a reliable narrator?

11. Were there any red herrings that misled you? How effective were they in building suspense?

12. If this story were told from another character's perspective, how might it change the reader's perception?

TIES THAT BIND - PROLOGUE

'It's been a quiet shift, considering it's the weekend, I mean.'

Bella glances at me, her voice light but laced with a cautious optimism that makes me uneasy. I'm a big believer in the power of tempting fate and referring to our shift as being *quiet* is doing just that.

'Don't speak too soon.' I take a right off the main road. The scenic shortcut over Otley is the route I drive by habit, especially at times like now when sunrise is imminent. The station isn't far, but I've learned better than to assume a shift is over until I've completed all the paperwork and walked through the door at the end of it. Due to holidays and sickness, we already started well before our usual clocking-in time of eleven pm so I want to get out on time and sink into bed before the rest of my house starts stirring.

'I hate finishing at this time,' Bella slumps into her seat. 'I prefer the evening finishes when we all meet in the pub.'

'Oh, I don't know. After that one we threw that crowd out of last night, I'll quite happily settle for a nice cup of tea instead. The state of them all was enough to put *anyone* off alcohol.'

'Yeah, it was a right dive, wasn't it, Sarge?' She pulls a face.

'It was a case of wiping your feet on the way *out*.' I laugh. 'Anyway, those two lads going at each other will be regretting it this morning as they wake in the comfort of our cells.' The image of their blooded faces fills my mind. 'With sore heads for all the wrong reasons.'

Bella's laughter suddenly stops short as a huge bang echoes through the emerging dawn. I don't just hear it – I *feel* it resonate through me. Then all is quiet again, save for the hum of our engine.

'What the *hell* was that?' I ease off the accelerator, scanning the road ahead.

'Over there, Sarge!' Bella's blonde ponytail swings out as she twists in her seat, her eyes locked on a spot beyond the treeline. 'Pull over – quick!'

I swerve our patrol car into the Surprise View car park, slowing as we crunch our way over the loose gravel. 'Shiiit.' Against the backdrop of the evening sky, thick plumes of smoke curl into the air. The source – a small vehicle, looks to be crumpled against the dry stone wall at the far end.

'Jeez.' Bella's hand flies to her mouth. 'How have they managed that? In a car park, of all places?'

As we reach it, I bring the car to a halt and throw open the door, my hand already on my radio.

'Keep well back,' I order Bella, as I scan the scene. "We don't know if this is going up in flames. Let's assess things first—then I'll call it in.' This is why the newly-qualifieds are always paired with me. I'm calm under pressure and always remember to explain the procedure to those shadowing me.

'Oh my God.' Bella's voice is barely a whisper. 'There are people still inside.'

I resist the urge to ask her what she expected since the crash has only just happened. I should also remind her that this is what all her training has been for. But that would be insensitive. After all, the first time is always the worst. I'll never

Ties That Bind - Prologue

forget my first road traffic accident when I had to stand by, redirecting traffic while all four deceased passengers were cut free by the fire service. I didn't sleep for several nights after that. But that was on the M1, not in a sunrise car park at a tranquil beauty spot.

I reach for my radio and tilt it to my face as I circle the scene. 'This is Unit Twelve, Sergeant Shepperd.' I wait for a moment. Why do they always take longer when we're calling in something urgent?

'Come in Unit Twelve.'

'We've got a serious one-vehicle RTA at Surprise View Car Park, Otley.' I glance at the mangled bonnet. 'Substantial front-end impact and smoke present. Two casualties are trapped inside, and a third has been ejected. Requesting immediate backup, ambulance, and fire service. Over.'

'Received. Stand by.'

Bella is still frozen in place, her eyes fixed on the motionless figure sprawled in front of the crash site amid the shattered stones.

'Ambulance ETA four minutes. Fire service, six.' The radio crackles.

I nod toward the casualty on the ground, my voice steady. 'Four minutes, they're saying, Bella. Four minutes too long. We need to intervene.'

She doesn't move.

'Come on, I've got you.'

She still doesn't move.

'There's no time like the present to put that CPR training into practice.'

Find out more on Amazon

INTERVIEW WITH THE AUTHOR

Q: Where do your ideas come from?
A: I'm no stranger to turbulent times, and these provide lots of raw material. People, places, situations, experiences – they're all great novel fodder!

Q: Why do you write psychological thrillers?
A: I'm intrigued why people can be most at risk from someone who should love them. Novels are a safe place to explore the worst of toxic relationships.

Q: Does that mean you're a dark person?
A: We thriller writers pour our darkness into stories, so we're the nicest people you could meet – it's those romance writers you should watch...

Q: What do readers say?
A: That I write gripping stories with unexpected twists, about people you could know and situations that could happen to anyone. So beware...

Q: What's the best thing about being a writer?
A: You lovely readers. I read all my reviews, and answer all emails and social media comments. Hearing from readers absolutely makes my day, whether it's via email or through social media.

Q: Who are you and where are you from?

A: A born 'n' bred Yorkshire lass, now officially in my early fifties. I have two grown up sons and a Sproodle called Molly. (Springer/Poodle!) The last decade has been the best: I've done an MA in Creative Writing, made writing my full time job, and found the happy-ever-after that doesn't exist in my writing - after marrying for the second time just before the pandemic.

Q: Do you have a newsletter I could join?

A: I certainly do. Go to www.mariafrankland.co.uk or click here through your eBook to join my awesome community of readers. When you do, I'll send you a free novella – 'The Brother in Law.'

ACKNOWLEDGMENTS

Thank you, as always, to my amazing husband, Michael. He's my first reader, and is vital with my editing process for each of my novels. His belief in me means more than I can say.

A special acknowledgement goes to my wonderful advance reader team, who took the time and trouble to read an advance copy of I Don't Like Mondays and offer feedback. They are a vital part of my author business and I don't know what I would do without them. A special mention to Pheadra Farah who suggested one or two poignant additions - for example, the very last line of the book!

I Don't Like Mondays is my twenty-second full-length novel and it becomes harder and harder to think of first names for my characters. Therefore, I'm really grateful to members of the group who offered their own names up for me to use! They are:

Cathy (Cathy Christopher)
Brad (Put forward by Carina Ann)
Samantha (Put forward by Deborah Voss)
Daniel (Put forward by Linda Russell)
Mel (Mel Copley)
Harry (Put forward by Mags Charles)
Emma (Emma Byrne)
Bob (Bob Fendt)
Teresa (Put forward by Susie Smith Coburn)
Zoe (Put forward by Nan Bell)
Austyn and Matthew (Put forward by Dan-Sharron Moodie Sullivan)

I will always be grateful to Leeds Trinity University and my MA in Creative Writing Tutors there, Martyn, Amina and Oz. My Masters degree in 2015 was the springboard into being able to write as a profession.

And thanks especially, to you, the reader. Thank you for taking the time to read this story. I really hope you enjoyed it.

Printed in Great Britain
by Amazon